GILDED
BUTTERFLY

GILDED BUTTERFLY

LESLIE O'SULLIVAN

CITY OWL
PRESS

GILDED BUTTERFLY
Rockin' Fairy Tales, Book 2

Cover Design by MiblArt. All stock photos licensed appropriately.

Edited by Lisa Green.

For information on subsidiary rights, please contact the publisher at info@cityowlpress.com.

Print Edition ISBN: 978-1-64898-212-5

Digital Edition ISBN: 978-1-64898-211-8

Printed in the United States of America

PRAISE FOR LESLIE O'SULLIVAN

"*Gilded Butterfly* is a unique and magical mashup of fairy tales, Shakespeare, and lore, unlike anything I've read before. At its heart, is a beautiful story about family, the destructive power of chasing fame and money, and the healing power of love. The twists, turns, and magic sprinkled throughout create an engaging story that brings a new kind of fairy tale to modern Hollywood." — *Megan Van Dyke, author of Second Star to the Left*

"*Pink Guitars and Falling Stars* is a fast paced and very engaging read, with a constantly evolving main character and a colorful cast. The adventure wraps up nicely, and ends with a hint of what is next in the Rockin' Fairy Tales series. This is a great read if you are looking for an action-packed modern fairy tale with aspiring rock stars who fall from the sky." — *Paranormal Romance Guild*

"Leslie O'Sullivan's narrative style in *Gilded Butterfly* celebrates truth, love, and heritage, and reads as pure poetry from the opening line until the end." — *InD'tale*

"As full of heart and soul as the music it describes, *Crimson Melodies* drew me in with a fresh take on a classic tale, masterfully combining celebrity and monster romance vibes to give me everything I wanted and more!" — S.C. Grayson, author of *Beauty and the Blade*

"Submerging readers into a fantastical world, *Wild Azure Waves* is a love story swimming with music, mysticism, and magic." — *InD'tale*

"*Pink Guitars and Falling Stars* is an interesting take on the story of Rapunzel...O'Sullivan has definitely nailed the initial animosity between Justin and Zeli. As they become closer, the relationship jumps off the page and morphs beautifully. There are awesome love scenes with a lot of description which pull the reader right in and keep a tight grip... A fascinating remix of a popular fairy tale with some very sexy differences. One to add to the e-reader and to be read list!" — *InD'tale*

"With wickedly clever wordplay, fresh and lovable characters, and an utterly unique take on a classic fairytale, *Pink Guitars and Falling Stars* is one of the swooniest romances I've ever read. You'll be cheering for B.A.S.E. jumper Justin to help Zeli escape her tower in the heart of Hollywood's twisted music industry and fall equally hard for their chosen family on the Boulevard. A romantic, heart-in-your-throat read!" — *Sarah Skilton, author of Fame Adjacent*

"Submerging readers into a fantastical world, *Wild Azure Waves* is a love story swimming with music, mysticism, and magic... Villains deliver with evil schemes and diabolical characteristics that readers will hear their sinister chuckle every time they are on the page. Leslie O'Sullivan's whimsical fantasy tale is an interesting take on sorrow, second chances, and soulmates." — *InD'tale*

"*Pink Guitars and Falling Stars* reads like glitter and stardust, like a song of the heart set free and realizing every dream." —*Fairrryprose*

Hot Set is a 2023 Holt Medallion Winner for Mid-Length Contemporary

Pink Guitars and Falling Stars is a winner of a 2023 Gold Author Shout Reader Ready Awards "Top Pick."

To my mom, Sidney,
who wove Shakespeare into my life.

ROCKIN' FAIRY TALES

BY LESLIE O'SULLIVAN

Pink Guitars and Falling Stars

Gilded Butterfly

Wild Azure Waves

Crimson Melodies

Emerald Spire

Thou Nature, art my goddess; to thy law
My services are bound.

King Lear
Edmund, Act 1 Scene 2

1

CONFAB

WINDSHIELDS ARE A DARK DESTINY FOR BUTTERFLIES. AS I WIND UP the drive to Midas Lear's Waterfall Palace in the Hollywood Hills, my windshield becomes one such destiny for a vibrant blue butterfly. The poor critter traveled to Hollywood in search of fame and fortune with plans to name its cover band *Wing Spread*.

The driver's side glass of my deep blue, Tesla model 3 had other plans. In a single fatal moment, the band, *Wing Spread* became *Smush,* which sounds more like a pop-up night club than a cover band. In Hollywood, it's all about the name.

I pull as far off the road in front of the mansion as the narrow drive allows. There are those who would mock me for bemoaning the death of a bug. In my humble opinion, sadness should be mandated when something lovely is destroyed. I, Adair Holliday, am to blame for a drop of beauty gone from the world.

I retrieve an index card from the leather messenger bag my half-brother, Desmond, gave me last month on my thirtieth birthday with the directive: *"Time to upgrade from your folksy backpack look, Adair."*

Pigs will soar on golden wings before he passes up an opportunity to "improve" his little brother. Desmond, the result of our father's indiscretion, didn't come into my life until a few years after grad school when Dad folded him into the "family business of show business." Thus, *Project Adair* is on overdrive as Des makes up for lost big brother time. It's annoying in an endearing way.

With respect, I scrape the white card under the butterfly. "Sorry, buddy." My heart is as crushed as this blue beauty. Desmond, the more pragmatic of we Holliday brothers, would be first in line to diss my reverence. He'd hit the wipers and be done with it.

Across the road, I pick my way down a steep bank landscaped as a butterfly garden to the shore of a narrow stream fed by cascading water features of the mansion. It's ironic the intentional flora attracts winged beauties only to threaten death via windshields and waterfalls.

Before me, the final brushstrokes of a California sunset reflect off Midas Lear's Waterfall Palace, three stories of glass framed with stacked stone walls. The president of Golden Pipes Records runs his music empire from this Frank Lloyd Wright's *Falling Water House* meets Irish castle.

Spray from the waterfall spilling from the cantilevered stone shelf at the mansion's base dots the butterfly's wings. I crouch at the water's edge to release the creature and its paper ship into the current, a Viking funeral in miniature. The card flips, sending broken blue wings beneath the surface.

A bend in the stream disappears into shadows underneath the peppy blossoms of overhanging purple and pink crepe myrtles. Were I slightly metaphoric, I'd define the waterway as a parallel to the new turn my life is about to take. Maybe the fact I'm figuratively pondering means I possess a drizzle of the poet in my soul. A good showrunner needs such drizzle in the ole creative toolbox.

I'll leave poetic musings to Midas Lear and his three red-headed daughters. Rubata, Glissanda, and Chorda Lear will be my trio of responsibilities when I step into the executive producer spot on their reality TV show, *Kickin' It With Midas,* after we shoot tonight's season finale. I'm primed to step up my creative splash on the Golden Pipes Network.

I emerge from clusters of crimson columbine and lilac to the roar of an approaching engine. Desmond's vintage red Ferrari 360 Modena zips around the corner, screeching to a stop inches from my toes.

"Shit, Adair. You nearly ended up on my windshield."

The timeliness of his comment is not lost on me. I decline to share deets of my Viking butterfly funeral. "Cooling my jets for a sec by the water."

Des shakes his head. "Cooling your jets? My little brother, crowned prince of outdated idioms and clichés."

I celebrate and perpetuate the resurrection of sayings I've absorbed from the classic and not so classic movies and television programs I adore. More than one person has accused me of time traveling to the present from a black and white 1960s sitcom.

I tap a finger to my chin. "Are colorful phrases ever outdated?"

Rubata, the middle Lear sister, springs through the open pop top of the car. Her dyed cherry-red hair clashes with the Ferrari's paint. She raises her phone to grab a selfie with a green, white, and red striped bag. "Gelato. I gotta gelata," she sings and waves a handle bag stamped with the *Gelato Buono* logo.

I dive to catch the phone she tosses to me.

"Adair, get a shot of me with the gotta gelata and the car." Rubata holds the bag next to her cheek and puckers her lips. As I snap pictures, she flips her hair and kisses the bag. "Did you get the shot? Wait, switch to video of me singing *gotta gelata, gotta gelata*." Through the window, I catch her gold painted toenails dancing across Desmond's shoulder. "Oooo, Desi, feed me gelata. That'll look sexxxxy." Rubata opens her mouth and performs an indecent sweep of her tongue.

I pretend not to be uncomfortable with her overt sexuality. "You should be in hair and makeup, Rubata, not on a sugar run. And it's gelato, not gelata."

Lips matching the color of her hair, shoot a salty pout. "The sesh will wait for me, Mr. Gelato Buzzkill. I'm the star."

"We're live tonight," I remind her.

"Whatever. X-O, doll." She slides down inside the two-seater with a squeal when her generous bust catches the rim of the pop top.

Desmond holds out his hand for Rubata's cell. "This is my girl's golden day, so save your shade, Little Brother." He revs the engine. "You do understand what I mean by shade, or is that term too hip for your grandpa vernacular?" Rubata slides an arm across Desmond's shoulders and leans close to stick her tongue in his ear. A smile brightens his face as he shivers. I back away to avoid squashed toes as they fly up the hill.

Rubata is two hundred percent flirt. My fear is she'll pull a kissy move on Des outside the grounds of the Waterfall Palace that'll supply Paparazzi fodder for weeks. It's time for a brotherly chat about discretion when galivanting one-on-one with a Lear sister. His *little brother* snark will be topic number two. Desmond dismisses the moniker as brotherly banter, but it hits a clunker note with me. Younger brother or not, I'm a blink away from being his boss.

Irritation with Des fades as I drive through the stone tunnel next to the Waterfall Palace that leads to sound stages, Golden Pipes's recording studios, and business offices. I've grown a thick skin when it comes to my brother's arrogance and verbal jabs. Dude hasn't had an easy go of it. Our father took his sweet time even acknowledging Des. I'm sketchy on the deets, but apparently, Desmond's mother pulled shady shit with threats against my mother and I. Restraining orders were involved, and Hamilton Holiday tapped out on his older son. Dad and Des didn't click until adult Des initiated contact. I do want my brother to feel *Kickin' It With Midas* is a family business. He is talented, and when I'm in charge, I don't plan to take his skill set for granted.

I pull into my producer spot and watch Desmond's production

assistant, Matty, wedge the gelato bag under his arm while making a pathetic attempt to stretch a cloth cover over the Ferrari.

"Matty, let me take the..." I raise my arms to the sky and add boom to my voice. "Delectable nectar of the gods off your hands."

He laughs at me. "Adair, you're a character in search of a sitcom."

I grab the bag from him. "A character in search of a sitcom... Genius! I love that idea." I sling an arm over his shoulder, and the car cover slips from his grasp. "Write something up. I imagine a vibe like Pirandello's play *Six Characters in Search of an Author*, but hilarity will ensue."

"I wasn't pitching."

"Always pitch. Being a P.A. is not an end game."

Matty blushes and gives the Ferrari cover his full attention for half a second before turning to me. "Rubata wants one scoop of rum and one scoop of chunky chocolate delivered to her dressing room. Not in the same bowl. They can't touch."

I swing the bag. "I'll sic craft service on her, and Matty, when you are ready to pitch, I'm all ears."

The sound stage buzzes with the music of anticipation. Cameras, cables, monster-size lights overhead, audience bleachers —damn, I love it all. I could live on a sound stage with its unfinished walls and million possibilities. When it's not amped up for a show the way it is tonight, the place still has a presence. The ghosts of performances past linger. A sound stage is never empty, even when it's empty.

I duck into the kitchen and surrender the gelato with Rubata's directive to our craft service team. Halfway across the stage to the control booth, a meaty forearm lands on my shoulders. I'm flanked by two near giants. The owner of the forearm, Midas Lear, booms his welcome. "Ladies and gentlemen, the luckiest son-of-a-bitch on the planet, Mr. Adair Holliday!"

Hamilton Holliday, my father, gives a slow clap. "Man of the hour."

Both men are over six feet and missed their calling as linebackers. The similarities end there. Late into his sixties, Midas still boasts a crown of red-gold curls and a smile as broad as a half-moon. My father is pure silver fox, complete with the sly and hungry outlook that made him a success in the insanely competitive entertainment industry. They came up together in the music biz ranks, Midas in the spotlight and Dad behind the scenes.

"I beg to differ." I bow to Midas. "The newest Rockin' and Rollin' Pantheon inductee deserves that honor."

Midas returns the bow with a sweep of his arm, then with uncharacteristic reverence, rests his palm on the cover of a large glass case in the middle of the throne room set that holds the real star of tonight's show, the Golden Guitar. "Our parting is imminent, dear old friend."

He spins to smack me on the back. "You're a lucky bastard, Adair, to deal with my three beauties instead of this old buzzard." Lear pounds a fist to his chest.

Over Midas's shoulder, Desmond stands in the shadow of a fabricated turret at the edge of the set, his expression tense. Damn. He hates the word bastard.

I wave him over. "Join us, Des."

He approaches, stiff as a toy soldier come to life. Desmond cultivates the vibe of being slick and tough-skinned, but there are more places than he admits where arrows pierce his armor. The unwanted bastard issue is the cruelest sting.

Midas aims a thick finger my way. "Remember, Adair, Golden Pipes's number one goal is to beat the shit out of Rampion Records." He spreads his arms wide. "If I could mount a cannon on the top of my Waterfall Palace, I'd blast Gothel's fucking Rampion Records Tower to dust."

"I believe Justin Time and Zeli took care of that for you," I say.

Midas scowls. "Those two talented shitiots should be under contract to me. They have no clue how ruthless the music business can be."

I beg to differ. Justin and Zeli survived Gothel, the essence of ruthlessness.

Midas snorts. "At least I stuck it to Gothel one last time with overpriced rights to their precious *Summer Number One* hit, *Just in Time*."

Did he, though? *Just in Time* went viral and platinum after Rampion's annual pro-am singing competition last summer. Once they took the helm of Rampion Records, Zeli and Justin turned the *Summer Number One* contest into a weekly television show watched by everyone with a pulse on the planet. Their current revenue makes Midas's grudge victory for the song look like fool's gold.

Midas drops a lion paw on my shoulder. "With you handling the *Kickin' It With Midas* franchise and me kicking asses full-time at the record label where I belong, we'll bitch slap Rampion back into second place."

I swear Midas's eyes glow when his competitive side is online. He loves kicking asses almost as much as he enjoys getting his own ass kissed. "Yes, my liege," I say with a salute. Behind me, Desmond stifles a grunt.

"Keep this show's hot damn magic golden, Adair," says Midas. The formidable force of nature struts away to bark orders and profanity at his personal entourage.

"I predict ninety percent less explicit language bleeps with Midas off the show, eh Hamilton," says Desmond with a forced laugh. It hits me as sad he addresses our father by his first name instead of Dad.

Dad responds with a percussive *humph* and then jerks his chin toward the far end of the studio and the control booth. "Let's walk and talk, Adair."

Before I catch up with Dad's long-legged stride, I glance at my brother. The lost expression in his eyes is hard to take. Hamilton Holliday can be a real ass. "He means you, too, Des."

Desmond blows by me to take a place at Dad's side. Looking between the two, it strikes me how one is a near perfect copy of the other. Desmond is leaner but matches our father in the intensity of his chocolate gaze and sharp features. His licorice black hair echoes the shape and flow of Dad's silver-gray waves. I inherited my mother's roundish features and cinnamon curls.

Dad flicks a finger between Desmond and me. "Adair, bring Desmond up to speed on the rebrand for next season ASAP."

Des looks sucker punched. "Rebrand? You've already made decisions?" He's pissed. Our father has a knack for setting Des off. I'd like to believe he doesn't do it on purpose. Sometimes, I wonder. We Hollidays could stand improvement as a family.

"Of course, I did," huffs Dad. "I needed to guarantee a fresh direction for the show before I step down. I'm not going to leave a flaming shit brick on Adair's porch and walk away."

I share Desmond's bristle at Dad's inability to take his hands off the controls. In mere hours, *Kickin' It* will be my baby. The next incarnation of our show is mine to shape. It's time for Hamilton Holliday to cut the cord and make room for my perspective.

I walk next to my brother. "Let's get through tonight, Des, and tomorrow, I'll deal you in on Hamilton's new vision for the show."

Desmond scowls. "Oh, do make me wait, Adair."

I raise a hand. "Nothing is in cement, but here's the gist. I continue to steer Chorda's story line as well as running the overall ship. You'll have exclusive producer credit on both Rubata and Glissanda's segments."

His scowl grows barbs. "Second string."

I shake my head. "That's not the intent."

Hamilton ignores the rising tension. "Even with the app expansion, our numbers, especially on streaming, still trail Rampion. Adair, stoke the bonfire on the Golden Pipes app. People are posting their *Sing with the Lears*, *Walk the Carpet like Rubata and Glissanda*, and *Be Your Own Statue of Gold* pics and videos all over social media. Brainstorm more interactives along those lines."

I whirl my hands with manic energy. "Midas plans to lure smaller labels under the Golden Pipes umbrella with promises of creating new shows for them. The app has the potential to explode with that additional material for tie-ins."

Dad fans an arm in the direction of the throne room set where a crew staples plastic vines along cracks in faux stone walls. "Remember, the key is never let *Kickin' It* grow stale. This show is the cash cow. Fatten her up, don't let her go dry."

I open my mouth to answer. Desmond pre-empts me. "Why plan anything for next season before we know tonight's outcome? The renaissance for *Kickin' It* depends on whoever inherits Midas's Golden Guitar in the choosing ceremony tonight. That sister gets the brighter spotlight, and the other two become backup."

Our father slows. "Adair and I sketched out contingencies, but I think we all know which way tonight will go." His fingers tap against his thigh while his gaze drifts up to the catwalks. "When Chorda carries the show's focus, she'll have to shed her low-key artist image and hit a few Midas level notes of bombast."

I issue a non-committal grunt. Dad speaks of featuring Chorda as if she's fully on board for the upgrade. Far from it. A low-key artist is exactly how she defines her image, one who stresses that hiding behind a lens disconnects her from fans. Next step in her mind is not increased exposure on *Kickin' It*, but a live tour away from her constant *camera in the face* existence.

I know this as her confidant not her producer. My confidant side gets it. My producer side loses sleep over it. Per her wishes, I promised to keep mention of a tour and sabbatical from the show under wraps until she's ready to discuss details with her creative team. Tonight's outcome may force the issue. I'm confident that together, Chorda and I will find mutually agreeable middle ground.

The stage manager darts over to our walk and talk to grab Dad. While the pair deals with the latest issue, Desmond leans in, his voice tinged with a growl. "There's no guarantee the guitar will go to Chorda." He punctuates words like upper cuts, putting me on the defensive.

I strike back. "Chorda is the clear favorite."

Does Desmond truly favor one of the older Lear sisters to Chorda? Rubata's kiss to Desmond in the Ferrari flashes through my mind. Is there something legit between them? I shake it off. Rubata kisses everyone, even me.

"Face it, Des, Chorda is the true musician. She sings and composes. Everyone expects the Golden Guitar to be drawn to her gifts. The other two perform beautifully, but they don't write music."

Desmond laughs. "Someone's buying into the myth the guitar chooses who it will play for." He waves me off. "This mystical choosing ceremony is Midas's ruse for ratings—no magic involved."

"Careful, Desmond." Simmering anger in our father's voice ends the discussion as he reengages with us. "The Lears believe what they believe. Don't question them."

"Of course," says Desmond, his face stained ten shades of red. "I'd never challenge a Lear."

Our father checks his watch. "We go in an hour."

While Dad heads for the booth, Desmond takes deep breaths through gritted teeth. "Did your pal, Chorda, finally snow you into believing the sisters' fantasy about being Irish witches, and that Midas controls the destiny of a magical guitar?"

Desmond's just weathered Dad's typical lack of warm fuzzies toward him. Now is not the time to let him bait me into an argument. "It's not my place to question personal narratives. What I do buy is the version of the truth fans will believe when the guitar goes to Chorda."

Desmond raises fists, no longer tempering himself in our father's absence. "I hate to burst your kumbaya bubble, Adair. Midas's magical bullshit is about boosting his image, Rubata's cosmetics, and Glissanda's clothing line."

"Hey! We're making good television here, not just advertisements." I jab a finger at him. "You're part of that 'making good television'."

True, the more popular the show, the better for both Lear and

Holliday personal enterprises. Who gives a rat-a-tat crap if the Lear sisters fancy themselves witches and think Midas's Golden Guitar is imbued with mystical powers or not? It doesn't matter if I believe it. The Lears do, and our audience buys it.

Desmond's shoulders sag. "At least someone thinks so." He runs a hand through his hair in a move identical to our father. "It's a real kick in the ass to be cut out of you and Hamilton's strategy session for *Kickin' It's* future."

"Don't take it to heart. Chalk the move up to Dad's ego. Consider all decisions tentative for now. Your input matters to me, Des."

Desmond's eyes brighten, and he stands straighter. "Good to know." He gives me a brotherly thump on the shoulder. "Thanks for that, Adair." He tugs on his suit coat, and with dare I say—a grateful smile—heads for the booth.

I've had a glass-half-full to Desmond's glass-half-empty life. It'll soon be in my power to boost his career, maybe a top producing spot on one of our new shows as well as his segments on *Kickin' It*. His work speaks for itself. Chorda is still the show's favorite, but under Desmond's savvy and creative eye on Rubata's and Glissanda's segments, their likeability factor has soared. I won't discount him the way our father does. It's important the rest of the world sees in Des what I see.

Chorda's voiceover fills the studio with the sound check. She and I co-wrote the updated narrative of the Golden Guitar myth for tonight's season finale. The youngest Lear sister spins the tale with a reverence that could convince the most stalwart skeptic the legend is absolute truth. We've shared a thousand secrets growing up. Chorda's never strayed from her belief in the family legacy of the guitar.

My mouth sneaks into a smile. The sound of Chorda's voice and the dance of her perfect lips when she sings, or speaks, or sighs are what I believe in. The depth of my appreciation for the alluring woman Chorda has become is one secret I plan to keep to myself.

2

WIND FROM THE EAST

I'M AN UNWILLING PARTICIPANT IN A GAME OF HIDE AND SEEK.
Neither Desmond nor the Lear sisters are here, and our warm-up
band is halfway through their set to rev up the studio audience. We
go live in forty-five minutes. The three starlets of the show
managed to give my battalion of production assistants the slip.

I leave the sound stage, jog across the parking lot and through
the gate to the Waterfall Palace's rear entrance.

The security guard waves. "Hey, Adair."

"Hey, Grav. Are the sisters inside?"

The ex-Marine and drinking buddy of Midas walkies his staff.
There's a chorus of nos and one "try the garden."

"I'll send someone down there," says Grav.

"I got it," I say and head along the winding pathway to the series
of terraced gardens behind the mansion. The sisters' lives change
tonight, so stealing a few pre-show moments together makes sense.
The Golden Guitar will only play for the destined successor to
Midas's fame and musical accomplishments. To use Desmond's
term, the other two will be relegated to second string.

The Lears gravitate to their tiered gardens. The landscaping boasts trees and flowers from their native Ireland back when they were the O'Leary family.

I wish there was some comfort I could give to make the choosing ceremony easier for the Lear women. What I can offer is my creative contribution as our generation rises together into the new phase of *Kickin It*.

I wind along the pathway down through each terrace. There's no sign of a single redhead. Where the hell are they? At the bottom of the third level, I stop. Before me stand two massive, upright stones with a capstone balanced on top, a dolmen. Midas calls the formation his portal to the Sidhe, the otherworld of Irish folklore. It's a forbidden gate. Midas brought me down here when I was a kid and warned me about the shit that could happen if I crossed through. Even now, the sight of it under the first sliver of a waxing moon gives me shivers.

I'm about to turn back when I hear the murmur of female voices below. There's a faint yellow flicker on the underside of the dolmen's capstone. What if Midas is right, and a single step through his off-limits gate zaps me into an immortal kingdom from faerie stories?

Desmond would call me a chicken shitiot and walk right through the portal.

One voice rises above the rest in a chant, first in Irish and then in English. "Come to us, beloved Bríg. We bear you gifts of reverence and love."

Chorda.

It's eerie how similar the sisters' speaking voices are. Yet, when they sing, their voices are as different as doves to a lion.

The other two join Chorda. "A trio of steadfast hearts welcome you to our circle."

Yep howdy, all three sisters are down there. There's no choice but to wrangle them to set. I close my eyes, step through the dolmen, and smack into a tree.

"Shi–"

I bite off the curse as the sisters' voices continue to fill the night. I'm in the same world in front of the same oak tree that's always been on the other side of the portal. The path curves around the tree, which is not in a freakin' fairyland.

I've got a few minutes to spare before I break up the party.

They continue. "Strengthen our sisterly bond so we may withstand the challenges of this night."

I wipe bark crumbles from my hair and peek around the trunk. The sight snaps my eyes wide.

At the bottom of a steep path, a flat terrace, larger than the garden levels above, stretches wide. A circle of seven rectangular stones, each about the size of a fire hydrant, fills the space. Within the circle, I make out the faint outline of a yellow triangle made of what appears to be flower petals. Each sister stands at one of its three points, facing inward. In the center is a low stone table with a line of green candles along one edge and white ones on the other. A small glass bowl is positioned between the dual highways of candles. At its bottom, a handful of lumpy green rocks reflect candlelight.

The sisters turn to the east and chant to the willow centered there on the terrace. They finish and turn to the rowan tree situated on the north side. I see what's coming and duck behind the oak as they focus on the western tree.

"Mighty hawthorn, we ask for your spiritual energy, protection, and hope to light our way."

I attempt to blend with the trunk, hoping not to be caught snooping when they turn my way. The sisters face the oak and intone a plea for confidence, optimism, and the ability to cope with difficulty. Stillness does not meet the quiet that follows. Instead, wind howls in from the east and raises goose bumps on my arms. This time of night, a steady onshore breeze from the Pacific usually dominates the air, not an odd microburst from the opposite direction. The rogue wind tears straight through my clothes, piercing my skin to the center of my bones.

My heart flip flops as I peer around the trunk. The sisters once again face the middle of their triangle configuration. The wind gains strength to whip Rubata's cherry red, Glissanda's strawberry blonde, and Chorda's auburn locks toward the west. The blow feels wild enough to rip every strand from their heads.

As if on command, the sisters' hair begins to undulate in perfect synchronicity, three harmonies underscoring a silent melody line. My heart beats in rhythm to match the up and down repetitions of the movement. Each subsequent peak of their wind-driven locks rises higher until all three crest in a trio of arcs pointing to the sky. I hold my breath, waiting for their hair to drop back to their shoulders. Every strand remains suspended in mid-air. Before me is a version of the Hokusai woodblock print of *The Wave* come to life. We're in the thrall of a song I should know but can't remember.

A final, powerful gust rages through the garden. The dance of the triple red tresses comes to its end and nearly knocks the three women off their feet. Candles fall and go out, except the centermost white pillar. An ear-splitting whistle of wind pierces the air, then calm returns to the terrace as the Lear sisters catch their balance.

A strand of gold about two-fingers thick in Chorda's auburn hair catches the candlelight and flickers. The story goes, when she was a baby, Midas held her in his arms to play a lullaby. A string from his Golden Guitar snapped and tangled in Chorda's hair. Ever since, the golden streak has been part of her mane.

I've always believed the story was hooey, a publicity ploy. It's more likely the golden strand is Chorda's birthmark like a guy I knew in grad school who had a patch of white at the crown of his dark brown mop. The white spot never left no matter how short he cut his hair.

My gaze locks on Chorda. The golden strand radiates a faint glow as if a low level electric current runs through it and bathes her features in muted saffron. She juts her chin to the sky, daring the elements to challenge her. Her portrait of beauty and strength overwhelms me. How can I do her true presence justice on a reality television show? My world tilts, and the oak steadies me.

A knot of anxiety throbs in my chest. I try to write it off as nerves about the sisters' tardiness and tonight's show, but weird energy surrounds me. Midas's warnings about the dolmen might technically be a lie, but I did witness something after walking through its passage that was none of my business.

These sisters believe they are witches. Dialing up a good luck ritual isn't that out there for a Lear. So, the wind kicked up when they chanted words. Wind can kick up any time in L.A.

The priority here is getting the three in studio, but I'm too entranced to call out. Below me, the sisters walk a circle from stone to stone, joining their voices in an atonal hum. They stop at each stunted pillar in turn to press a palm to its top. All three seem know the exact beats of when to move and when to pause. It's a synergy born of family connection and beliefs.

I slink around the tree and away from the ritual ground and try to land on whether their trancelike movement under a sliver of moonlight is ethereal or creepy.

I've never experienced such a bond with my own scattered family. At times, I question if we Hollidays even deserve the title of family. My father, mother, half-brother, and I are four separate entities, each in their own orbits that occasionally overlap. I feel as if I'm ignorant to the essential components of what family is supposed to be.

I give my head a shake to snap out of my own issues to appreciate the positive takeaway here. Chorda is in the thick of it with her sisters, asking trees for sisterly bonds. That reads to me as a renewed commitment to the show, not a loophole to escape.

Casual chatter erupts as Rubata and Glissanda near the oak. They're too close for me to bolt away unnoticed, so I stay put. Once they pass, I'll cut over and climb terraces to beat the sisters to higher ground and hail them. I'm such a shitiot. If I'd hollered for the sisters when I first hit the top of the gardens, then I wouldn't be in this sitch.

"Put the candles and malachite in the trunk, Chorda," yells Glissanda from a yard away, her face blue in a cell phone's light.

"I'll clean up after the show. I don't want to be late," Chorda calls from below.

"Oooooo, I'll be late for Daddy's partay," whines Rubata for what she assumes are Glissanda's ears only as she slides a finger over her own phone screen.

"Oooooo, he might pluck the golden hairs from my head," says Glissanda, matching her sister's low, mocking tone.

My face heats at their diss of Chorda. I detest the way the pair playoff their mean girl tendencies as jokes. In the last few years, they've ganged up more often against Chorda. Any time I bring up how much it bothers me, she shuts me down. According to Chor, unsavvy male that I am doesn't "get" how sisterhood works. She insists they'd die for each other, and minor bickering means nothing.

Rubata's voice could sour sugar as she shoves her phone in Glissanda's face. "Look, Chorda is still the fave." She presses a fist to puffy lips. "I'm sick of everyone saying the guitar will play for Chorda because of her stupid golden stripe."

Glissanda shoots a poison dart look down to Chorda and chants. "Da's favorite. Da's favorite. Next person who throws that in our faces will get their eyes plucked out."

I hear Rubata's influence in the ugly rumble of Glissanda's threat. Her public face is 'kissy, kissy, love, love, my family is everything, and buy my new line of whatever sexy clothing is in season'. Hints of viciousness in the eldest Lear sister would be a huge fan turn-off. We do everything possible to cultivate her image as the benevolent and wise older sis while Rubata is painted as edgy with a dash of generous.

Tonight, I see none of their benevolence or generosity, just thorns. It drives me bonkers not to leap out of hiding and pour water to douse their bitter flames. My opinions need to stay on lockdown. It's my duty to make every sister shine no matter how rough and scratchy they are in real life.

Down below, Chorda, ever the pleaser, scurries to gather ritual goodies off the stone table and plop them into a wooden chest near the hawthorn tree. The woman is a fan favorite by virtue of being herself. Her natural sweetness and choice to see the best in others are what drive her popularity. As her producer, I'll help her see how that strengthens, not weakens, her bond with fans.

Rubata sniffs. "Desmond says there's no way Chorda will win. She's too *meh*."

I sink teeth into my bottom lip.

They reach the oak without a glance my way. Rubata tosses a hank of cherry hair over her shoulder as she speaks. "You got that right, honey. Desmond said his money's on me."

Glissanda stops next to my hiding spot.

"Desmond doesn't know shit," says Glissanda. "He wants to get into your yoga pants." She grabs Rubata by the shoulders and studies her face.

Rubata squirms.

"Ha!" squeals Glissanda, delighted with her catch. "You and Desmond have bumped nasties."

Damn it, Desmond. If Rubata slaps him with harassment, brother or not, I will fire him.

Rubata lifts a handful Glissanda's hair and lets it fall in sections. "Guess he got tired of strawberry blonde."

Holy crap, Desmond's messed with both sisters?

Glissanda bats Rubata's hand away. "Stop fishing, Sister. She strikes a chest-and-ass-out pose. "And point of factoid, no one gets tired of this." Glissanda smacks her own ass.

Rubata wiggles her surgically enhanced behind to bump her sister's. "Maybe strawberry blonde is Adair's favorite flavor."

"Puh-leeze," says Glissanda, finger-combing hair back into place. "I don't do goofy." They giggle at my expense.

Rubata wiggles a pinkie below her waist. "And I don't do anything less than thock."

Glissanda laughs, copying Rubata's insult to my manly attribute but then switches to her thumb. "Skinny can hide a nice package." They share a laugh at my expense. Glissanda flicks her wrist. "I suppose we have to kiss up to Adair when he takes over the show from Hamilton."

Rubata executes a full body roll, shaking off the suggestion. "Puh-leeze, back atcha. Mr. Goof is a pushover. He won't give us trouble."

Goofy, a pushover, and questionable girth, is it? My overheated face probably glows as bright as Chorda's golden streak. I stretch my collar for more air. I'd love to jump out and advise them on the perils of speculation regarding their new boss's anatomy.

I practice restraint. Point one: they're not wrong about the goofy. Although I prefer approachably charming. Point two: I don't give a flip over who the Lear sisters invite under their covers unless it will adversely affect the show. Point three: This pair will never get a gander at my respectably ample manhood.

I run my tongue over my bottom lip. I'm a liar. There is one Lear sister I wish would keep a vacancy in her bed. It's a shitiotic wish. Chorda considers me a bud and on-call sounding board to analyze her parade of short-lived boyfriends. Listening to her relationship woes is never fun, but she's done the same for me. That's what friends do.

The sisters check on Chorda down in the circle. Glissanda runs a finger over the small tattoo of a gold guitar on Rubata's upper arm. "Did Bríg put a chill on our victory spell during the ritual?"

Rubata claps a hand over the tattoo. "Nope. My tat was toasty the whole time. Yours?"

Glissanda lifts her foot and a golden cuff on her ankle with a guitar etched into its surface peeks from under her gown. "My personal summer sun kept shining. Your tat and my cuff would be icy if Bríg screwed with the spell. This is our night." She fusses with the shoulder of her glittery, diaphanous gown. "Even so..." Her gaze locks on the ritual table. "What if the malachite turns against us? You know that crystal can go either way."

Rubata squeezes Glissanda's cheeks between her fingers, making her collagen puffed lips even more ducky. "You worry too much, bee-ach. Our goddess, Mórrigán, gave every sign she'd tip the malachite's power in our direction at Da's ceremony."

Glissanda slaps Rubata's hand away. "Don't hate on me for being caush."

"Over-caush. Mórrigán lit our talismans when we summoned her last night, and they're still charged. A goddess guarantee— doesn't get more hella perf than that. We can't lose." Rubata swipes a finger across Glissanda's forehead. "Ditch the stress, doll. You'll crinkle with wrinkles."

Glissanda grabs Rubata's right hand where a gold ring with a green and black, oval stone sits on her finger. She lifts her own right hand with an identical ring and taps it to her sister's. "Did you give Chorda her malachite ring?"

Rubata's lips curl into a predatory smile as she sing-songs. "For you, Chor Chor. Matching rings as bling to cling around our zingy sister thing."

Glissanda frowns. "Tell me you didn't bust out that rap when you gave her the ring."

Rubata twists her ring. "I could have, but I chose vanilla verbiage. 'These rings represent our unbreakable sisterly bond. They'll remind us to focus on the strength we share no matter what happens tonight.'" She flips her hair. "I may have promised a binding spell. Sisterhood trumps Golden Guitars, blah, blah."

Glissanda shivers. "Chorda will believe the ring bond, but what if Bríg senses it's a ruse?"

Rubata waves her off. "Chill, babe. The rings and ritual thing tonight scream Team B. That goody goody goddess will lap up our fauxvotion. She'll never know she's lost her influence over us or our powers."

Glissanda glances at Chorda and shakes her head. "Itty bitty sissy is clueless we've pledged to our true goddess and left Bríg to her."

"Best decision we ever made," says Rubata. She grabs Glissanda's wrists. "This is war, and the Golden Guitar is victory. Let Bríg and Chorda spout pastoral prophesies. The Mórrigán's power will come through and give us the guitar."

Their talk of spells, talismans, and goddesses prickles my skin with the sensation I'm being watched, and not by a Lear sister.

Glissanda dots a finger to her bottom lip. "Still, Chorda's hair glow freaks me."

Rubata grunts. Her expression is so volatile, I expect her to spit in the dirt. "It did blaze like a fucking lighthouse."

Glissanda kisses the corner of Rubata's lips. "Faith, sister. The Mórrigán will be with us tonight."

Rubata adjusts her breasts higher in the gown. "I'm still going to put a big ass carnelian stone in my bra. A little extra luck never hurts."

"I'll wear clear quartz crystal in mine."

"May the luckiest boobs win," says Rubata.

"You or me, Sister, it doesn't matter. We share the spotlight fifty-fifty."

Rubata links arm with Glissanda. "And the spoils. After tonight, the Golden Guitar will do the work. We sing what it writes and look hot."

What it writes? They seriously believe they'll look at the instrument and demand it makes music. Is that what it does for Midas? I shake off the insane notion.

Rubata's phone pings. She checks it, then spins so her gown wraps around her waist. "Sweet. I'm over ten K hits on my pre-show post."

I'm afraid her tibia is going to snap twirling in stilt-high stilettos on the path and make a mental note to up injury insurance on her.

Glissanda starts madly texting. "Not for long, doll." She finger-punches her screen. "Oh, yeah. My Golden Guitar yoga pants giveaway will kick your social media ass."

"So says you." Rubata waves her phone above her head and wobbles on her ridiculous shoes. "Golden Guitar bronzer giveaway is live." She *pffts* at Glissanda. "And what's up with the new shiny shit you're using for yoga pants? It makes my lady parts sweat."

The two stroll up the path, dueling with their phones.

I burn in the wake of their toxicity and rest my forehead against the tree for quick self-talk. Rubata and Glissanda have their own followings and loyal fans. Merchandising and marketing benefit their clothing and make-up lines and, therefore, the show. They are an integral part of *Kickin' It's* success. Dropping them in the middle of a forest without a map is not an option.

I jump when the phone vibrates in my pocket. As silently as possible, I press it to my ear. It's my father with the inevitable backing track of Midas running through every expletive in English and Irish.

"Be there in a jiff," I whisper and end the call.

Something slides across my neck and sends a jolt through my heart.

Chorda Lear digs her chin into the hollow between my neck and shoulder. "Gotcha."

3

THE FAVORITE

PETALS TICKLE MY EAR. I SNATCH THE SUNFLOWER FROM CHORDA'S hand and beat it against my heart. "Holy jeez, Chorda. I hope you've got defib paddles in your wooden storage box down below."

She slinks from behind the oak. Even though there's plenty of space to get around me, she brushes her body lightly against mine to move onto the path. My thoughts shift from rituals and stone circles to the points of contact between us.

Her golden streak hovers inches from my nose, its glow doused. I'm tempted to slide my fingers down its length. Is it warm? Would it give off a faint shock the way a metal doorknob does after you scuff your feet across the floor? What if it turned my finger gold? In all the years of our friendship, I've never been invited to touch her precious strand.

Chorda steals the sunflower back to bop me on the nose. "You are a sneak."

I bat it away. "I am a producer in search of my delinquent cast."

Chorda tilts her head to one side and studies me. "How shall I punish you for trespassing?" A sly smile sneaks across her face. "You deserve a *geas*, a very tricky spell that'll stick with you until I consider you properly chastised."

I grab her hand and tug her up the path. "Whatever *geas* thingy I deserve, hit me with it after the show."

She feigns shock and places a hand over her heart. "Don't play fast and loose with a *geas*, Adair. You just gave me permission to spell you." She *pffts*. "That flies in the face of your 'witchcraft is hooey' philosophy."

"*Geas* or spell me. Whatever gets you to set on time."

A V-wrinkle deepens between her eyebrows. "Have I ever been late for a show?"

I force a speedier pace and try to lighten the mood. "Will this *geas* make me grow a curly piggie tail?"

Chorda's loud exhale tells me my joke landed, thank goodness.

"I'd never give you pig's tail, Adair. Monkey or maybe donkey, nothing porcine."

We reach the top tier of gardens. "How kind of you."

Chorda slows and rests her hand on my arm. "Seriously, what did you think?"

"Of?"

"Of the ritual. I know you saw most of it. You must have questions."

"You saw me?"

"I felt you." She stills, waiting for my reaction.

This isn't the first time Chorda's tried to draw me into a conversation about her dedication to witchcraft. It's the perfect time to stick to my policy of topic avoidance. The trick is not to make her feel I'm blowing her off.

"It's okay to ask about the ritual even if you think it's hooey." She slows. "It matters you understand that part of me, Adair." We thread through parked cars. "You're entitled to your opinion, but it would be easier to stomach if it was an informed opinion."

"Can we do this later, Chor?"

She waves me off. "Only with the promise that if you choose to label my craft hooey, you'll do it to my face. I didn't appreciate hearing your opinion from Desmond."

Desmond is not my favorite person right now.

I take both her hands in mind. "I'm a jerk for calling your belief system hooey to you or anyone else. I grant you permission to double *geas* me for spying and smart-assery."

She squeezes my hands. "Sounds fair." Her gaze lingers on mine. "No questions?"

Chorda clearly wants me to understand what I saw in the garden. There's very little we don't share, but I've never been comfortable talking about her witchcraft. It's something that could turn into a real hot button issue in our friendship.

"About what you saw down in the grove? Adair, it's important for me to believe you are capable of having an open mind."

Her hands glide up my forearms, bringing her close enough for me to enjoy the heat flowing from her body. If she were any other person here under the thin curve of the moon, I'd slip my hands to the small of her back and ease our bodies together. For a follow-up, my lips would tap a tentative kiss on her temple. Next, my mouth would savor the soft skin in front of her ear. I'd linger longer and longer on each kiss, tasting the curve of her jaw until I reached the corner of her mouth. Her scent and the tiny breaths she'd take with each new approach would make me bolder. My lips would brush against hers, asking. If her answer was yes—

"Adair?"

I snap out of moonlight fantasy.

"If you won't ask anything, at least tell me how you felt when you watched us." Her limeade green eyes widen, waiting.

We've stared each other down countless times. It's different tonight, more intense. Is this a test? Fear grinds at my spine. If I fail, will our connection be damaged?

"It frightened me." My admission is a surprise. The sisters called to that Bríg person as if she'd pop into their midst. What if asking favors of trees had cracked the ground open and they'd fallen in? I may not understand or believe in otherworldly forces, but if I'm wrong, I imagine displeasing them isn't good. My skeptical mind can't dismiss the inexplicable sense of danger lingering in the air surrounding their ritual.

Her expression softens, so I continue. "The circle, the four trees, and the way you all sounded unnerved me. I felt there was a wall between us I couldn't cross. What if you needed me, and I couldn't get to you?"

Chorda throws herself into my arms. "Adair, I will never be out of reach."

I pull her to me. "That's all I need to understand right now."

"Are you open to hearing more?"

I can tell she held back from saying *finally* at the end of her question. We've been close for so long I hear her missing words as clearly as the ones she speaks.

"I'll always be open to you, Chorda." I kiss her cheek and step away. We are friends who've become colleagues. I need to tamp down inclinations in any alternate direction. I reach for the sound stage door.

"I'm going to hold you to your word," she says and taps my chin with her fingertip.

I've stepped in it now. Chorda took my *open to you* as the official go ahead she's tried to wangle out of me for years to hear her out about witchcraft. I gear up to backtrack but stop when her smile fades.

"Wait." She clutches the door handle.

"It's time to go in, C."

Chorda backs away from the door. "I'm afraid."

That's valid. The Golden Guitar choosing ceremony is about to change the dynamics of her life. The sisterhood of the three Lears may face a monumental rift, testing family bonds. They've known this day would come their whole lives. That doesn't mean it's welcome. I silently seethe over Rubata's and Glissanda's acid tongued comments about Chorda winning.

I always assumed the Golden Guitar would choose Chorda, or rather Midas would orchestrate the guitar to choose Chorda. She is his favorite. Personally, I wish he did a better job of hiding it. In truth, animosity between sisters lends drama to the show.

My vision, once Chorda claims the guitar, is to gently convince her to agree to a Chorda centric rebrand of *Kickin' it With Midas*. I'll continue to play into the influencer status of all three women with their music, make-up, and fashion. The show's push will be to propel Chorda into the spotlight she deserves instead of always taking a back seat to her sisters' media glory hogging. I don't want to kill her dreams of a tour. We could work it into her story line. There's room for compromise.

Chorda interrupts my mental flow. "I'm afraid it will choose me." Her shoulders sag. "The responsibility...the obligation..." She shakes her head. "I'll be the one trapped in a glass case, not the Golden Guitar."

I grip her shoulders. "I believe the Golden Guitar is supposed to choose you. You're the most dedicated artist of this Lear family generation. Your sisters have talent, but you dig deeper. Choosing you is the single destiny that makes sense for the Lear dynasty."

Chorda burrows against my collarbone, claiming a handful of my shirt. "There's no guarantee destiny ever makes sense."

I wrap my arms around her. "You won't be alone. I'll be right here."

She pulls away to meet my gaze. "Are you afraid of taking over for your father?"

I wasn't before she asked. I've been racing toward this goal. Chorda's question thrusts me into a beat of self-reflection. Once we step onto the sound stage, a new phase begins.

"I welcome the challenge."

"I asked if you are afraid."

Damn it. I'm petrified. How does this woman always know how to cut through my layers into the quivering mass of strawberry jelly at my center?

"Yes. Not afraid of moving forward. Afraid of not being everything to everyone I need to be."

She squeezes me tighter and whispers in my ear. "Let's be afraid together."

"Deal."

Chorda pushes me away with a laugh. "I've got it, the perfect *geas* for you." She raises a hand to the moon. "If Adair Holliday loses faith in his worth, may his best friend help him find it."

"And here I was worried a *geas* was a scary spell."

"For now, it's a cause-and-effect promise. I am capable of switching it to something scary. Like..." She nibbles on a fingernail, not hard enough to mar her sparkly polish. "If you ever make me cry, Glissanda gets to dress you for a year."

"Harsh. Stick to your first *geas*."

Chorda grabs my hands and shakes. "Done." She lets go and flings her arms wide. "Let's do this." With the confidence of a gladiator, Chorda Lear shoves open the door to the sound stage and marches in, her gait in perfect time with the band. She claps her hands above her head, grabbing the beat of the song.

I pause in the doorway to watch as she greets the audience. Perhaps I'm bewitched after all.

4

THE GOLDEN GUITAR

MIDAS LEAR SITS ON HIS THRONE, EVERY BIT THE MUSIC MOGUL. HE commands a room, or in this case, a castle set. His gilded perch is in the shape of a curved electric guitar. Diamond studded frets rise behind him, dazzling in the powerful beams of overhead stage lights. His bulky frame fills the royal chair. He stares directly into the camera, prepared to intone his lines with regal resonance.

Glissanda, Rubata, and Chorda stand in a line stage right of the platform holding the throne. The two older Lear sisters strike poses overflowing with attitude choreographed to feature their figures in the most flattering way, a hip cocked high here and a chin lowered just so to flash doe eyes to camera. Chorda projects zero affectation. She stands poised and dignified.

I watch from the floor, not the booth. This isn't the night to be one step removed.

The opening voiceover rumbles through the massive sound stage.

Across the River Boyne, two supplicants stood in judgment before the goddess. "It is I," said the first, "who, dear goddess, shall pledge you the worthiest gift." The first supplicant drove a fist into the water and cleaved the Boyne into two branches. "The might to part the course of a river will live within the flesh of those in my line who come after. I dedicate clan and kin to you, Oh Bríg."

The second supplicant said not a word but opened his mouth to gift the goddess with notes so sweet and pure, their kind had never before graced the Earth. Birds and beasts flowed in a great host to linger within the beauty of the song. The goddess kissed the singer, Michael O'Leary, on each cheek. Where her lips touched his skin, a golden glow lingered for a heartbeat before fading.

I'm so caught up in the familiar fable, Desmond's nudge startles me. He jerks a chin at the monitor. "Rubata overdid the collagen. Duck lips."

I switch my gaze between monitor and the middle Lear sister. "I don't see a difference. She looks gorgeous as usual." I lower my head to focus on the voiceover.

Desmond continues to interrupt. "Correction. She looks gorg," he says.

"What?"

"Gorg for gorgeous." He sneers. "She insists her *thing* is not finishing words. It's ridiculous."

Rubata's idiosyncrasies are a *discush* for another time. "I need to listen to the new intro."

Desmond huffs. "He who wrote it already knows what it says."

"Des, I promise we'll do drinks later at *Sunset and Vinyl* and talk." I leave him so I can concentrate on The Golden Guitar myth rework Chorda and I wrote. We read it aloud countless times, but material always sounds different live.

A guitar of purest gold was then passed from the goddess Bríg into the keeping of Michael O'Leary. "This vessel will bestow the gift of creativity to flow through one in each generation of your family. Accept it with my promise but take heed. Only the worthy, the truest spirit will wake the vessel. If the false-hearted dare touch the sacred instrument, they shall be gilded in sorrow evermore."

Kickin' It With Midas's catchy opening theme thunders through speakers. As the last note fades, Midas rises from his musical throne.

"Welcome to my Waterfall Palace, you sons of bitches."

The studio audience goes insane. They leap to their feet and call out to Midas.

He signals the fans to sit. "Asses in seats, people." The sisters wear tolerant expressions as they indulge their father's antics, each woman's look resonates with its own unique base note. Glissanda's holds the slightest hint of haughty and *get on with it*. Rubata manifests her signature loop of boredom over anything not focused on her. Chorda's face is the only one shining with genuine affection for the patriarch.

Midas struts down three steps, one for each daughter, and hits center stage. "It's time to put these old pipes out to pasture." He wiggles fingers near his throat.

The audience erupts with a chorus of "No" and various expletives, the chosen language of the monarch. One of the perks of Midas owning the Golden Pipes Network is his control of censorship. Between Midas and his fans, there is a constant barrage of curse bombs peppering every episode. If we bleeped per regular network standards and practices, we'd have to change the name of the show to *Bleepin' It With Midas*.

"I am fucking honored to be inducted into the Rockin' and Rollin' Pantheon." Midas Lear drops into a courtly bow for the audience, cueing another explosive reaction. Lights chase over the stage, setting the accents of metallic gold paint on the scenery aglow. He turns to his daughters and honors them with another bow. The sisters curtsy as rehearsed. As not rehearsed, Glissanda and Rubata skip over to Lear. Each chooses one of their father's cheeks to dot with a kiss.

Through the headset, I hear heated conversation in the booth and turn down the volume. Characters going off script is part of the show's DNA, but tonight is multi-camera live, a throwback to variety shows of the past with less wiggle room. It's the farewell Midas orchestrated for himself.

The two older Lear sisters vamp back to their places. Chorda never leaves her mark. She smiles and nods to her sisters. When I look to Midas, he's staring at her. My gut twists. Crap, he's waiting for her to gush over him, and she doesn't get it. Chorda is a rule-follower. She won't be spontaneous and buck the blocking from rehearsal.

I wave my arms, trying to get her attention. When her gaze flicks to me, I motion for her to give her da some love. She scrunches her face, trying to decipher what I'm telling her to do. It finally dawns on her, and she turns to Midas. It's too late. He steps forward, arms crossed. The man is clearly pissed. The entire exchange lasts a few beats before he continues.

"The moment has arrived for me to pass the legacy of the Golden Guitar to one of my beloved daughters."

Rubata and Glissanda clap their hands and run through a series of split-second poses intended to translate as sexy excitement. Chorda maintains poise, a loving smile for Midas on her lips.

Midas shakes a thick finger at the audience. "Make no mistake, I'll still be around. You shitiots can't get rid of me that easily. My energy will be on launching the Golden Pipes Record label into the exosphere. Listen up, all you bastards with dreams of "Kickin' it" in Musicland. Do you have "it," an indefinable talent to blast you onto the charts?" He points two fingers at his own eyes and then at the audience. "I'm looking for you."

Lear crosses to the glass case housing the Golden Guitar. The instrument is an exquisite piece of art in addition to being the vessel per the myth that brought Midas Lear—aka Michael O'Leary the umpteenth—fame and fortune. It's an unusual shape. The body of the guitar echoes the outline of a harp rather than the hourglass figure of acoustic guitars. Rising from the body is a standard neck with frets and tuning pegs of rose gold. The entire wooden body is gilded with a layer of 22 karat yellow-gold leaf stamped with a Florentine pattern. Its golden strings are a shade lighter than the body, the same color as the streak in Chorda's hair.

I listen for the cue to raise the lid of the glass case. Magic in five, four, three—

Midas waves his hands over the lid, and it not so magically pops open thanks to a hidden mechanism. He reaches inside with gentleness that's not part of his everyday operating system and lifts the Golden Guitar above his head. Like a priest blessing the sacramental host in communion, he offers it to his congregation of fans. Once again, they raise the roof of the sound stage.

"Today, I bequeath to you, one of my daughters, the greatest damn treasure of gold in all the world." He brings the guitar with him as he takes the throne. "In the scope of time, beauty lasts a day, but gold is forever. Whosoever presents me with the loveliest tribute song will take this vessel of fecking fame and fortune from my hand." Midas lays the guitar across his lap. Behind the throne, between two golden turrets, is an LED screen replica of a medieval tapestry that takes up the better part of center stage. It depicts three maidens kneeling, each on their own step, at the feet of a mighty king on a throne of gold. Replicas of tonight's tapestry images will splash across Glissanda's clothing line of show themed merch on the *Kickin' It* app for immediate purchase.

Since Midas refers to his mansion as a palace, I figured, why not go whole hog with the royalty trope. Besides Glissanda's show tie-in fashions, Rubata will launch a new line of lip glosses, lipsticks, or liners. I can't keep it straight. We branded her new products with upper crust monikers and catch phrases like *Kiss the Duke of Burgundy, Bend the Knee Blush,* and *Princely Purple.* I can taste the sweetness of my percentage.

The stage lights dim until the only bright spot is Midas and the three sisters who each perch on a step beneath the throne, copying their positions on the tapestry screen above. Their costumes are soon-to-be trending gowns from three top fashion style makers who contribute to Glissanda's line. Each unique fabric design pays homage to medieval motifs.

Midas reaches out a hand. "Glissanda, my first born."

Glissanda crosses to Lear's side and takes his hand. The woman moves as if she's walking the runaway at New York Fashion Week. The oldest Lear sister is her clothing brand personified. I picture girls everywhere dying their hair strawberry-blond and strutting down school hallways doing "the Glissanda."

The tapestry backdrop, my brainchild, uses stylized animation from a camera feed to mimic the action happening onstage.

Midas kisses her hand. "Whatcha got for me, babe?"

Glissanda snaps her fingers and holds her palm out flat. An extra in jester's motley prances on stage and hands her a mic. I wince at the cornball bit, but Midas insisted. A spotlight tinted rosy pink catches both Glissanda live and LED tapestry Glissanda. She drops chin to chest. Soft light picks up the chainmail watermark on her gown. When her music, a torchy ballad, plays, she slowly raises her gaze to the audience and begins to sing.

"Da, my da,
I do love you more than I have words
Da, my da,
You are dearer to me than eyesight"

Glissanda covers her eyes, something she never did in rehearsal. Great, the drama queen improvises.

"Space"

She pinwheels an arm. I think I hear her gown rip.

"Liberty"

Glissanda brings her palms together around the mic and bows.

"Beyond any riches or rarities."

Are you kidding me? She rubs fingers together in the sign for money. If she wanted choreography, we would gladly hire a pro. Her moves are laughable.

"I love you sooooooo much.
Da, my da."

Oh, Lord, she's trying to sound operatic. It's not working.

"*Da, my da.*

I love you as much as life itself.

Da, ah, ah, ah, ah..."

I squeeze my eyes shut. Please don't climb that scale one more rung. It will be the screech heard round the world.

"*I loooooove you more than fame, health, beauty, or honor.*"

One hand rests over her heart. Her voice slides between the same two notes. She beats a fist against her chest for emphasis as she musically lists each item. There are titters in the audience. Glissanda is so melodramatic, I expect a mustache twirling villain to come out and tie her to railroad tracks.

"*Da, my da,*

My love for you is too deep to keep speaking of it.

I shall keep it as a treasure in my heart.

Da, my daaaaaaaaaaaaa"

Glissanda bows. Lear claps for her, along with the audience. It's hard to miss the muffled bursts of laughter hiding within the applause. I join in, semi-stunned at her campy performance. The woman can sing. Why she attempted a bizarre hybrid of torch song and opera defies logic. Play to your strengths when the stakes are this high. Don't go off book. She tossed dignity out the window in her desperation to appeal to Midas. That can't be what the Golden Guitar is looking for.

I shake my head. Did I just give the guitar credit for the choosing? I'm off my nut.

Glissanda throws kisses to the bleachers and swirls back into place. Chorda sneaks a look in my direction. She doesn't give anything away but stares at me, widening her eyes for a split second. We share a moment of amusement at Glissanda's gushtastic tribute.

Midas calls on Rubata. Her heels clickety-clack in a rhythm as she approaches her father. Her gown is covered in a motif of daggers, each with a different ornate pattern on its hilt. Its off-the-shoulder design reveals the guitar tattoo I saw in the gardens. When Rubata gets close to Midas, she abandons the strict tempo of her strut for a balletic turn and sweeps into a bow. Lear kisses her hand as he did with Glissanda and motions to center stage. With a snap, Rubata stands and resumes her clickety-clack beat to where the mic lays in the center of the spotlight. She flicks a toe under the mic and sends it flying upwards. The audience erupts when she catches it and winks at them over her shoulder.

Rubata's song is upbeat with a hip hoppy/rap flavor. She's snappy jazz to Glissanda's moody.

"Hey there, Da,
I'm gonna match Miss Gliss
With a different riff
That's mighty spiff
What she said
Of your golden head
Is righteous stuff
But a little too puff
What I'm gonna say
Is up to snuff"

Rubata moves, snaps and clicks in an entertaining and catchy performance. People are dancing in their seats. I pat the beat of her song on my thigh. This is audience gold. I check in with Chorda. She twitches her shoulders, getting into it. Lear sits statue still except for one index finger tapping out the tune on the body of the Golden Guitar.

"I vow to ditch
Any joy or bliss
That doesn't hold
Your name in gold
There's just one thing
From you my king
To make me sing
Oh daddy, oh daddy, you're never a baddy, I've haddy my limit with

anyone callin' you shabby, my daddy, I'll stabby the rabbley who won't shut their gabbys, I'll shout like a cabby about
>*My daddy's love*
>*The rest can shove*
>*Off!"*

Her mic drop, swivel, and ass shake kills. She gifts the crowd with her signature pout. I may owe Desmond one. Her lips are on the ducky side, but it works for her persona. The stomping and cheers from the bleachers are an honest-to-goodness showstopper. The tapestry projection strobes as Rubata's image returns to its position. The stage manager flaps his arms, a human pelican ordering the audience to chill. The applause signs blink *quiet*. Booth chatter goes crackers as the director shouts for all hands to get our train back on the track.

Midas grins like a dragon who's doubled his hoard. I wave my arms to catch his attention and gesture to the audience. He places the Golden Guitar on the throne and descends the three steps to drop a kiss on the crown of the strawberry blond and cherry heads of his two oldest daughters. Our king takes center stage, and a mere slashing of his hands through the air quiets the audience.

I try to catch Chorda's eye to flash an encouraging smile. She stares at the floor. Her skin blanches swan white. Even from here, I see her shake.

Lear holds both arms out to his youngest child. The moment he does, the audience starts a quiet chant.

Chor-da

Chor-da

Their support brings the last sister to her feet. She tucks into her father's arms for comfort.

The scene breaks me a little. I know how much Chorda loves Midas. She's daddy's little girl.

I flash on a scene from our childhood repeated more times than I can count of Chor and Midas down in the gardens making music together, a pair of creative kindred spirits. She'd beg for time with him to learn what makes a song tick, and he always joyfully obliged. The other sisters never sought that deep musical connection with their father. They were content with singing. Now, Glissanda and Rubata overdo it to vie for Lear's attention from the favorite.

The Lear and Holliday families share that dynamic.

Lear and Chorda face one another center stage. Their mirror images waver across the LED tapestry. The scenery pulses almost imperceptibly with golden light. The big moment draws closer. Chorda will sing and Midas will lay the Golden Guitar in her arms. She'll caress its strings, and it will play for her. The legacy will be passed on. Chorda and I will spin her career into a mountain of gold.

Midas strokes the golden streak in his third daughter's hair. "And now, my joy, my sweet Chorda, what will you sing for your da?"

Does a fat tear drip down Chorda's cheek? Why? She practiced her tribute song to Midas with me as an audience. It's beautiful and shines with truth absent from her older sisters' ass-kissing ditties.

"Nothing," says Chorda.

Lear cocks his head to stare at her. "Nothing?"

A second tear chases the first. "Nothing."

Midas roars with laughter. "Darling, you kill me. Leave it to you to tease the old man. Nothing gets you nothing." He places the mic in Chorda's hand.

"Da, I agree with Glissanda. It's impossible to speak the depth of what's in my heart. I do love you in every way a child should love their father, but my sisters' sentiments feel overblown and insincere even for our show."

My eyes blink a mile a minute, my nervous tell, trying to digest Chorda's slam of her sisters and *Kickin' It With Midas*.

Midas stalks to his throne. He clutches the Golden Guitar to his chest. "Tread carefully, Chorda. Sing."

She sets the mic on the bottom step. "I can't. Da, you love me, and I love you. I honor you, but it's not true to say I love you more than my senses, or any other love I might find in my life. My song is simple, but without flattery. It's not what you want to hear."

"Sing me a fecking song, Chorda, or you'll never touch this guitar." Midas's face is on fire.

This is bad. So bad. There are gasps and murmurs from the audience. Their odds-on favorite for the Golden Guitar may as well have set the instrument on fire.

Desmond bumps my shoulder. "I told you passing on the guitar on was Midas's call."

Chorda throws her shoulders back. The interlocking lily pattern embroidered on her gown is as rigid as her stance. What is she doing to us? To the whole *Kickin' It With Midas* franchise? She must sing for Midas. It'll be a shitshow if the guitar goes to Glissanda or Rubata and it doesn't play. Or will it? Is Desmond right? Is the *Golden Guitar plays only for the worthy* a ruse?

I'm gut-twisting scared. There's no scenario short of Chorda giving in that can save the show.

"If a simple *I love you* isn't enough for you, Da, then keep your guitar."

Midas Lear shakes the Golden Guitar with such violence, I fear the instrument might snap. "I will not dishonor the gods of my forefathers and make a mockery of this ceremony. I swear by the sun, every phase of the moon, and the planets that rule our destiny, no one will claim the guitar tonight." He storms to the glass case and replaces the guitar inside.

Rubata and Glissanda glare at Chorda.

"From now on, Chorda Lear, I strip you of my name. You are no daughter of mine. Get the hell off my stage and out of my life, you ungrateful disappointment."

My heart crumbles at the sorrow on Chorda's face. "Give the guitar to one of my sisters, Da."

Lear charges Chorda but stops short. He shakes a fist. "It stays in the case until I decide how to fix this fucking outrage." Midas whirls in an arc, taking in all three sisters. "Anyone who dares to touch the Golden Guitar will pay the price."

As Chorda runs off stage, I catch the flare of her golden strand a second before it dims.

Desmond steps in front of me, a smirk on his face. "And scene."

5

EXIT STRATEGY

I MANAGE TO RALLY THE STUNNED STAFF AND GET THE STUDIO audience ushered out in record time before Midas truly erupts. At first, he sat on the throne with his head in his hands, wailing about serpent's teeth and thankless children. Now, he paces back and forth with my father at his heels, muttering God knows what with occasional bursts of "cluster fuck" and "shitshow."

A dozen people scream in my ear about viral social media and the mob gathering down at the gate of the Waterfall Palace. I put a P.A. on getting more police presence so shuttles with the audience can get out. I wish we could let those busses leave via the secret entrance at the rear of the property, but we'd have to blindfold a few hundred people. The crew is still on nail-biting standby. There's enough tension on the sound stage to spark a chain of aneurisms.

We can't salvage the Golden Guitar choosing ceremony tonight. Midas is too enraged to come up with an alternative ending fans will accept. Since this circus and its monkeys are about to be mine, I take it upon myself to call a wrap for tonight. Midas will never allow this fiasco to be his farewell to *Kickin' It With Midas*. Cameras will roll again soon.

When the hubbub subsides and everyone regroups, I'll closet with Dad and Midas to plan how we paddle out of these frothy rapids Chorda whipped up.

My worries over Chorda are on multiple levels. Her current state of mind must be brimming with pain. Her allegiance to the show after tonight is a big, fat, multi-colored gif of a question mark. An ugly thought claws me. My future success is directly tied to Chorda's involvement on the next incarnation of the show. It's tough not to be stressed out about the big picture. Of course, I don't want my friend falling apart, but I can't put the show in jeopardy either. I slap my priorities back into place. Chorda's well-being comes first.

I dash down a hallway off the sound stage to her dressing room. The trip proves fruitless. She's gone.

Matty, Desmond's P.A., rushes past me holding the gelato bag. I grab his sleeve.

"Do we have eyes on the sisters?"

"Rubata is at the palace. She needs her gelato ASAP."

"What about Glissanda and Chorda?"

Matty shrugs, and I let him go, envisioning Rubata's ire if her gelato melts. The security guard at the sound stage door is my next target. I bust out my official mover-shaker tone. "I'm looking for confirmation all three sisters made it to the palace?"

He murmurs into his headset and then nods. "Safe and sound."

The tension in my shoulders clicks down a notch. Chorda is free from the pandemonium. I don't want anyone bagging on her. The woman chose truth and the roof fell in. I hope she's okay. *Shitiot, Adair.* Of course, she's not okay.

Desmond jogs over to me. "Hamilton wants you on set."

It's time to grab a shovel and start cleaning up our shitshow.

Midas sits on his throne, cradling the Golden Guitar. The theatrical lights are dark. Work fluorescents light the space in their ghoulish tint. Lear's eyes are red and swollen. From angry tears or sorrow, there's no telling. I suspect it's a combo of both.

My father stands near his friend, looking ten years older than he did an hour ago. Associate producers, writers, production assistants, and other various crew members congregate nearby, awaiting a cue for next steps.

Our liege lord ignores everyone. He begins to hum one of the ballads that made him a standard at proms and weddings. The notes become words. Slowly, he adjusts the guitar and strums the strings.

Silence.

Midas stares at the instrument. He presses thick fingers into the frets and attempts to play.

Nothing.

He holds the harp-shaped body near his lips and whispers. Sitting tall, he positions the guitar once again. With a deep breath, he tries to belt out the song. His voice is clear and rich with its characteristic resonance.

The Golden Guitar is mute.

I brace for Midas to go off. Instead, he deflates. "What has she done to me?"

He can't put this on Chorda. She never touched the guitar. No one touches the guitar unless they take it from Midas's hand, or so the legend goes. The golden statue of an Irish chieftain next to a fountain near the Waterfall Palace's main entrance is rumored to be a poor, ancient fool who touched the Golden Guitar without permission.

To believe that's true, I'd have to buy into the Golden Guitar myth. Which I don't. Well, I didn't before Midas's guitar went dead. I'm on the verge of waffling. There must be some other explanation. Witchcraft and myths are storytelling, not truth telling.

Lear carries the guitar, his wounded comrade, and sets it into the case. He walks off set, out the door, and into the night. My father follows. No one speaks for an awkward stretch until Hamilton returns.

"We're finished here," he says. "Head out. Check email later tonight for tomorrow's schedule."

Everyone obeys until only we three Hollidays remain center stage. Dad puts a hand on my shoulder. "Midas doesn't want me to step down until the repercussions of tonight are behind us. I'm sorry, Adair." He rakes a hand through silver locks. "I don't know if I have enough left in me to deal with this."

I get Midas's need for Dad to handle the blowback from tonight. It's still a gut punch. Subtext: neither Lear nor my father think I'm capable of mopping up a sewage spill of this magnitude.

"Midas wants us to prolong the season with new segments featuring the sisters as filler. We'll take another shot at the choosing ceremony after his induction into the Rockin' and Rollin' Pantheon."

I'm afraid to ask my next question. "As in, all three sisters?"

The bags beneath my father's eyes darken. "Midas doesn't want to give Chorda"—He crooks fingers in air quotes—"a red ass second of coverage. He's steaming over the stunt she pulled."

White hot panic laces through me. "She didn't play things exactly his way, so he banishes her from the show? She doesn't want the damn guitar. End of story. Give it to one of the others." I lay a hand on my father's shoulder. "You know he'll talk to Chorda, and they'll make up. She's Daddy's little girl."

Desmond chimes in. "Not anymore." He waves his cell at us. "Rubata says Midas ordered Chorda out of the Waterfall Palace tonight."

"What!"

My father crumples onto the bottom step of the set. "It's true. I convinced him to let her relocate to the Malibu house."

I rip off my headset. "Excluding Chorda is not in the best interest of the show. She's the favorite. Our audience will insist on knowing the follow-up to her—"

"Defiance," says Desmond.

He's right. Potential fallout sickens me. No one openly defies

Midas Lear without scars, not even his daughters. Rubata and Glissanda may whine and cajole, but they don't oppose. Tonight's fiasco could tarnish my golden future, along with Chorda's.

Desmond steps up. "I can handle forward motion here in studio to produce Glissanda's and Rubata's filler segments. Hamilton, if you're not stepping down, that leaves Adair free to go with Chorda and craft a story line for her at the Malibu location."

I flashback to the eager and wide-eyed Desmond who joined the family's producing team. For the first time in a long time, that Desmond is back. He's energized and stepping up, characteristics I feared had been beaten out of him by the less than generous helpings of approval and encouragement our father tosses his way. This resurgence of my brother's creative confidence arrives at the perfect moment.

Desmond leans on the Golden Guitar's glass case. I cringe at the irreverence of the pose. I need to give him pointers on reading a room.

Our father shoots him a look.

Desmond steps away and braves Hamilton's scowl. "We'll load Adair up with the equipment he needs to produce his Chorda segments in Malibu. He and I will put our heads together on the best way to finesse her story back into the show. I'll keep production on the rails from this end. Midas will be none the wiser we're creating new Chorda material."

Desmond's brainstorm has merit. "I don't need to relocate. I'll take a daily crew out to the property to shoot and supervise the edits here at the studio."

Des shakes his head. "That's not–"

I cut him off. "Right. If I travel between here and Malibu, questions and possible leaks to Midas open wide."

Our father looks from Desmond to me. "It's essential to keep Chorda's involvement off Midas's radar, or he'll shut it down. Until we convince him otherwise, he wants her cut out completely." He rubs a hand down his face. "We risk losing a significant audience share if Chorda vanishes from the show."

I shake my head. "This is dicey. We need to explain my absence."

Dad wears a mask of utter exhaustion.

I snap my fingers as the solution flashes in my mind. "I'll tell Midas I'm off to promote the new features on the Golden Pipes app while Desmond and I produce the filler segments."

My father presses a thumb to the underside of his chin and slowly nods. "Okay, Adair. That will allow you to stick with Chorda. She trusts you. If we lose her from the show because of this, our numbers are fucked. Keeping her committed is on you."

Now I'm fighting a two-headed beast. The father/daughter rift will validate Chorda's desire to distance herself from the show, and persuading Midas to reverse his banishment scenario is key to getting back on track.

I slump onto the step above Dad. Come tomorrow, I was supposed to be the one leading the rebrand of *Kickin' It With Midas*. Now, I'm charged with being a solo act to shoot and edit clandestine footage of Chorda, persona non grata, that will only see the light of day based on Midas Lear's whims and temper.

I speak to the floor. "How much of a break do you see before new filler episodes air?"

"The story is hot," says Desmond, looking between Dad and me. "I think we should cash in. Right?"

My brother tenses, waiting for approval to prove he's a viable part of the conversation.

Dad stands. "The Rockin' and Rollin' Pantheon broadcast is less than two weeks away. I want a solid lead up to Midas's big night. We'll go into reruns for a few days until the fresh episodes are set for air. It's a rush job, boys."

No rest for the weary. "Okay," I say in my best take-charge tone. "We start tomorrow with reruns of the Irish vacation episodes while we shoot the new stuff."

"Perfect." Our father points at both of us. "I want you two to produce rough cuts of episodes ASAP, one version with and one without Chorda. I'll oversee final cuts. The writers will get you outline proposals by tomorrow night with new scenarios. It's imperative to keep the *Chorda Done Him Wrong* narrative at the forefront. We'll need to fabricate over-the-top strokes for the other sisters as B story lines for balance." He fires off a message on his cell to the writers as he thinks aloud. "We could go the false arrest route, staged car accident, or fan break-ins to the property." Dad snaps his fingers. "Maybe trumped up legal snafus with Rubata and Glissanda's businesses."

None of our writers will be getting shut eye tonight.

"As always," says Dad. "Improvise within beats to find spontaneous gold nuggets. Ratings and revenue are key."

"Des, you work with the writers for Rubata and Glissanda's segments," I say. "I'll create Chorda's story line and make sure no content leaks of my footage make it to the studio for anyone to see." I scan the stage for unwelcome ears on our discussion.

My father nods, every wrinkle on his face more pronounced from overhead lights. "Yes, and I'll work on getting the angry bastard to bend on Chorda."

I spin a finger in the air as creativity sparks. "I'll target Midas's soft spot for her with my new material. Once Chorda's given a longer forum to explain her reasons for not singing to Midas, he'll cave." With possibilities brewing in my brain, I will give Chorda hope that tonight's damage can be repaired.

Dad claps me on the back. "Find a way to keep her on the show, Adair." His shoulders slump. "I'm going to go bathe in whiskey and break things." He checks his watch. "Looks like I won't be catching my flight to Ireland tonight to meet up with your mother."

A diminished Hamilton Holliday heads for the exit and then retraces his steps to us. "Production meeting at ten tomorrow. Keep everyone guessing about Chorda's story line. Don't confirm any speculation. Lay low, Adair."

When his gaze flits to me, I read the depth of his exhaustion. From the day I stepped on a sound stage, he warned me a career in television is factory work. The production line never stops. Success means continually churning out product. Constant pressure ages you before your time.

His hand weights heavy on my shoulder. "Adair, it isn't for lack of trust that I'm not stepping down. I owe it to Midas to see this through."

I answer with my own weary smile. "I know."

Dad shifts into boss mode. "If we can hash out the narrative on the filler episodes and schedule a new ceremony time by tomorrow, these old bones might be able to jet off to Midas's place in Ireland for a week." He rubs the back of his neck. "Lord knows I need the reset. I'm counting on you." He pauses. "Both of you."

Finally. The look on Desmond's face at our father's inclusion almost makes this whole mess worthwhile. We three Hollidays together will keep *Kickin' It With Midas* afloat. My new reality comes into sharp focus. Chorda and I may still be on the cruise, but we're trailing behind in a lifeboat.

"His honor, Hamilton Holliday, has left the building," says Des, dropping down next to me on the step. "You, brother, are one lucky son of a bitch."

"How's that?" I scratch my scalp until it stings. "Not only did I lose taking over the show tomorrow, I'm booted out of studio."

He grabs my upper arms. "You scored the grand prize, shitiot. The whole freakin' planet wants to know why Chorda snapped."

I bat his hands away. "She didn't snap."

Desmond reclines, resting elbows on the top step. "Call it what you will. Aren't you curious why the woman may have pissed away her future?"

Said curiosity burns a hole in my gut.

"You have the opportunity to spin her story any way you please. This is award level shit, Adair." He stretches his fingers in a series of bursts. "Chorda Lear, the tainted daughter. How will she survive?

What happens when there's nothing but an empty tin bucket at the end of her Lear rainbow?"

"Stop. It'll be a tragedy if they can't reconcile, not award level shit."

He pinches the joint between my shoulder and neck. "Picture it, Adair. Chorda's story will tug at a million heartstrings. Midas will smell ratings and how they can add gold to his treasure vault. He'll be all over reconciliation when it comes with capital gain."

"That's exploitative."

Desmond laughs. "That's reality TV. The name of the game is exploitative."

I rub the spot he pinched. "Chorda will hate it."

"If you're not into it, let's swap sister segments. I'll go dark ops in Malibu, and you deal with Thing One and Two here at the Palace."

The thought of Desmond in Malibu alone with Chorda curdles the steak dinner in my stomach. I try to think the best of my brother, but when it comes to Chorda, especially after witnessing the dalliance between Rubata and him, I'm not there yet.

"Chorda will want it to be me." I want it to be me.

"Done. We'll placate Lear. He'll get an ego stroke from his Pantheon induction. His majesty will hand off the Golden Guitar in a new choosing ceremony, and the show will go on." He bumps my leg. "The wreck of a ceremony is nothing more than a final hiccup before you take over for dear ole dad."

Hiccup? It's acid reflux. "Elephant in the room, Des, the Golden Guitar stopped playing for Midas."

Desmond pops down the stairs. "The old fucker was faking for dramatic effect."

"I don't think so."

"No one gets the last word when Midas Lear is onstage. It was his tragic, sweeping gesture to illustrate how deeply his sainted Chorda wounded him."

Right now, the question of the Golden Guitar's silence is not my priority. Chorda is. I need to find her and see what shape she's in.

First, I'd better order up the goods for a remote studio and arrange for it to be transported to the Lear Malibu property tonight. I've got to start shooting tomorrow. I'll mentally rough out story lines, but my instinct is to go organic and unscripted. No scripts, no leaks.

"Why are you still wearing a sad, little clown face?" says Des.

I'm glad he embraces being on Team Holliday, but his sarcastic edges need sanding if he wants to continue playing in the big leagues. "I need to talk to Chorda, but I've got equipment to wrangle."

He skips toward the booth and edit bays. "Go track down your chickadee. I'll deal with the edit hardware and send it to Malibu. You handle the talent."

I suspect handling the talent means something very different to him than it does to me.

I call after him. "I appreciate it, Des. Send me a video link to the production meeting tomorrow."

Des turns, chewing on his lip. "Not so incognito. What if Midas makes an appearance and grills you about Chorda?"

He's right. "Text me during the meeting as things take shape. I'll make sure my assistant, Gabby, is there."

"Will do."

"Des, you're all that and a bag of chips."

He rolls his eyes. "You are so the opposite of hip, Little Brother. Next, you'll be bringing back *jumpin' Jehoshaphat*." Des raises an arm in farewell and disappears into the control booth.

I'm alone on the sound stage. Suddenly, the exterior door slams open. No one walks in. A gust of wind rattles paper-laden clipboards lining the studio wall. Fresh memories of the strange wind that rose during the sisters' ritual and Chorda's glowing golden strand of hair fill my mind, and I shiver.

6

IVY

GRAV OPENS THE MASSIVE GLASS SLIDER AT THE REAR ENTRANCE TO the Waterfall Palace. He's been the guard at the palace since I was a kid and still rocks his military haircut along with a don't-screw-with-me attitude.

"Ceremony went south, I hear," he rumbles in his deep bass. "The girls screeched past me like a freight train with faulty breaks."

"All three?"

"Chorda first. She flew straight upstairs. The other two headed for the kitchen." Grav pinches his chin. "Didn't like the look of Chorda. Weepy, you know. Not her." He jerks a thumb at the enormous living room that looks more like a grand hotel lobby than a home.

The décor has an autumn vibe with its palette of earth tones, mostly burnished oranges and golds, always the gold. There are splashes of green from potted palms and a creeping vine accenting the massive oak front doors. One wall is splattered with Midas's gold records and dozens of other golden trophies. A half-dozen arrangements of chairs and couches flanked by glass-topped, gold claw-footed tables are artfully positioned throughout the space. Castle-worthy gold-flecked stones frame walls of glass that form the front of the mansion. Beyond these windows, the main waterfall cascades in a curtain bathed in the glow of yellow-gold spotlights.

The family rarely lingers here. It's the hangout for parties, receptions, interviews, and *Kickin It* segments. The next floor up, with its more casual yet still designed to the nth degree common space and bedroom suites, is where the Lear family nests.

Grav clamps a hand on my arm. "You and Chorda are thick. Gal needs a friendly shoulder."

"We all do tonight. Thanks, Grav."

If I'm lucky, Chorda is alone. I'm walking in blind with no idea how much she knows of her father's post-show edicts. I may be the bearer of more bad news rather than comfort.

I take the gilded floating stairs two at a time. Next to me, an indoor waterfall splashes down into a pond filled with the kin variety of koi, golden fish. These fish eat a more specialized diet than the Lear sisters. When we were kids, Chorda named every one of the koi. I swear they'd swim up to her when she called so she could tickle them under their fishy chins.

At the top of the staircase, a narrow waterway circles a sprawling room with a wall-sized flatscreen and overstuffed couches in multiple shades of gold. Abandoned Yoga mats line up in front of the TV. The indoor stream splits at the far end of the room to meander down a quartet of hallways. Eventually, it spills out the front of the palace in lesser waterfalls. I take the leftmost hall to Chorda's bedroom suite. To my surprise, her door is open. I hear the sisters' voices tripping over one another.

Chorda's voice pushes through sobs. "He can't send me away. The moon—"

Her sadness rips through me.

"Oh my God," says Rubata. "If you say the moon is waxing one more time, I'm going to stuff a pillow over your head."

It's the content, not the tone, that says Rubata. Someday, I'll figure out how to tell the sisters' speaking voices apart.

"Forget the waxing moon, little sister. You fucked up. You had one job. Sing your perfectly sweet song for Da."

Ah, there's Glissanda—slightly less nasal than Rubata.

"It felt wrong to add to the gushfest after you two sang." Chorda's voice holds underlying gentleness absent from the other two. It's the voice that plays in my head when I want to see the best of the world. Hers, I always recognize.

"Gushfest! Judge much?" says Rubata, slurping what I guess is her gelato.

I hear Chorda release a big breath. "Bad choice of words."

Gushfest is generous. I haven't checked social media yet. I'm sure fans are having a field day with Rubata and Glissanda's hokey, on-the-nose musical offerings to Midas.

Glissanda clucks her tongue. "Da demanded we blow sunshine up his ass."

"He thrives on bluster and praise. We delivered," says Rubata. "You didn't."

"I didn't mean to criticize." Chorda sounds miserable.

"Sure you did," says Rubata. "That's your thing, Saint Chorda. School us on how we can be better people."

Rubata is definitely the most nasal.

"Oh, we have *things* now, Ruby?" says Glissanda. "What's mine?"

"Puh-leeze," says Rubata, then breaks into an imitation of Glissanda that's not too far afield from her own voice. "I'm an earth mother. I'm connected. The trees tell me what clothes to design." I hear a finger snap. "Do you know how cray you sound?"

"Dial down your tarty party, Rubata," says Glissanda. "You're as bad as Saint Chorda."

"Fine, slap me with hashtag Saint Chorda because I care about the integrity of our family," says Chorda. "I felt too exposed, sharing private feelings. I couldn't do it. Da already knows how much I love him."

"Ugh, you're such an ivy, Chor Chor," says Rubata. "If you'd been born a holly like Gliss and me, you'd never let an inflated sense of loyalty screw with what's rightfully yours."

Born a holly? Ivy? These sisters speak a language unto themselves.

Harumphs and snorts tell me Rubata and Glissanda's attitudes are about to devolve the sisterly convo into a snippy argument. Tonight, the goal seems to make Chorda as miserable as possible.

"This can't be the way Bríg intended the night to be," sniffs Chorda. "The Golden Guitar should go to one of you."

"Ba-ríg," says Rubata. "Our do-gooder goddess."

"Ruby," warns Glissanda. "Show some respect to Bríg."

I sneak closer and catch a glimpse of Glissanda stroking Chorda's hair, avoiding the golden strands. "Lil' sis, Bríg knows you're spesh to us," she coos. "You need to wise up about how to play Da. Your image is going to need a good zhuzh after tonight."

Glissanda's voice is overly saccharine. The sisters' words from the garden come back to me.

Itty bitty sissy is clueless we've pledged to our true goddess and left Bríg to her.

There seems to be a goddess smack down Chorda isn't clued in on. As if there is such a thing as a goddess smack down or a goddess.

I seize the break in the sniping as my cue to walk through the doorway.

"And speaking of do-gooders," says Rubata. She hovers over a carton of gelato to lick a goo-covered spoon.

"Did you come to help Chorda pack?" says Glissanda, switching her attention to the cell in her hand.

"I won't leave. I need to stay here and talk to Da," says Chorda.

"Bad plan," says Glissanda. "Even at his best and most logical, Da's default is rash. He won't listen, hon." She licks a finger and smooths her eyebrows. "Disappear for a while and let him chill."

Chorda's face scrunches. "How is that better than going to him right now and fixing things before they get worse?"

"Oh, puh-leeze," say Rubata and Glissanda in tandem.

"Don't ever poke a music mogul beast in mid-roar," says Glissanda. "Unless you want to lose a finger. Give him space, baby sis."

Rubata clicks her tongue. "Da could stand to be a cooler character like Grant Gothel."

"Gothel?" I blurt. My eyes pop wide at Rubata's compliment to Grant Gothel. "He was such a *cool character* the night of the *Summer Number One* last year when he threatened to kill Justin and Zeli. Prison's cooling him off real good."

Rubata's gaze pierces Chorda with accusation. "Disloyalty drives people to extremes." She upends the gelato carton to catch the last of the melt. As the middle Lear sister checks her phone, a thin line of chocolate drips down her neck.

I bite my tongue to avoid getting into a cage fight with Rubata over Grant Gothel's lack of character.

Rubata aims her supersized lips at me. "Bad night for you, too, Adair. We hear Hamilton's ass is staying in the captain's chair." She cackles. "Adair...chair. Rhyming is my jam."

Chorda's expression breaks my heart as I watch her take on the guilt of my delayed promotion as well as the botched choosing ceremony.

Glissanda lets out a shriek. "Ruby, help! I lost a social thread." She waves her phone at Rubata. "Fix it."

Rubata snaps her fingers and flattens her hand for the cell. "Give it. You need to learn how to work your own damn social media, Gliss."

Glissanda skitters to Rubata. "You're the techie." While Rubata slides a finger over the phone, Glissanda starts listing off other fixes she needs, then sets hands to hips, frowning. "Ruby, how do you know my password?"

Rubata snorts.

I hit my limit. "If the two of you don't mind skedaddling, I need to talk to Chorda."

"Yes, Gliss, let's do skedaddle." Rubata laughs. "How old are you, Adair, eighty?" She sets the empty carton of gelato on Chorda's bedside table next to two others. There are multiple drips of tan and chocolate down the front of her gown.

Glissanda and Rubata close in on Chorda. The two raise their palms. The three sisters clutch hands, three identical rings click together.

"Lear, Lear, and Lear," says Rubata.

"Sister, sister, sister," answers Glissanda.

Chorda finishes their chant. "Always, always, always."

Glissanda kisses Chorda's hair, and the two elder sisters scuff through the door in bare feet. Someone pinches my ass. I don't give them the satisfaction of yelping. Before I shut the door, Rubata whispers to Glissanda, "The night is going our way. *Mórrigán* is on duty."

I'm up to my eyeballs with goddess talk as those two credit their celestial BFF with the night's disaster.

Chorda fusses in a bathroom as big as my Sunset Boulevard condo's kitchen. She slams things into an oversized, silver-handled bag, and spins to face me. "Are you here to deliver the official reprimand from Hamilton?"

The youngest Lear sister has a very long fuse. When it does burn down...fireworks. While she's this hot, her reasoning clicks off. Years of practice taught me minimal responses are the way to go when she hits her limit. "No."

"I ruined the ceremony. Now, I live with the consequences. I'm off the show." She abandons the bag and zips into her room-sized closet. "Goodnight, Adair."

"Not leaving."

"Apparently, I am." She tries to slam past me with an armful of clothing.

I grab her wrist. "Chor, slow down." I want to pull her into my arms. I want to smooth her hair and promise her I have a fix for tonight. I want to feel her settle against me and trust I can help her through this. I want her to raise her face to see the honesty on mine and allow me to dab a reassuring kiss on her plump, collagen-free lips.

She yanks out of my grip.

"You're not off the show."

My statement slows her down. For a heartbeat, I swear disappointment shines in her eyes. "Did my father change his mind?"

I lower my head to scratch the nape of my neck. "Not exactly."

The onslaught of angry tears replaces that shimmer of disappointment. "What did he say?" She studies my face and finds nothing to give her hope.

"There's opportunity here."

She glares. "Don't you dare ask me to capitalize on what happened tonight."

"I'm not—" I stall. *Oh crap.* That's exactly what I'll be asking her to do.

With a single nod of her head, Chorda jams the clothes in her giant bag and storms out of the room.

Damn. I meant to bring her hope, and I compounded her misery. Convincing her to stay on the show without Midas's blessing will be my Waterloo, especially when she had one foot out the door already with her dreams of touring. I sit on the edge of her bed and collect my thoughts. Chorda must stay on *"Kickin' It"* for the good of the show. Not leaving works in her favor as well as mine.

I slide my hands over her satin bedspread. I'll drive her out to the Lear's Malibu place and give her fireworks a chance to sputter out. Her normally rational mindset will take over. Once she hears my plans for her filler segments, the situation will seem less bleak. We've always been able to untangle knots in our lives together. The current mess may be a doozy, but we'll handle it.

I launch to my feet and hurry down the stairs after her. No Chorda in the formal living room. I check the kitchen to find an empty gelato bag and two pairs of impossibly high platform heel shoes.

Grav will know where Chorda went. *Oh, God.* I hope she didn't go full-steam-ahead and decide to tackle Midas right now. He's probably halfway into his five-thousand-dollar bottle of Jameson Vintage Reserve. Ugly is all that could come of a father/daughter tête-à-tête tonight.

I skid to a stop in front of Grav.

He points to the side of the house. "Garage."

I fly down the steps to the family garage. Chorda's car is gone. I sprint to the studio parking lot, jump into my Tesla, and rip down the winding drive. A small crowd lingers at the front gate, waiting for signs of the Lears. Through its metal bars, I watch the taillights of Chorda's thunder gray Volvo Polestar streak around the curve.

7

THE POOLS

It's fortuitous neither one of us is pulled over for reckless driving, especially Chorda. She tears up the road like a madwoman, blowing through yellow lights in a blur and taking turns fast enough to tip onto two wheels. A handful of cars that scream Paparazzi shove between us. I'm ass-clenching scared she'll try to outmaneuver them and the jaws of life will be involved.

I lose her on Pacific Coast Highway, a route next to the ocean where the privileged dwell. Thank Chorda's fancy goddess we're closing in on the Lear Malibu property. Midas named his Malibu estate Garinish after an island in Bantry Bay over in Ireland. He loves to tell stories of the days he lingered writing music in the gardens on Garinish Island when the Golden Guitar first came to him. One of Chorda's hiatus-fun-for-Adair-and-Chorda schemes is to kayak Irish waters out to Garinish so she can dip into its creative well like her father.

It's a straight shot from PCH to the Lear security gates. Not a single hair on a Paparazzi head will get past Midas's security. I wind up the short hill between the highway and the turnabout in front of the guard gate. A pair of cop cars works in tandem with Lear security to shoo press diehards away from the gates.

Hoots and catcalls take aim at me as I'm waved inside.

"Adair, what's the fallout from Chorda's *screw you*?"

"Is Midas on his way to have it out with her?"

I keep my window up and avoid eye contact with the press beast.

It's a bit of a trek to get from the security gate to the beach property. First a short hill climb, culminating in a steep crest sparking the sensation you'll launch airborne straight into the Pacific. After a scary tip downward, I navigate a block-long series of one lane switchbacks to the roundabout in front of the main house.

My heart punches ribs with every curve, letting up a smidge when Chorda's car isn't dangling off a cliffside. These hills form a natural barrier to keep prying eyes off Lear land. A finger of lesser bluffs tapers down to the waves to form the northern boundary of the grounds. The main house sits in the middle of the property above a narrow stretch of sand, separating it from the ocean.

A formidable gold fence defines the borders of Midas's seaside kingdom. Inside the spike-topped fence lies a strategic line of postcard-perfect California fan palms that rise from a five-meter-high border of Paparazzi-proof, Mountain Mahogany shrubs. Its butter-creamy flowers shine gold in the light of lampposts. Even though the mahogany is too thick for the heartiest of monster lenses to penetrate, Midas added one last protective layer of holly bushes to his perimeter. Lear holly, thanks to botanical stick-to-it-iveness from the gardening staff, produces gold berries instead of the traditional red. There's a thread thin scar on my right arm from the time Chorda and I attempted to harvest the gold berries for some nefarious prank against her sisters.

Rubata made a crack about being born a holly back at the Waterfall Palace. I assumed the family's affinity for trees and plants is part of their Irishness and connection to the land. I make a note to ask Chorda about plants and secret witch code.

Bringing up that subject will rope me straight into the witchy conversation I'm not real keen on diving into. I roll my head to crack my neck. I need to get over it. A convo about Chorda's craft is inevitable. I promised to give her the chance to open my mind a smidge. A promise to a friend is sacred currency.

On final descent to the house, the Pacific shines black beneath me. A solitary boat patrols beyond the breakers. Midas keeps security on the water as well. No one can troll close enough to shore for shots of the family. The Lear oceanfront oasis is blissfully secluded and designed to thwart the most innovative sneak. It's semi-tragic the way the Lears must hide within a cocoon to function the way most families take for granted.

My car bumps onto a large circular drive of bricks before the ocher stucco and glass house. The entire property is landscaped with the caveat that every flower must be yellow or gold. The Lear greenhouse employs full-time botanists to work on hybrid flora.

I lurch out of the car and nearly roll my ankle on the edge of one of the bricks stamped with an image of the Golden Guitar. Chorda's car stands alone out front. Around the corner of the house, I spot the SUV that belongs to Bibs, friend to the Lears and housekeeper. She's been with Midas since he and his wife, Deedee, whom I always thought of as an aunt, moved here from Ireland to start Golden Pipes Records. Dad says Midas was a lesser son of a bitch when Deedee was alive. We lost my honorary aunt to a stroke the year Chorda and I started junior high. Mrs. Lear never saw Midas's golden dreams come to fruition. I've always wondered who Midas Lear would be if he hadn't lost the love of his life.

Bibs lives in one of the bungalows on the property down a short path from the house. I'll claim one of the others for my remote studio.

I lean into the car, pop my glove box, and retrieve a key to the front door. I snatch the bouquet of sunflowers I bought at the grocery store and my duffel from the trunk. My packed bag used to be for unplanned overnights or weekends with my ex-girlfriend, Caity. I maintain it from force of habit more than wishful thinking. Tonight, besides extra clothes, I tossed something else in the duffel

I already feel guilty about. The button camera, seedy member of the spy cam family, is stuffed inside. It goes against my conscience to use it, but a fellow in my situation with a show to save must be resourceful.

Dim light leaks from the windows. Instead of barging in, I ring the bell to avoid startling Chorda. I left messages I was incoming but got zip in reply. I also let Bibs and the main gate know an equipment delivery would follow in my wake. I'll tell Chorda in person about the remote studio when I share my plan for her new segments.

I unlock the door and let myself in. As soon as I step into the foyer, lights blaze on.

"Chor?"

She doesn't answer.

"Bibs?"

Glissanda redid the inside of the beach house last year in shabby chic with a dash of New England yacht club. There are too many lobsters and blue and white life preservers for my taste. Midas's platinum records line the walls here. There's a chair rail of muted gold, and the exposed wood beams are whitewashed with a golden sheen. The man loves his gold. At least its more understated out here than at the Waterfall Palace.

I skirt around a pair of long, blue-and-white striped couches and through an archway into the kitchen. Lights pop on to greet me. Stainless steel and gold-veined white granite define the space. I grab a vase from one of the low cabinets, dunk the flowers in water, and set them on the center island. My cheek tingles where Chorda dusted it with her sunflower earlier. I hope a dozen will bring her a little bit of joy now.

"Chorda?"

I make my way to what Chorda and I dubbed the dolphin room, a long narrow space down a couple of steps from the living room that runs the length of the house. Its ocean-side wall is glass. Cushy gold and white chairs offer a perfect view of the Pacific. Chorda loves to do her writing here. As kids, we'd spend hours waiting for dolphins to appear in the water, count seagulls, and make up stories—or in Chorda's case, songs—about mermaids.

At the far end of the room, I spot her overstuffed bag. Her gown is tossed on the arm of a chair. A rogue image of her naked silhouette strolling along a moonlit shore pops into my head.

I smack my cheeks and shove the lovely, yet inappropriate image down deep.

I do love Chorda Lear. There is a clear delineation between loving a friend and passionate love. Friend love is a steady, pleasant state of affection. Lover love is a hot pulse of flame. Naked fantasies about Chorda fall onto the wrong side of the divide.

The glass door to the deck is open a crack. I know where she is —the tide pools. It's where we'd escape her sisters or our fathers' tempers, a place of peace. The perfect spot to hear the sea sing its quiet song.

I dump my bag next to hers and grab for the door. I don't move. My mind explodes with potential next steps. Will Chorda be glad to see me, or will she shove me into the surf? Is she ready to talk about tonight? The future?

My intention is to create a narrative for the next set of shows showcasing Chorda as the beautiful person she is. Honesty, loyalty, and love will be the heart's blood of her segments. I must convince her to open up on camera.

I lay a palm on the doorjamb. Will remorse be enough to keep the audience on Chorda's side? I believe raw truth is what will feed fans. I agree with Desmond. Reconciliation is the sweet spot. I stare at my duffel, torn whether or not to use the button cam to capture raw truth.

I dig into the bag for the button camera and slip it inside my dress shirt. I'm doing this for the show, not personal gain. A foul buzzer sounds in my head. My personal gain and the show's fate are knotted together. Ignoring what a masterful Chorda story line will do for me is denial, a kissing cousin to a lie. With a silent vow, I swear not to use footage from the spy cam Chorda hasn't approved. I will craft a story to tear at the heartstrings of her fans and pray she understands why I didn't want her inhibited while I captured it.

I skirt the patio and infinity pool to tap down the wooden stairs. At the bottom, I kick off my shoes, roll my khakis to the knees, and make my way across the sand. A hundred yards from the house, craggy rocks rise in a natural fortress before marching into the surf. Around its base, a series of small tide pools glisten under the first sliver of Chorda's waxing moon. Before stepping around the boulders that shelter the pools, I switch the camera to night mode in the hope of getting shots I can use.

Chorda perches with her back to me on a natural rock stool surrounded by tide pools about the size of a golf green. She watches waves spit droplets of foam over the top of the seaside boulders that protect the series of shallow pools. Away from city lights and without a brighter moon for competition, starlight reflects off the surface of the water like silver glitter.

"Chor?"

Her shoulders rise at the sound of my voice. Slowly, she turns. I wait for her to speak first. I'm the intruder here. She pats the space beside her on the rock.

I make my way around some pools and through the center of others where I won't step on anything alive to reach her. Fine spray from the sea dampens the rock. When I drop onto the slippery surface, I slide against her, hip to hip. We sit, listening to the waves sizzle against the rocks.

Chorda rests her head on my shoulder. I wrap her in my arms.

"I'm sorry, Adair."

"You don't owe me an apology."

She pulls away. "Don't say I owe my father an apology."

Her anger proves how shaky the ground between father and daughter is.

"Never."

Let the lies begin. The apology angle was going to be my lead. I screech into a course correction. "What happened tonight is nothing we can't fix."

She points to the house. "If you're here to fix me, you can drag your ass right back to the city."

There's a catch in her voice, the tell she's fighting tears. I recapture her in my arms. "You don't need fixing."

It takes a few beats before Chorda relaxes. "You stand alone in that assessment." Once again, her head finds its way to my shoulder. "The ceremony was wrong. The Golden Guitar should have nothing to do with flattery or hyperbole. The legacy is about sensing creative investment and dedication."

Here we go again with the legacy and the Golden Guitar's magical power. Chorda is into her magic one hundred percent. I must tread lightly and not shatter the path of eggshells between us.

"Back in the day, how did your Da prove he was the worthiest talent?" Fingers crossed this is a good tale for Chorda's story line. I rub her shoulders and then turn to make sure the button cam will catch her face.

"He worked like a dog at his music, paid his dues in pubs and busking on the street. He sang about beauty and genuine emotion. Da painted with words and melody. He spoke to the soul." Chorda leans back on her hands and studies the stars. "When the time came for Granda to step aside for the next generation of O'Leary artists, The Golden Guitar only played for Da. It understood his desire to create truth. He told me I must always do the same with my music."

I picture the golden statue in front of the Waterfall Palace, the alleged cursed chieftain who dared to touch the guitar without invitation. "What happened to his brothers and sisters when they held the guitar?"

Chorda wrinkles her nose. "Nothing. It didn't play."

"There isn't a hidden gallery of O'Leary golden statues?"

She laughs. "Your questions make me wonder if you're still flip-flopping between belief and non-belief in our Golden Guitar mythology."

I nudge her with my shoulder. "I prefer to stay on everyone's good side."

She returns the nudge. "My glass half-full guy." We share the silence for a moment. "No statues, just disappointment. Granda handed each of his children the guitar. A direct exchange from the artist who holds the current claim on the instrument is a brand of permission."

"That's how they avoided the golden whammy."

Her voice is sharp. "Stop it, Adair. There's no whammy. The guitar's silence is devastating enough."

"I'm sorry. Misplaced humor. Bad habit."

Our feet dangle side by side in the water of the largest pool. I toe a sea anemone and it tightens around me.

Chorda rubs her toes over the top of my foot, and sings "Ahhhhh," as the next wave knocks on our hideaway door. She studies the sky and the reflection of stars in the pools. "Everything looks different in starlight, doesn't it?"

The catch has left her voice. The woman is more resilient than I could ever be. I take in her lovely profile, the curve of her generous breasts, the feel of her legs snugged against mine.

"Heightened beauty from the cosmos," I agree. If we weren't in business together and she wasn't my best friend, I'd trade our leg tangle for a taste of her lips.

"I am sorry I ruined the show for you, Adair." She kicks at the water. "I'm not sorry I ruined my part in the show." Her kicks become furious, and she splatters us with fishy smelling tide pool water. "I'm ready to be rid of reality show popularity. It's crippling." Now she's up and stomping from pool to pool.

It's a visual bullseye. I adjust my chest/camera angle to catch it all. Even if I don't use her words, the image of a wild woman splashing through the tide pools is captivating.

Chorda sinks onto her knees into one of the deeper pools and leans forward on a rock. Her cutoff shorts and low-cut, blousy top are completely saturated. The camera and I see an alluring portion of her breasts and raised nipples for a quick beat before her hair trails over them as if they caught us peeking.

"I have to own what I've become, a reality show and social media commodity. Ask Rubata and Glissanda. Our worth is judged by an algorithm of likes, comments, and shares." She twists and sits on the craggy rock not facing me. "With every scene we film, another piece of me evaporates into public consciousness."

I'm shocked how oppressive *Kickin' It* has become to her. It's clear, her desire to step away and go on tour is more than fear of fan disconnect.

She kneads her temples. "Except for the damned praise song for Da, I haven't been able to write anything new in months. The show drained my creative well."

"Chor, I wish you'd told me you feel this way. We could change things."

"Criticizing the show is a slap in your face." She inhales deeply, chest rising.

If her gaze wasn't on the sky, she'd catch me distracted by the gorgeous curves accentuated by her damp clothing. I force myself to search the stars with her.

"I played along even though it was chipping away at me since the show isn't solely about me." She holds her arms up to the moon. "Before you found me out here, I asked Bríg for guidance and strength. I'll need both to step away from *Kickin' It With Midas*."

Bríg better nix that plan, or she'll make my shit list. Can I be smote for wanting to kick a goddess's ass?

Chorda steps carefully around the pools to stand directly in front of me. Her hands rest on my knees. "I managed to write the song for my father because I do love him."

The catch in her voice makes a reappearance. One of us is about to break into tears, and if I can't talk her into staying on the show, odds are it will be me.

"I found grace in writing his song. It gave me hope I hadn't lost my gift."

"But you didn't sing it to him?"

She shakes her head. "Not like that. I ache for him to hear it, in its truth, its simplicity. Not in a fabricated competition with Ruby and Gliss for who loves Da best."

My dear friend opens the door for me. "You can still sing it for him, Chor."

She drops down sideways onto my lap. I know there's no subtext or flirtation involved with her position, only trust. It takes all my self-control to respect that.

"Someday. If he forgives me."

I thread an arm around her. "Hear me out. Let's back off a bit from the walking-away-from-the-show talk and lean into the tour angle. It'll give you a breather, a chance for fresh perspective." Tour footage storyboards dance in my head.

She shoots off my lap and nearly falls. I grab her hips to steady her.

"Did you not listen to a damn word I said?"

Reconciliation scenarios join tour storyboards. "I did hear. You want to make up with your father, right?"

Chorda narrows her eyes. "Of course."

"Instead of walking away, think of the show as a vehicle for that. We'll plan your segments together to show you're not an ungrateful child just because you didn't play his game. The story we tell will be on your terms. When the time is right, you'll sing him your song."

"My segments?" A tight mouth joins her squinty eyes.

"Hamilton and Midas want fresh filler episodes between now and whatever second choosing ceremony your father decides on for the Golden Guitar."

A glimmer of hope sparks in her eyes. "Da wants to hear my side?"

Yikes. This is shaky ground. "I believe he will be interested in your explanation about tonight." There, a speculation instead of an out and out lie.

She covers my hands with hers. "I don't know, Adair. The song I wrote for him is meant to be sung without the stakes of the Golden Guitar hanging over it. That's my truth. He needs to know I don't care about legacy. I care about him."

I can't hedge anymore. She deserves more than my weak-ass speculation. "The nasty truth is he refuses to speak to you, Chor. Curating your story line with the specific purpose of reaching out to him is your bridge."

Chorda squeezes my fingers. "And if he won't watch these segments or bans them from the show?" Her tears are golden beads sliding down a thread of moonlight.

Screw Midas's ego. How could he hurt Chorda like this?

"He loves you. Pride stands in his way. He'll get over himself." My mind gallops through a narrative. The loyal daughter who yearns to reconcile with her hard-hearted father. The fanbase will revere Chorda as an angel, not a sharp note in the Lear symphony.

She presses her legs against mine. "I don't know, Adair. Mending things with Da should be off camera." She flicks her wrists. "He's done me a favor. It'll be freeing to shed the crap that comes with being on the show."

I bring her hands to my lips and drop a friendly kiss on her knuckles. "I promise to clear crap out of your way. We'll make the show work without sucking you dry."

She shakes our hands. "If I go with your idea, forget any groveling or admission of being an ungrateful child."

This is promising. "I understand." I'm trying hard to keep focus on our convo instead of the heat rising everywhere the skin of Chorda's legs touch mine.

"I will be who I am, not who people want me to be despite consequences to my popularity."

"Absolutely."

"My sisters can keep the show as their vehicle to sell shit."

Red alert. I can't let that one go. "I'll never reduce *Kickin' It* to an infomercial. It's always been more to me. Think of the new talent we've showcased and—"

Chorda flaps her hands. "Sorry, I was harsh." She chews on her bottom lip. It swells ever so slightly with the ministration.

I appreciate how the natural plump suits her.

"My yes will mean we share creative input on my segments."

I rip my gaze back to hers. "You got it." I do intend to involve Chorda, but I may need to tweak the story here and there to prevent hurting her reputation even more or widening the gap between Chorda and Midas. I've got emotional objectivity she lacks.

Worry tightens my shoulders, anticipating pushback from my father and Desmond. They want to key into a portrait of Chorda's remorse and the hardships of living outside Midas's golden sphere.

I need to stick to my vision. Her story must be about heart. Her truth, honesty, and loyalty will be what keeps fans devoted to their favorite. I'm sure I can convince her to sprinkle in a dash of what Desmond and Dad want. We'll make it fit around her chosen narrative. I can please everyone.

Chorda moves her feet between mine, pushing my knees slightly apart. Her tears are gone. "If it was anyone else, Adair, I'd walk away, but you're my oak."

The beautiful woman between my thighs sparks nervous chatter. "I'm an oak? Since we're on the topic of botany, what's with the ivy and holly talk tonight from your sisters at the Waterfall Palace?"

Chorda giggles, a beautiful sound. "Celtic tree astrology."

I shake my head. "Of course, it is. I walked right into that one."

Chorda lays a hand over my mouth before I continue. "You're an oak, a champion for others, nurturing, generous."

I smile against her palm. She brushes a floppy strand of hair off my face. Her touch is silk. I want more of it.

"Gliss, Ruby, and Da are born under the sign of holly, high-minded, competitive, ambitious."

"No kidding?" I tilt my head and will my fingers not to stroke her face. "And you?"

"I'm an ivy."

I raise my eyebrows. "And?"

"Guess." She bumps my leg with her hip.

"Hmm." I meet her gaze. "Charismatic?" She smiles, so I keep going. "Compassionate?"

"And I hold my own when shit starts raining from the sky."

"I never doubted that." I give her a light squeeze with my knees. "Thank you for trusting me with your story, Chor."

She moves closer, and I force myself to breathe. This is nothing more than a friend seeking comfort. Our bodies make contact. I focus on her face since the wet clothes plastered against her skin leave nothing to the imagination. Chorda wants a hug, reassurance she's not alone at rock bottom.

It would be more awkward to avoid the hug. I'm terrified she'll discover the camera under my shirt. Her breasts conveniently supply the perfect alcove for my sneakery to stay hidden. I count to five and break the hug. The cold tide pool water dampening the crotch of my khakis could be doing a better job of discouraging my burgeoning hard-on.

Instead of extricating herself from a front row seat to my arousal, Chorda slides hands over my shoulders to clasp behind my neck. Breath warms my face. "Thank you for following me out here."

"Always."

She squeezes me into a second power hug, pressing her fantastic shape against me. My mind is at war trying to convince my body our wet hug means nothing beyond friendship. It's not a threshold into something new between us. Chorda needs me, and my job is to be emotionally available and not to physically ache for her.

It's a relief when she's the one to let go before she registers my body rigidly disagrees with my mind. I need to hide my hard-on as much as I need to hide my spy cam.

Chorda's hands are still on my shoulders. She leans in for a slow brush of lips across mine. Damn, her soft mouth makes me hunger to plough through any metaphoric threshold.

We've cheek kissed for years with the occasional corner-of-the-mouth peck. For sanity's sake, I must assume Chorda briefly kissing me is a minor extension of our usual practice. The lingery nature of this contact must be the closeness she needs tonight to feel better.

I imagine catching those lips to savor the warm tingle jumping from her mouth to mine. I mentally lasso the sensations and attempt to flick them away. Chorda is a toucher, a hugger, a kissy girl. I'm mistaken to believe this is a real kiss. She's looking for a guarantee that, in the face of the monumental disaster with her Da, the rest of her world is steady. I'm steady. This is all the kiss I'll ever be allowed from her, a friendly lip brush.

My excellent rationalization is blown to smithereens with the second approach of Chorda Lear's lips. They press against mine with no intention of a fly-by. She lingers. Her hands on my neck increase their pressure. The best move is to pull away. Instead, I sink into the heat and insanity of what's happening. This should be a quick kiss, a kiss without desire or expectation.

That's all it has a right to be, but it's not.

Her mouth moves ever so slightly. What do I do? Surely, she doesn't expect me to respond. Am I to blame for bringing us to this point? Did I encourage her by staring at her deliciously plump bottom lip?

Neither of us breaks. Neither of us moves. Dangerous currents jump between our lips as we still in the moment of a previously untested connection. Her lips are damp from the mist. I long for her to open so I might steal a deeper taste to discover if her tongue is sweet or salty from the sea air.

She shivers, and I snap out of our shared shitiocy. With the slightest push of my mouth, I end the kiss with a gentle smack. A kiss neither of us took further. A kiss that can't happen again.

A kiss I'll relive a thousand times.

"Feel better?" I ask, gently guiding her away from me so I can stand. What else do you say when you've almost genuinely kissed your best friend, and it felt freakin' fantastic? I tell myself it was about the comfort she needed, not desire.

"I do. That was nice," she says.

Even in the scant light, I catch her flush. I take her hand like the friend I am. A friend, I'm her friend. She needed a sweet, little nothing kiss, and I'm happy to oblige. I discreetly tug at my pant leg to allow my crotch breathing room. We leave the tide pools behind and head to the house.

The porch light catches the golden streak in her hair. Chorda reaches for the stair rail and smiles. "Maybe we should do it again sometime."

8

CHORDA TAKE TWO

CHORDA LEAR WANTS TO KISS ADAIR HOLLIDAY AGAIN. GOD KNOWS, Adair Holliday's mind is stuck on a single note like a skip in a vinyl record with the desire to kiss Chorda Lear again.

Adair Holliday and Chorda Lear may, under no circumstances, kiss.

Malibu, we have a problem.

When I reach my temporary digs in the bungalow, the crew already set up a mobile edit bay for me. I stay up late to upload the footage of Chorda from my button camera. God, her splashing and confessing dark feelings about the show are gripping.

My attempt at work fails to shove the sensation of a sodden-clothed Chorda Lear body out of my kinesthetic memory. Between the sheets of the bungalow's king-sized bed, memories of starlight and tide pools make for forbidden dreams.

At dawn, I throw open the door to the bungalow, hoping the cool morning breeze will snap me out of impossible fantasies. A small bowl with a puddle of milk at the bottom sits next to a plate with breadcrumbs on the small brick slab of a porch.

"Chorda Lear, you madwoman," I laugh. She's left offerings of bread and milk for the good folk, her Irish faeries, outside my bungalow to ensure my welcome. The gesture is as endearing as it is wacky. My guess is the bread and milk ended as a midnight snack in the belly of a passing raccoon.

Goose bumps and shivers send me into a hot shower to pep me up for our first day of shooting. As soon as I turn off the water, my phone pings with a video call. It's my father. I sling a towel around my waist and answer. His face has aged another dozen years. "Everything okay?"

His breath rattles. "I'm too old for this shit."

I've heard his song before. I wait for the familiar chorus.

"I'm tapped out, Adair. Last night was supposed to be the end. I had freaking chest pains thinking about cleaning up Midas's latest toxic dump."

I start blinking too quickly as I process. "Chest pains?"

Dad flattens a hand over his heart. "I allotted enough energy, creativity, and tolerance for Midas's bullshit to take me through the choosing ceremony. My reserves are dry. Mentally, physically I'm stretched to the limit."

I'm shaken. Hamilton Holliday doesn't have limits.

He presses heels of his hands into his temples. "To keep Midas from going completely off the rails, I'll stay on in name only until we stick a pin in this season, but the show is yours."

I grab a second towel to wipe the streams of water pooling into my eyes from wet hair. "You're handing off to me?"

"I am, but we'll maintain the façade I'm still on duty."

My fingers dig into the towel. "So, I'm in charge, but not in charge?"

Dad scrapes hands through his hair. "Basically."

"From out here in Malibu?"

His gaze shifts to the ceiling the way it does when he's calculating a solution. One finger writes in the air while he thinks aloud. "Desmond stays in town while you button up Chorda's story line. I've already sent over a production meeting agenda and instructions on how to proceed with the filler episodes, air dates, and an outline for the second choosing ceremony. It's idiot proof. Not even Desmond can fuck it up."

I wince at the insult to my brother.

His eyes lock on to the phone screen. "Cover my ass next week, Adair. I'm going to Ireland. From there, I'll plan how to break it to Midas that I've stepped down without him having a second core melt down." He shuts his eyes for a long moment before looking at me. "Son, if I don't disappear, *Kickin' It* and Midas are going to kill me."

"Are we looping Desmond in?"

He fans the air in front of him. "Not yet. I want him to think he's still answerable to both of us for now."

I hate subterfuge and Dad's lack of trust in Desmond. What's the point of family if you can't rely on them? "I agree to disagree with leaving Des in the dark, but I'll do it. For the record, you underestimate him."

"Maybe I do."

Hamilton Holiday is a granite pillar. Seeing him on the verge of collapse is unnerving.

"I'm ready to take this on, Dad. Drink whiskey, eat good Irish beef, and avoid Midas's calls. We'll train him to trust me."

A layer of stress melts from his expression. "Thank you, Adair."

"Love to mom."

He hangs up before the second 'm' in mom without anything resembling a warm fuzzy farewell.

The dozen spreadsheets worth of plans that occupied my brain last night before my promotion was cut off at the knees reenter my gray matter in a high-speed data dump. It's going to be tricky to set everything in motion and maintain the ruse of Hamilton's hand on the wheel. I'm ready. It's time for Midas to put on his big boy pants and accept me.

Dammit, why didn't Dad figure this out before I was banished to Malibu? It would be so much easier to pull strings from the studio.

I lean against the bathroom counter to think. If I had stepped into my new position last night, Chorda would have been friendless and alone at the tide pools. I tap a fingertip to lips remembering the soft heat of hers pressed against mine. That is not something I'm willing to have missed. I'm here with her now. Priority one is to take the week, play the game Hamilton Holliday is still in charge, and get enough footage to craft Chorda's story line. When we're finished, I'll walk into the studio and don my executive producer cape. The power that comes with the title gives me control to guide *Kickin' It With Midas* where my vision wants to take it.

I NEVER TIRE OF THE LANDSCAPE AND MAJESTY OF THE MALIBU CLIFFS jutting out over the Pacific, as long as I don't get too near the edge. Their scale is grand and their dominance ancient as they defy the ocean's attempts to batter and sculpt. What was it like to be one of the first to come across the end of the continent? Did the beauty of these rocky fingers reaching for the horizon inspire or terrify as one peered over the edge at the treacherous drop?

"Napkins?" asks Chorda as the car weaves toward the trailhead at the top of the sea cliffs near the Lear estate.

I open the center console. Chorda laughs, unearthing my sandwich bag stuffed with a stash of mismatched fast-food napkins. "Quite the collection."

"I can't throw away perfectly good napkins."

"Goddess forbid," says Chorda, snatching my water bottle to soak a napkin and dab the drop of coffee she dribbled on the front of her gauzy aqua blouse.

We're both in beach casual today. I like to think our attire illustrates the safe and breezy friendship we've worn for years. I'm rocking a polo instead of a T-shirt, so the button cam has a peep hole. I debated this morning whether to keep wearing the thing. I'm paranoid Chorda will hold back as my handheld camera rolls. I can't risk missing off-book moments that might perfectly capture the tale of estrangement and reconciliation my friend needs me to paint.

Yes, my friend, my lifelong friend—not the woman I'm dying to steal a long, slow kiss from. I need to bury such inklings under the floorboards where no one will find them. To my great relief, Chorda's made no mention of kissing, past or future. I need to concentrate on her shiny new narrative not the intoxicating buzz I felt when our lips touched.

Her phone rings. "Hi, B... Fine... Thanks. I want you to keep them... I've got tons of pics of us on my phone... I appreciate the call. Bye." She groans. "Enough already."

"B? The latest ex?" I use *tone* when I speak of Chorda's last discard.

"He offered to buy me dinner and gift me all the framed pics of us from his apartment."

I'm gratified she also uses *tone*. "Told you ole Butch was a clinger."

"Batch."

"I don't acknowledge that as a name. I choose to refer to him as Butch. In fact, let's stop referring to him at all."

Chorda laughs. "I should block his number."

"You should, but you won't. You're too nice."

She walks her fingers across my shoulder. "Maybe we should hook him up with Caity."

With a quick dip of the head, I trap her fingers and make the sound of a buzzer. "No misdirection, Ms. Sneaky. The Butch block is still on the table. I vote yay. You broke up with the guy over six months ago. Build a wall." Butch/Batch was a needy puppy. It was a happy day when she let him off the leash.

It's always a happy day for me when Chorda detaches from a boyfriend.

Chorda tugs at my hair. "Did you block Caity?"

"No need. I'm sure she blocked me."

Chorda plunks her rainbow painted toenails on the dash. "She did not. You handled the breakup like a gentleman."

My head falls against the headrest. "After wasting over a year of her life when the whole time I knew we had an expiration date."

"Stop it, Adair."

"Stop what?"

"Belittling yourself."

"I only do it with you. To the rest of the world, I'm Mr. Confident." I throw thumbs up over the steering wheel.

She rubs my arm. "I'll keep your secret."

Oh, if she knew every secret I'm keeping, this conversation would go a very different way.

A flurry of texts buzzes up my watch like a swarm of stinger-clad insects.

"What the hell?"

I glance at the time. It's nearly eleven, the production meeting back at the studio is in full swing. The texts share the theme: *Is Desmond in Charge?*

Chorda yips when I stray into the oncoming lane due to my lame attempt at automotive/communication multitasking. "Pull over if you're going to text, Adair."

We bump onto the dirt shoulder, and I dig out my cell to call Gabby, my P.A. "Step out of the meeting." The background buzz disappears as she slips away. Dad set the agenda for this meeting. Desmond should just be a mouthpiece. Judging from the texts, the mouthpiece isn't doing his job. "Gabs, what in blue blazes is going down at the meeting? I'm getting a shit ton of under the table texts from multiple department heads."

Chorda chuckles and whispers, "Blue blazes."

Hey, if the old tyme saying ain't broke...

She pokes me. "Put it on speaker, Adair."

I hold up a finger to put her off. Speaker phone is a no go. Chorda doesn't need to hear negative volleys at her that might arise after last night's fiasco.

Gabby pants into the phone after clearly sprinting away from the meeting. "People are losing their shit because it's Desmond and not you or Hamilton calling the shots. Add Midas MIA, and it's a hot mess."

"Hold the fort. Midas is missing?"

Did Midas flip out over Desmond acting as Dad's in-studio proxy and refuse to show?

Chorda grabs my arm. "My father is missing?"

"Gabs, define MIA."

"Not technically missing. Lear is at the Waterfall Palace. He won't come down for the meeting."

"Hamilton probably already briefed him on the agenda. He's trusting the Hollidays to handle things."

Midas keeping distance will work to our advantage. It'll be easier to slip in the Chorda scenes if he isn't micromanaging. I mouth, "He's home," to Chorda and she loosens her grip.

Gabby's voice is strained. "Everyone expected you or Hamilton. What should I tell people?"

Skipping today's production meeting is a rookie error. For appearances, without Hamilton on scene, as the new showrunner, I should spearhead the meeting. I agreed to his shadow scenario too quickly in my Chorda-centric brain. "What did Desmond say that was so inflammatory?"

"He said Chorda is stepping away from the show. No one believes him. It's not true, is it?" The strain in her voice rachets up. "I'm getting bombarded. I don't know what to do, Adair."

My thoughts collapse like the result of a bad Jenga move. Desmond may lack finesse, but he is telling a version of the truth. For this to work, Midas needs to believe the production team accepts his edict of banishment for Chorda. I should have foreseen the dip in everyone's comfort level when Desmond stepped into Hamilton's shoes instead of me. Dad and I blew it by not announcing my fake app promotion tour up front.

"Go back to the meeting and put me on speaker."

"Got it."

"Gabs, sorry I put you on the spot."

The first thing I hear is Desmond raising his voice against the onslaught from the production team.

"I've got Adair on the line," says Gabby in a loud voice she's usually too shy to use. The room quiets.

"Hey team. Apologies for not making the meeting. As I'm sure Desmond let you know, Hamilton and I are dealing with fallout behind the scenes while I go ahead with the promotion junket for the new Golden Pipes app upgrade release. I expect everyone to dip a toe in the *Dress Like Gliss* feature. We'll both be out of studio for most of the week. Desmond has the wheel for now as we forge ahead to create filler content. Des, a word."

The background rumble ticks down a notch as Desmond commandeers Gabby's cell and clicks off speaker. "Go ahead. I'm in the hall."

"Look man, I am so sorry to feed you to the lions. I should have passed the baton to you publicly."

"No big thing, Little Brother." He gives a nervous laugh. "Didn't expect such sharp teeth. I appreciate the call, but I promise you, I've got this handled."

Clearly, he wasn't privy to the under-the-table texts. "I'm sure you do. We knew it would be a rocky road to hide Chorda's segments from Midas's radar. Any suspicion we're keeping her on the show?"

"Not so far. They're semi-freaking over a possible shift to a Rubata/Glissanda vehicle."

"Everyone loves Chorda."

Chorda huffs at my comment.

"Is she on board with the grand scheme?" asks Des.

"Are you on board, C?" I hold the phone up to her.

"I'm on board."

I squeeze her knee. "We're shooting today. I'll finish rough cuts ASAP. Unless you need me to come in."

"No." His reply is clipped and adamant, but then he mellows. "It's cool, Adair. We caught the team off guard is all. Make magic with Chorda."

"Okay, Des. Be large and in charge."

He snorts. "You need someone to write you snappier dialogue."

"Give Gabby her phone."

Chorda pinches my arm. "Is everything okay?"

"Hey," says Gabby.

"Gabs, be my eyes and ears. Assume I'm in charge."

"Thank, God."

I hang up and Chorda jumps on her phone.

Rubata answers the face-to-face on the first ring. "How's the beach?"

I try to remember the last time Rubata didn't sound smug.

Glissanda joins the party. "We thought about coming out there with you, hon, so you wouldn't be alone, but Desmond insists we stay put to shoot new segments."

"It's fine. Adair and Bibs are with me."

Rubata snorts. "Of course, the boy wonder is holding your hand."

"I'm calling to see if you know why Da wasn't at the production meeting," says Chorda without comment on Rubata's snark.

"He hasn't left his room since last night," says Glissanda.

Tension lines crease Chorda's forehead. "Except for his dawn swim you mean?"

"Nope," says Rubata. "Skipped it. Da's still sleeping."

Concern colors Chorda's voice. "He never misses his swim. It's his time to commune with Manannán mac Lir. Da would never ignore his god."

"Depressed people sleep," says Rubata. "Hmm, and why is he depressed enough to skip his morning ritual? Oh, right, because of you."

"Harsh, Ruby," says Glissanda.

I grab the phone from Chorda. "Have a nice day, ladies," I say and end the call.

Chorda snatches it back. "Butt out, Adair."

I strangle the wheel. "I'm wearing my producer hat right now. I want my star in an optimistic frame of mind as we shoot your segments, and Rubata's shade is not conducive to that." Desmond would be proud of my correct usage of *shade*.

She stares out the front window at a clump of pricky pear cactus. "If there's room left for optimism."

"Do I want to know who Mr. Man MacLear is? I take it he's not your father's swimming coach?"

Chor blows out a hot stream of exasperation. "Manannán Mac Lir," she says, correcting me. "The god Da pledges to is a sea god." Her gaze locks on my face, waiting to see if I'll regress to my customary avoidance.

I am a heel. Chorda wants to share an uber important part of her life with me, and I keep putting her off. "I will honor my promise not to avoid the subject of your supernatural family values. Once our scenes are finished, we'll sit on the beach all night if that's what it takes for you to rattle my thick skull with gods and goddesses talk."

She leans with her back against the car door to aim a full volume stare at me. "You won't excuse your way out?"

"No excuses."

Chorda slaps her cheeks and hums. "I need to focus."

"What will it take to clear your head?"

She inhales deeply, and a delightfully dreamy expression settles across her features. "The promise of a mango smoothie from the *Beach Shack*."

"Your wish is my command," I say and pull back onto the road.

Chorda giggles. "You are so corny, Adair."

There are no other cars at the dirt parking lot of the trailhead. Good omen number one for a private day of shooting. The trail is steep, but it boasts a kickass view of cliffs and the water. There are plenty of flowering plants to gently frame my subject.

I love that Chorda wore tropical print tennis shoes instead of on-trend sandals or her onscreen nosebleed high heels. It humanizes her. She trots ahead of me down the trail. Chor's confidence balances my squeamishness at being one false step away from falling down a cliff. Her hair is drawn up in a high ponytail, the golden streak sliding parallel to her face before it disappears into a scrunchie. The sun brings out the gorgeous reds in her auburn locks. I surreptitiously start the spy cam.

"Hey, Chor, why does Rubata dye her hair lollipop red? Isn't it the same color as yours?"

She shoots me a sly look. "She doesn't use dye. It's a spell."

I stop to avoid crashing into her and sputter. "She colors her hair with a spell?"

Chorda laughs and skirts around a bend in the path. "No. I just wanted to enjoy your skeptical ass reaction. We don't waste craft on hair color."

I'm grateful her mood lightened after the call to her sisters.

"I owe you for that one." I intend the threat to be friend-zoney. It comes out flirty. *Lock it down, Adair.*

"You name the currency, and I'll pay up," she says with a shoulder shimmy.

She matches my flirty tone. I enjoy it more than is healthy. Chorda and I work together. Chorda and I enjoy the trust bond of friends. Our power balance on the show could be construed as uneven with me in a boss role. I can't add any more nuances to our relationship than the best of friends. Too many snake pits wait for me if I stray off our well-trod path.

"Head down there," I point to the large flat overlook that boasts an excellent panorama of the Malibu coastline.

We kick up dust on the way down. It clears quickly.

Chorda moves to stand beside me, sides touching. "It's beautiful."

I move away to fuss with equipment. "Beautiful scenery for a beautiful lady." Thankfully, the scenic spot is wide enough to quell my acrophobia into a workable percentage.

She gives me a shy smile that does more than the morning sun to boil my insides. Am I imagining this new flavor of attention that she seems to be giving me?

I motion to a low stone wall at the edge of the overlook. "Sit there. Stretch your legs and lean back a bit."

Chorda settles herself and tilts her chin up to catch the sun. I roll camera. She languishes for a few minutes and then finds the lens.

"Tell me about your music?"

She places her hands on the wall and leans forward. "What are we going for here, Adair? Is this an interview? Do you want a stream of consciousness?"

We should have talked more specifically on the car ride over. I crave spontaneity, and she wants direction. Middle ground is called for. I lower the camera.

"You want the world, especially your father, to see an authentic you, right?"

She nods.

"Can you share life snippets that've never come out on the show?"

Chorda eyes me playfully and lifts her blouse above her belly button.

I'm sure my face matches the color of the red bottlebrush bushes near the wall. "Too much sharing."

She grins and fluffs her shirt into place. "You're the boss."

I don't like her calling me the boss. It alludes to a dynamic already giving me fits. "I prefer partner."

Why does every word out of my mouth sound suggestive today? It's the damn tide pool kiss. I need to relegate that moment to the rear view, pronto.

Chorda straightens her legs and then repositions to lounging casual. "I'm giving you a hard time, Adair."

If her shirt had risen an inch higher, that's exactly what she would've given me. "Why don't you talk about what inspires your music?"

I see a muscle in her jaw twitch. "Nothing at the moment."

"Then talk past tense. Maybe it'll shake something loose."

Chorda makes her ponytail dance. It's carefree, reminiscent of high-school Chorda before fame took too big a bite out of her soul. Jeez, we're only thirty. How can those days feel a lifetime ago?

"Do you care if I close my eyes?"

I lift the camera to my shoulder, hyper aware of the button cam's faint vibrations against my chest. "Any and everything you do is right, Chor."

Her smile centers me. There's nothing flirty or suggestive about it. It's a smile that says, *I trust you, my friend.*

Instead of closing her eyes, Chorda fixes her gaze on the cliffs at the far end of the bay. "The first song I wrote was about the Van Gogh painting, *Sunflowers.*"

I wonder if she noticed the sunflowers I put in the kitchen last night.

"I've always loved actual sunflowers, but the painting disturbed me." Her hand flows through the air as if she's painting. "Sunflowers are bright and honest. Did you know sunflowers are associated with good luck? That's why we covered the ground with their petals last night for the ritual." She pops off the wall and blocks the camera lens with her hand. "Don't put anything about the ritual on air."

I lower the camera. "I'll lose that bit."

Chorda sits sideways on the wall with her knees drawn up. "Van Gogh's sunflowers look sharp, as if you could cut yourself on the petals. They're nothing like my sunflowers. I wrote that song about perceptions and misperceptions, juxtaposition. Bright yellow beauty versus more jagged truths."

"Your first gold record."

She nods. "Not out the gate. It took months for it to gain traction. Da thought it was too dark, but it spoke to people."

Chorda rests a chin on her knees. "I haunted galleries, both mainstream and fringe. I wrote songs about paintings. Artists communicate with me through their paintings, sculptures, collages, weavings. I share my interpretations of their messages through music."

She swivels to face me. "The beauty of art is not in a single truth. It's in the collection of truths it gives to the world."

I'm afraid to blink or breathe in case I miss a single word.

"Music is time. Not a set moment, but an endless river to connect past, present, and future. Humanity flows parallel to music, to art. We relate and intertwine to tell the story of lives, of beginnings and ends."

Her words are grace, an offering to the sun. I hope she doesn't expect me to speak because I've lost words. I am the emotions she stirs with her openness.

"Music is memory. Music is wishes. Music is the path our spirit takes to both light and darkness. It's life."

She stands and glides over to a cluster of deep lavender flowers. Each complete bloom could fit in my palm. Their centers shine with a burst like a golden star captured by a circle of six identical rounded petals.

"This flower is called blue-eyed grass. So delicate and, at the same time, vibrant. Paintings, nature, it's all a contradiction, an eternal question we strive to answer with beliefs, stories, songs, paintings..." Chorda trails off as the sea demands her focus. A rising breeze makes her ponytail flare, the petals of her own flower.

I long to ditch the camera and press up behind her. Hold her. Rest my cheek against hers and stare at the ocean. I want to thank her for her words and the beauty within them. I treasure the fragment of her soul she shares with me.

I keep rolling. The insights are not mine alone. She means to share with everyone, especially Lear. They are both her truth and her peace offering.

Chorda points to the horizon. "Nature also speaks to me." Wind pulls her hair from the scrunchie. Strands blow across her face, giving her an untamed look. "Da thinks we've got an inside track on nature, being Irish." She trains hair behind her ear. "That's arrogance talking. Have you ever been out to Miaqua and heard *The Mermaids* sing their songs of the sea?"

I almost answer, forgetting she speaks to the audience not me. Miaqua is enchanting. Who would guess a repurposed aquatic research center in the Santa Barbara channel would become a world class concert venue? The sextet of blue-haired sisters, *The Mermaids*, who call the place home, sing the praises of sea and sky with a piercing, ethereal sound. Midas has tried to buy their small label for years to add to Golden Pipes Records.

"Their sound coaxes the soul into impossible places, the space between the crest of a wave and its crash to the shore, or a wind strong enough to raise a storm at sea. They don't sing about nature, they sing nature." She sighs. "My next journey is to write and sing about impossible energies."

It takes me a moment to accept my feet still touch the ground instead of drifting through this journey of that which is Chorda Lear.

"Any specific impossible energy in mind?"

She treats me to a gentle smile. "Love."

The word sets my blood on fire, and I burn. This woman and the essence of who she is will reduce me to ash since love between us is not in the game plan. We must live outside the boundaries of passion. If I wrote music, my song would be of the unfairness in the position life defines for Chorda and me. Trust is our tether. Compromising it could break us. Hell, I'm compromising it every time I slip the spy camera under my shirt. Yes, we're friends, but she's also my livelihood and my future. I am not allowed to want more.

"I dream of writing love songs as powerful as what Justin Time writes for Zeli." She hugs herself. "To be so raw and transparent is a level of truth I've yet to touch." Her expression is wistful, a gentle moonbeam on a sunny day.

"You have written that song, Chorda."

She purses her lips. "I don't think so."

"To your father."

Chorda shifts from a muse to one of the furies. "Turn the camera off." She lunges for it. "Now."

"Okay, okay." I stop rolling and lower the camera.

"Why bring my father into this moment?"

I windmill my free arm. "It felt right. The song you wrote for him is filled with the love you say you're trying to write about. The reason you didn't sing it on the show was to protect its truthfulness."

Her freckles dot skin as cherry red as Rubata's hair. Microbursts of pissed off are the only sounds she makes. After a stomp around the perimeter, she plops onto the wall, chin on fists. "It is that special to me."

I nod to the camera. "Tell them."

"It's none of their business."

My gut tightens. She can't close off this early in the game. "Make it their business on your terms. Share what you told me last night about wanting to reconcile with your father."

Her resistance brings me out of my momentary lapse into Chorda worship and back to business. I need Chorda's presence to be part of *Kickin' It With Midas* for all our sakes. Good gravy, a show featuring Rubata and Glissanda alone will last a minute and a half. Sure, they have robust followings, but those numbers are zip-wah next to Chorda's fanbase. I'll be the showrunner of a big fat nothing.

Together, Chorda and I can keep the show afloat. Once *Kickin' It* is on track, we all face a better future. I detest the status of everything being up in the air.

"You expect me to bust out the song for my father right now?" When I sit next to her, she jabs her thumb at the cliff.

"Because if you do, you're going over."

I stare down the cliff face to the very uninviting rocky shore and start trembling. "I am not asking you to sing it. Just explain why you couldn't sing it last night."

"To make Da hate me even more?"

I straddle the wall to face her and set the camera down behind me. "You know he doesn't hate you. This is your chance to tell the world his version of the choosing ceremony was a crock of shit."

She copies my position to face me dead on. "Do you honestly believe that?"

I slap the wall. "I do. After everything you've shared today, I believe more than ever the ceremony was ridiculous and the Golden Guitar rightfully belongs to you." I sweep an arm across the horizon line. "Rubata and Glissanda play and sing well with music someone else creates. That's a massive divide between you."

I hop off the wall to put distance between the drop and me. It's my turn to pound the ground. "What kills me is your father knows it. You are the true artist of your generation in the Lear family. Chorda Lear is not playing a character. The other two are so immersed in the characters they pretend to be on the show, they're turning into their own inventions." I shake my head. "They faded into caricature territory with those ridiculous songs at the choosing ceremony." I ball hands into fists. "What possessed your father to turn a family legacy into a dog and pony show?"

My jaw aches from tension. I'm fired up for Chorda's sake and the sake of the show. The debacle we're trapped in is one hundred percent on Midas Lear's head.

Chorda's voice is quiet. "Fame possessed him. It's his passion." She studies the waves below. "With all its trappings, money, attention."

"He's addicted to it. So are your sisters."

Chorda grabs the waistband of my cargo shorts and pulls me to the wall. "Don't mistake addiction for passion, Adair. Passion is in creating. I write and create a song. My sisters sing and create emotion." She runs a hand up my arm. "Either form is a way of gifting that passion to others."

I cover her hand with mine. "Will you repeat that?" This is exactly the tone I need to paint Chorda with bright, authentic strokes. The spy cam caught it all. To kill my guilt, we've got to recapture her words with her knowledge.

"Verbatim?"

"Whatever you feel." I retrieve my equipment and stand.

Chorda moves to the end of the wall next to the lavender flowers. She sits facing me, arms straight at her sides to support her as she leans into the shot. Her gaze locks on the lens. "I love my father." She narrows her eyes. "However, if he demands a praise song from me to prove it, he can go fuck himself."

The camera nearly slips off my shoulder. Thank goodness I've got superlative reflexes. "Holy shit, Chor."

She's laughing her ass off. "Too soon?"

"You're trying to build a bridge, not burn it." My attempt at rationality fails. I join her in cleansing laughter.

"Stop rolling."

"And lose exemplary blackmail material? Never."

Chorda lunges. Instead of the camera, her target is my waist. She throws her arms around me. "Your reign of evil ends now."

I lower the camera to defend against her onslaught and protect the equipment. The woman knows every vulnerable spot between my ribs. We tussle and laugh until we end up back on the wall.

She catches her breath. "I had to get it out of my system. I retract the *go fuck himself*. I said it for shock value." She thumps me in the chest dangerously near the spy cam.

I've got to stop wearing the thing. Too risky.

"I'm debating whether I should smash your camera or force you to sign an NDA in blood that no one other than the two of us will ever hear that comment."

"Cross my heart and pinkie swear it'll stay between us."

Chorda kisses my cheek. "Everyone needs a person they trust the way I trust you."

Guilt nearly chokes me. The button cam deserves to be smashed, along with my choice to use it in the first place. Shame on me. Screw its footage. I'm Chorda's person. I'd rather die than jeopardize that. I shift into producer mode. "Take two?"

We return to our marks, Chorda among the flowers and me framing a perfect shot. It must be a trick of the light, but I swear there are shadows beneath Chorda's eyes that weren't there when we started the day.

She speaks to the camera like the pro she is. "I love my father."

9

SPINNING

With the true soul of an artist, Chorda restates her fame/passion riff for my legit camera. Hallelujah, it's fab footage I don't have to hide. My initial plan to show Chorda the spy- cam material is flawed with a capital F. It paints me with the light of betrayal. New plan: Ditch all stolen shots and convince Chorda to recreate moments from the vandal footage I can't live without. I'll lie and say I recall those sweet moments from memory. A mega dose of self-loathing courses through my veins as I singlehandedly resurrect the term *cad*. My end game may be noble for both the show and Chorda, but I'm stepping in serious shit to get there.

For a hot second, I ponder sharing the illicitly gained shots with Desmond to illustrate the tone I want for Chorda's segments. That crosses the line into pure shitiocy. Sharing the button cam stuff with anyone increases disaster potential. Only after I erase every unsanctioned second is there a crumb of hope I'll shed the rotten stench of dishonesty coating my skin.

We wrap for mango smoothies. The bulk of the afternoon is spent at the Beach Shack seaside café over shellfish in an impromptu strategy session to map the rest of *Chorda Take Two*.

Now, magic hour has arrived. Chorda strolls through the

gardens of Garinish in a lacy white sundress embroidered with a delicate stitching of hunter green ivy. Through my lens, soft ambient light in these precious moments after the sun dips below the horizon gives Chorda a goddess vibe of her own. She speaks of family, loyalty, commitment, and vision as she delves deeper into her creative process.

"Did you know flowers have meanings? It's not their beauty alone that inspires me, but their symbolism too."

Chorda is not only musically gifted, she's philosophical, intelligent, and engaging. She's perfect. If I didn't already love her, this vision in the gloaming would bring me to that place.

Chorda pulls the branch of a tree to inhale the fragrance of the tiny citron buds dotting its length. As she speaks, her hands trail over other leaves and petals that make up the garden. "My family enjoys a unique relationship with nature. Our connection goes far beyond appreciation and admiration. I call to the trees, to the flowers, to the wind, and they answer. These forces gift their songs to me. I revere their messages and translate that energy and essence into my music."

She lifts her unpretentious acoustic guitar from a bench of woven wood and eases its strap around her neck. With a creamsicle sunset as backdrop, Midas Lear's favorite daughter sings the love song she wrote for her father.

"Five droplets of gold break off from the sun
As they touch the sweet earth, threads of family are spun."

She sings of belonging, of connection, of bonds that should be incapable of breaking. I hear love for her father, sisters, and mother up in the stars.

The song of what a family should be breaks my heart. I've never known this joy Chorda sings about. I want to experience the wonder of being part of the warp and weft of family she weaves into a beautiful pattern with her lyrics.

The streak of gold in her hair feeds off the waning light and glows. Chorda is of this garden, its rarest beauty.

As she sings the final note, the changing sky shifts her into silhouette, and she becomes part of the newborn night.

If Chorda's song doesn't transform Midas, his heart is truly stone.

She sets her guitar on a white Adirondack chair and rolls her shoulders. "Did you get what we need?"

I set my camera on the other chair and open my arms to her. "You are freakin' amazing."

She tucks in for a mutual squeeze with a side dish of rocking to and fro. I keep the button cam positioned between her breasts. "*We* are freakin' amazing."

I break first and spin in a circle with my arms reaching for the darkening sky. "Yes, we are."

We twirl for a moment like we're eight years old again. It's simple. It's silly. It's freeing. A reset to the essence of our friendship.

Chorda's balance wavers beyond twirl dizzy. She grips the chair but isn't any steadier on her feet. I'm afraid she's going to fall.

I reach a hand toward her. "You okay, C?"

She pinches the bridge of her nose and drapes herself over the chair back. "Head rush. Probably low blood sugar. I need chocolate."

"You always need chocolate."

She raises hands in surrender as she straightens. "Guilty."

Her first few steps toward the house are tentative and shaky. I rush to her side and thread an arm around her back. "This is more than chocolate wobbly." The smudges under her eyes have darkened. I'm not buying the blood sugar angle. It hasn't been all that long since we ate late lunch.

She steadies herself and pats the side of my neck. "Join me in the hot tub? I'll make us banana daquiris—no, Mai Tais. They're prettier. I think there are paper umbrellas left from Rubata's birthday luau."

My reset short circuits. The thought of sinking into a hot tub with Chorda on a deck overlooking a star sprinkled sky throws me right under a red flashing *restricted area* sign.

She grabs my chin in her fingers. "I know that look. What's freaking you out, Adair?"

I circle her wrist to remove the fingers. It's too late. Her touch coupled with visions of hot tub drinking sends a shockwave from the pulse point on my neck to the front of my cargo pants.

"I think the stress of the last two days is catching up with you, Chor. As much as I'd love to share girly cocktails, I've got a hot date with my bungalow edit bay, and you should park it on the couch to watch those Jane Austen movies you love to torture me with."

I collect my camera equipment to hide other traitorous equipment inside my zipper that shows growing appreciation for team hot tub. "See you tomorrow?" I attempt a casual stroll toward my bungalow.

"Adair, wait."

When I turn back, the easy breezy Chorda is replaced with a portrait of melancholy. Twinkle lights in the trees reflect off a sheen of tears. Her mood downshift douses my rush of lust. I set my load on the chair and take her hands. "Tell me."

"What if it doesn't work? What if my father writes me off for good? I humiliated him on live television." A tear breaks free. When it reaches the corner of her lips, a second follows.

"I will make it work. The story we tell will give him the chance to forgive you without sacrificing his pride or yours." I start to lift my shirt to dry her face and remember the spy cam that I should have buried deep in a hole when she changed clothes. Instead, my knuckle catches her tears. "Love and honesty are on our side. And your song..."

The tingle of the spy cam against my chest challenges my statement. I may not be the picture of honesty, but Chorda is genuine in her desire to find a way back to her father.

She tips her face up to mine, her gaze on my lips. As soon as she rises onto her toes, I drop a quick peck on her forehead and step away. We can't risk a repeat of our lip contact from last night at the pools. It was too close. I am too tempted.

I sling the strap of my bag over my shoulder. "Will you be okay?"

Chorda stares at me too long before she nods.

"Goodnight, Chor. Eat chocolate."

"Goodnight, Adair." She grabs her guitar and saunters up the path to the main house, picking out a song.

I watch until I'm convinced she's not about to keel over.

As an afterthought, Chorda glances over her shoulder. "Love you."

"Love you too." I say with a casual wave.

We've said this a thousand times. Tonight, it holds a different charge. It's my issue. Chorda is the Chorda she's always been. I'm an arrogant goof to fantasize she'd ever be interested in me in any otherway than *my pal, Adair*. She's vulnerable. My girl needs comfort. I'm the comfort. Nothing in the contact between us since last night is intended to be sexual. Chorda is an emotional artist. Sensuality is part of who she is.

I open the door to the bungalow and look up to the house. Chorda leans on the rail of the pool deck and watches the sky. Her loose hair rides the night breeze.

Love you too.

Hell, it's in my DNA to be in love with Chorda Lear. If I'm truthful, it's been part of my identity from boy to man. Caity was my longest relationship. I never invested feelings in her the way I effortlessly give them to Chorda. Caity was a melody without a harmony, sweet yet incomplete. I tried to make it work with her. My heart always knew a vital piece was missing.

Chorda is my melody and my harmony, a song I may listen to but am forbidden to sing. I need to be her rock, not a shitiot wondering what it's like to lose myself in her kisses.

There's double the moon tonight from last night. Chorda taught me how to tell if it's a waxing or waning moon. *Left last*. In a waning moon, darkness seeps across its face from right to left. A waxing moon welcomes light to grow until the last sliver of the left side brightens and a full moon graces the sky.

A waxing moon brings possibility.

AFTER A FULL NIGHT IN MY IMPROMPTU EDIT BAY, I WALK THROUGH the gardens to clear my head. Chorda's segments are built and perfect. I start with glimpses of the youngest Lear sister to feather in between Desmond's material and then build Chorda's presence in length to lead up to episode four where we fold her back into the family, if we can soften Midas's arrogance.

"I love my father."

Her purity in that statement is a heartbreaker. I use the same shot to open every narrative. The first series of segments are a father/daughter history. I dug into the archives and found beautiful moments of Chorda and Midas. I included family love as well. I want the audience to see the Lears as a whole, not the sum of its parts.

The second series I've named in my head as *Chorda the Artist.* Her exquisite musings about making her art are a master class in defining inspiration. The transparency in the way she shares herself pulls you in, and you don't want to be let go.

The third series of scenes delve into her reasons for not singing at the ceremony, and her comments about Rubata and Glissanda deserving the honor. She's generous and loving. Chorda Lear's motivation for what she did is love. I defy anyone watching to try and make a different case. I believe Midas will splash through the shallow pool of his pride to understand Chorda's refusal was born of the purest filial love, and he'll reach out to her.

My finale is a love letter to Lear from Chorda, culminating in her song. When she looks straight into the camera, she sings without expectation of reward. I lose it every time I watch.

The only wrong note is how exhausted Chorda looks in our end-of-day footage. When I flip back and forth between early and later shots, the wilt is evident. It must have come on so gradually I didn't notice. Hopefully, Bibs's cooking and a good night sleep will pep her up.

Dawn breaks over the eastern hills in an abstract painting. Three separate, vertical cylinders of blue gray clouds pierce layers of lazy golden sunrise to join in a swirling mass of darkness far above the horizon. The composition gives me chills. Am I looking at nature's comment on the tempestuous relationship in the Lear family? I wonder if Chorda could interpret the sky with her witchy sensibilities.

As I watch, sky colors combine into a melted sherbet float.

My guilt is far from melted.

I cut two sets of segments last night. Version One is only footage Chorda knew I was shooting. It's effective. It tells the story. Version Two is a masterpiece. The rawness, the truth of what I captured from the button camera takes the narrative from heartwarming to heart shredding. It's a primal father-daughter tale, more myth than fairy tale. Irresistible.

I must be satisfied with the shots I gained in trust. I am satisfied. If one never saw version two, version one is plenty compelling.

Desmond spouted off about award-winning opportunities. I scoffed then, but I see what he imagined now in Chorda's truths.

I drop onto the wood bench and look up to the house. What if Chorda doesn't mind the button cam footage? *"Hey Chor, I've got good news and bad news. Our segments are killer. One little thing, you had no freakin' idea I was covertly shooting a shit ton of the material. My bad. Are we cool?"*

I jump when my cell rings. For a crazy second, my sleep-deprived brain wonders if it's Chorda responding to my confession. What's the range on witch sensibilities?

It's Des. I answer. "Are you up early or still up?"

"B. I shot kickass scenes of Glissanda and Rubata sisterly shit yesterday. I wanted to edit while the narrative was fresh in my head."

We both inherited the night owl gene from Dad. I run a hand through my hair. "Define 'sisterly shit'."

"You know, family torn asunder, rift too wide to cross."

"Melodrama then?"

"As only Rubata and Glissanda can do. Isn't that what we're going for here?"

I rest elbows on my knees. "As long as you keep a path open for Chorda. Don't let them take too many cruel shots at her. All roads must lead to reconciliation. Remember, Chorda is ultimately our heroine."

Desmond breathes heavily into the phone. "Think about this. If we lead with Chorda on a white horse, where's the conflict, the redemption arc? An unknown outcome for her is key to rope in viewers. Make her earn it."

I don't filter a negative growl in time.

"Come on, Adair, she pissed all over Midas. We'd be fools not to cash in on that drama. There's fan anger over Chorda's blunder out there begging to be validated."

I wiggle bare toes in the cool, wet lawn. "We're telling an aftermath story, not vilifying Chorda."

"A ton of negative shit that needs addressing flows through your *aftermath*."

I don't even attempt to stifle my yawn. "Send me your cuts, and I'll send you mine. We'll string the beads together this afternoon into a compelling narrative we agree on. I need to sleep."

Desmond pauses. I hear tapping in the background like a pen on a desk.

"Des?"

His voice is strained. "I screwed up, Adair."

I slough off fatigue. Confessions are not standard practice for my brother. "How?"

"You've got to understand what I did was not intended to be an end run around you, I swear. I've always been the Holliday third wheel, and I thought—"

"What did you do, Desmond?"

"I sent my cuts to Hamilton."

I'm on my feet. "Before I screened them? That's bullshit."

"I know. Damn, I'm sorry. Here me out." He doesn't wait for a response. "I thought turning in cutting edge footage was a way to prove myself to Hamilton."

"Are you fucking kidding me?" I slap a hand to my thigh. Very uncharitable phrases about daddy issues threaten to break free. I keep them on lock-down. This is an irritant, not a game changer. Desmond's asshole move can't hurt the show. Dad will just forward the footage to me.

"I was hoping to speed things up. The sooner we deliver the filler episodes, the faster Hamilton will tap out. He'll finally see the quality of my contribution to our partnership." He clears his throat. "You do see *Kickin' It With Midas* as a Holliday brothers production, right?"

Truthfully, I envision the show's future as an Adair Holliday production with a side dish of Desmond. That doesn't match the equality he's pushing for. I'm pissed and exhausted. Temptation to put him in his place and tell him about Dad's secret handoff nearly wins out, but the bald-faced neediness in his voice forces me to take a breath.

"Let's land on you screwed up. From here on out, we vet every second of footage together. We'll discuss your role on the show after we button up the filler episodes."

His pause is too long. I did not give him the reassurance he sought.

Desmond's voice is strung tight. "Whatever works."

I take the out. "That's what works for me. We'll talk later." I end the call.

I've seen news stories about sinkholes that appear without

warning. I can't shake suspicion Desmond's behind-my-back move may be the leading edge of a sinkhole.

I collapse onto the bench to watch the sky lighten. Staring at the hypnotic flight of a seagull circling above clears my head over Desmond's daddy kiss-up.

A deeper shadow fades across my heart. Dawn is the time to kill shadows and let what lies beneath catch the light. Desmond is not the cause of my metaphoric sinkhole. I am. The vandal, button cam footage of Chorda I watched all night consumed me. The truth I've kept at bay is a drip I endured for years. Now that pipe has burst, and I've got a flood to deal with.

I don't love Chorda Lear. I am in love with her.

Every word she speaks, every time she touches me, the way we freakin' fit in each other's lives and always have supports my conviction we may be entitled to a journey beyond friendship. Don't the best love stories begin with friends first, friends who trust?

I spring off the bench as another truth hits. Trust is essential here. I must trash the button cam footage immediately. The mere existence of every stolen moment is a guaranteed trust killer. Once it's history, I'll come clean with Chorda. Destroying every second in those files is the right thing to do, even though it's painful. There is so much beauty in those scenes. Losing them forever is like torching a Picasso.

My gaze drifts to the house. "Am I crazy, Chor?"

Will she laugh if I tell her the truth of my feelings for her? Will I build a mountain of awkward between us? Will there be the possibility of laughing this off if she's not in the same place as me? Will I ever be any less in love with Chorda?

Fat chance. My emotions are not the musings of exhaustion. I'm worn down to pure truth. There's not enough energy in my bones for denial.

I'd be a shitiot to ignore the subtle shift between us lately. What I nervously wrote off as need for comfort could very well be Chorda testing the waters for more. I'm the one resisting. She's pushing like never before for me to understand her beliefs, what makes her tick. Isn't that a brand of intimacy?

Her excitement when I caught her pre-show ritual, the way she bared the depth of her creativity and love for family yesterday at the shoot, and our kiss that wasn't a kiss at the tide pool adds up to something, at least to me. Sinkhole or not, I'm ready to take a risk these fresh nuances in the friendship may be our gateway to something great.

I trudge toward the bungalow. Perhaps in sleep I will find answers to the first step I need to take in being in love with Chorda Lear. I don't bother to shed my cargo shorts and T-shirt. I fall on top of the bed face first and grab a pillow to hug. As I trade consciousness for sleep, a word pings in my head.

Equals.

I've always considered Chorda and I equals. That's not the image we project to the world. To step over the friendship line, I can't inhabit a dominant position as her producer. An imbalance of power could be interpreted as me pressuring her to enter into a relationship. That's an image I can't live with.

My lip curls into the satisfied smile of an easy fix. We'll name Chorda co-executive producer. Her input is already a vital part of the show. She just lacks the title. The other two sisters won't give a flying f. Rubata owns her makeup empire, and Glissanda, her fashion. In addition to her music, Chorda's thing will be partnering with me to shape the next incarnation of *Kickin' It With Midas* once she does claim the Golden Guitar.

Midas is another complication. Without reconciliation, there is no show for Chorda. Even more iffy is Chorda's desire to stay with the show. Giving her a producer credit is simple. The big question is, will she take it?

10

WORK OUT

BLAZING LIGHT CUTS THROUGH THE DOORWAY OF THE BUNGALOW.

"Ah, proof you're still alive," says Bibs, banging the door the rest of the way open.

On the wall, my color-coded sticky notes storyboard of Chorda scenes flutters in the late afternoon sea breeze. Bibs's chubby frame casts a shadow over me. The setting sun turns her white-gray hair gold.

"I take personal offense you missed all three meals today." She holds out a plate covered in foil. "All you deserve is a brisket sandwich and potato chips." Bibs plunks the plate on my edit board. "Did you hear me? Potato chips, not my roasted rosemary potatoes."

"Thanks, Bibs." I stand and bow. "I am not worthy."

She waves a hand in front of her nose. "Lord-a-mercy, Adair. You smell like a sump."

For half a beat, I'm afraid she's going to drag me to the bathtub the way she used to after Chorda and me would come to the house covered in sand and tide pool slime. Instead, she fans the door back and forth to circulate air.

I love Bibs. She mothered the Lear girls after Aunt Deedee died, and even though I have a perfectly good mother, I was thrown in the mix as well. She never understood how my mom and dad maintain their marriage from different coasts. I'm convinced separation is how my workaholic parents stay together. Their current Ireland tryst is an example of how they keep things fresh.

Bibs never approved of a mother, who only mothered her son in the summer and at Christmas. She had no problem being vocal on the topic. Neither her ranting nor my situation bothered me. Bi-coastal Adair was my normal. I never felt deprived. Mom produces NYC theater. Dad produces TV. End of story.

Separate but together might work for my folks. It's not the marriage I wish for.

"How's Chorda doing?"

Bibs plants hands on hips. "If you'd rolled out of bed before sundown, you'd know."

I'm lucky I scored the brisket. "In my defense, I did work all night."

She huffs. "Ms. C is as bad as you, sleeping the day away. I had to shake the girl awake to get food down her an hour ago. She's as pale as a lily."

"Did Chorda tell you what we're up to?"

Bibs softens. "The short version. It's a fine plan. I have faith the two of you will make it work." She hardens and shakes a fist at the window. "I'd like to take Midas Lear and pitch him over a cliff."

I stand and move toward her. "I'll help."

She backs away, fanning the air. "*Whuff.* Eat your sandwich, shower, and keep that girl company. She's walking around in a daze." Bibs narrows her eyes at me. "There's such a thing as too much sleep."

Before she heads out, Bibs opens the windows. I step into the garden with her when she finishes. "I'll be up to the house soon. Thanks for the food."

Bibs waves as she skirts an orange/gold bird of paradise as tall as her head.

When I re-enter the bungalow, I get a whiff of what poor Bibs endured. The open windows coax in salty sea breeze to dilute *eau de Adair*. Thank goodness, Chorda didn't show up to check for a pulse.

Said pulse kicks up to a canter at the thought of Chorda. Desire pools low in my gut like the last bands of color clinging to the sunset horizon. What will happen when I tell her how I feel?

My breath quickens. Is she experiencing the same things I am? If I never speak up, I'll never know. Right now, Chorda Lear could be talking herself out of me since I've given her no reason to believe I'm into her. My silence might kill our chance.

I've got to take a shot. The moment Chorda gives me any go sign at all, I'll take the risk and tell her how I feel. If I am totally delusional and she doesn't see me that way, it'll be easy to put distance between us. I've got the material I need for the filler episodes. I'll head into town until my blunder has time to fizzle, then we'll pick up the friendship from where we left off while my heart withers into a petrified root.

I wish I knew a witch ritual to clear my mind and give me courage. Since I've got zero in ritual chops, direct communication and a neutral venue are my tools. I grab my cell and text Chorda.

Going to work out in an hour. Care to join?

She sends me an emoji of a flexing arm.

There's my green light. I'm going to open the Adair/Chorda can of worms.

After a grooming session this side of ridiculous for a dude heading to a workout, I stroll down the path past a gallery of yellow, gold, and yellow/gold blooming hibiscus flowers to the gym bungalow. Its huge picture window overlooks the ocean. Besides a pair of treadmills and an elliptical, there are machines to target every muscle group. A rack of free weights, Yoga mats, a huge flatscreen, and a massage table fill up the rest of the space. The sisters do video sessions with their Yoga instructor when they stay out here. My foray into Yoga proved I am not he of the flexible ilk. I stick to weights and machines. A few years ago, Midas added a sauna when he decided sweating off his Guinness gut was the path of least resistance. I think he and my father used it twice.

I beat Chorda to the gym. If I start to work out and she takes too long, I'll be too sweaty. Not the dashing image I choose to portray as my overture to love. Settling into the ab machine is my first move. Will a thin layer of glisten on my skin be a turn-on for C? The weights fall with an ear-splitting *clank* as I lose my grip. Guessing what turns on Chorda Lear knocks me off base.

"Too heavy for you, doll?"

I'm so focused on looking appealing to Chorda, I miss her entrance. So much for glistening.

"I'd be happy to adjust that for you," she says, strolling over to me.

I couldn't lift a feather as I take in her form-fitting, aqua workout shorts and matching sports bra. The curve of freckled alabaster skin from her ribcage to her waist is a showstopper. It's not often I'm privy to a view of Chorda's midriff, so I wonder if her ribs have always shown in such clear relief against her skin.

She leans against my thigh as she pulls the peg out of the machine and moves it to the top position. "Try this."

I slide off the seat. "That's your setting, lightweight." I gesture for her to take my place.

"I prefer to start with stretches." Chorda walks into the center of the half-circle of machines, splits her legs, grabs her ankles, and bends over so she's looking at me upside down. "How'd the editing go? Did we get good stuff?"

The glory that is her perfectly round ass leaves me momentarily speechless. I turn away to avoid gawking. "Beyond good, Chor. It's brilliant." I move over to a leg machine with a strategic pad to hide the result in my shorts from Chorda's stretch.

Before I fake a lift, she's behind me, draping arms over my shoulders and leaning in so her cheek is next to mine. "I knew it would be with you shooting it."

Is this touching my sign? I'm shaky. Where's the line between *friendly* and *let's keep going* touching?

Chorda rests her lips to my cheek and lingers. Next, those warm, damp lips travel to my neck for another kiss, followed by a slide up to my ear for a whisper. "Thank you." Her body presses against my back.

If this isn't a thousand degrees of *let's keep going*, I have no grasp on reality.

I capture Chorda's hands and rest my chin on them. "Up for a game of *What If*?

She digs her chin into my shoulder. "I like games."

"What if I tell you I very much enjoy our position?"

Chorda frees her hands and slowly rubs graceful fingers over my chest. "What if I tell you I very much enjoy doing this?" She peels off my T-shirt and drapes her hands over my shoulders to swirl fingers through the dusting of hair across my chest.

And *let's keep going* wins out.

I cover my hands with hers. "What if I tell you I'm scared shitless about how very much I want to you keep doing what you're doing?"

She laughs gently, pressing her lips to my shoulder. "What if I tell you I am too?"

I swivel to face her. She backs away ever so slightly to let me stand. When her fingers settle on my shoulders, I rest my hands on her hips. "What if I told you I'm feeling a new kind of pull toward you, Chor?"

Her smile melts some of my nerves. "What if I told you it's about time?"

"Are you? Do you..."

She lays a finger across my lips. "That's one strike. You're not playing the game right."

I laugh. "What if I asked you how you feel about me?"

Chorda curls a strand of my hair around a finger. "What if I asked you, isn't it obvious? You're so dense. I'm starting to suffer from flirt fatigue."

"This is a big step." *Step, hell.* I've been shot out of cannon.

She lowers a hand to smack me lightly on the ass. "Strike two."

The smack undoes me. I pull her hips closer until we're about to touch. Once we do touch, the evidence of how undone I am will press against her bare stomach. "What if I asked you if we are absolutely insane to put our friendship on the line?"

Chorda rakes her nails gently over my chest. "What if I asked you to say, 'what the hell' and see what happens when we upgrade from what we thought was written in our stars?"

I slide my hands around to the curve of her magnificent ass and pull her against me. A small squeak of, dare I say, pleasure pops from her lips from the double team of my hands and my arousal. "What if I do as you ask?"

"What if I kiss you, Adair Holliday?"

"What if I say, 'are we really doing this?'" I slide my hands up her spine and into her hair. "Should we do this? We can still back off." I hesitate and loosen the pressure between our bodies. I want to give her the option, but God knows I don't want her to retreat.

"Strike three," she says, giving a low, throaty laugh that unleashes a hot quiver of want up my center. "I win. I am going to kiss you, Adair. You can kiss me back or just enjoy the ride." Chorda presses against me until I fall onto the bench. She slips her body between my knees and brings her mouth to mine.

I enjoy letting her take the lead as she captures first my bottom lip to taste and then claims the top. I open to her, and we share breath. Her tongue is first to the party, with mine joining the dance in a beat. The kiss is warm, wet, and wonderful. We claim, release, and dive deeper with each return.

I kiss Chorda Lear and may never stop.

I've expended tons of energy on restraint to avoid fantasizing specifics with her. Such imaginings seemed a breach of trust. I'm wildly fantasizing now with every sweep of her tongue against mine. Chorda snatches my hand and brings it to her breast, giving permission. She's full and heavy in my grasp. I'm suspended in altered reality as my fingers wrap around this previously off-limits part of her.

"Touch me, Adair," she gasps between kisses.

I slide both hands up under her sports bra to caress and squeeze. Hard nipples press into my palms. My focus is split between her lips and the thrill of her perfect breasts in my hands.

My words flow through a moan. "You're so lovely, Chor. So lovely."

Her hand sneaks between our stomachs and down past the elastic of my gym shorts. Fingers graze the tip of my cock, which rises to challenge the boundary of my waistband.

Chorda whispers in my ear. "Thoughtful of you to dress for easy access."

I harden more under her touch. She straddles the bench, wrapping slender legs around me as she circles appraising fingers to explore my girth. I buck my hips, trapping her hand between us. If we continue one more second, tonight will go farther than it should.

"Chor," I groan. "We can't—." I twine our fingers to pull hers free. She uses the front of her skintight workout shorts as a swap. The shape of her beneath the thin fabric slides against my length. "Adair, I want you."

"Reckless," is all I manage, fighting the urge to rip down those shorts and enjoy the heat between her legs. My body tenses. As much as I want to take her right now, I also want longevity.

As if sensing the shift in my intention, she pushes backward off the bench. "Oh, shit. You're asking me to stop."

We both glisten with the layer of sexy sweat I was going for earlier. Panting, I force words out of well attended to lips. "Not want to stop...think we should...talk first."

Chorda's face flushes, and she yanks her sports bra into place. "I thought you—"

I find enough breath to speak. "I do." I make a bargain with my dick to send blood to my brain so I do this the right way.

Taking Chorda's hand, I lead her to the massage table where there's more room. We sit hip to hip, thigh to thigh. I take a deep breath. "We shouldn't turn the bungalow into a bangalow before we're clear about where this is going."

Chorda's laugh flares. "Did Adair Holliday make a sex joke?"

I shrug.

She catches her breath. "I'd expect it of Desmond. It's a new lane for you."

My insides roil at the image of Desmond cracking sex jokes in front of Chorda.

"I shouldn't make light of what we're starting here. This is huge, Chor."

She checks out my crotch again. "It appears so."

I guide her chin so we're eye-to-eye. "You know what I mean."

Chorda gives me a quick kiss. "I do, Adair. Believe me, I've pulled myself apart thinking about you and me together. I keep coming back to the idea we could work." She narrows her gaze at me. "Any argument you throw at me, I will destroy."

I lay a hand on her thigh. "I'm sure you can, but they're still legit. I need to protect you from speculation I'm dipping into the talent—literally." I let out a nervous *hmmm* at my second sex joke of the night. "A boss taking advantage."

Chorda lets out a snort she'd never allow free in public. "Wait, you think you're my boss. Oh, sweet Adair. I'm your boss. There's no *Kickin' it With Midas* without the Lears. We're equals, you big goof."

"You say that, but is equality truly the perception? Gossip and speculation, especially from your dear sisters and my brother, could spin the concept of us into ugly media hits."

Chorda flicks her hand at me. "You're overthinking and overstressing." The beginning of a smile raises a corner of her lip. "I appreciate you looking out for my image." Her expression sours. "If I still have one that isn't coated in shit."

I take her in my arms. "Nix such self-smack talk, C. The Golden Guitar ceremony is going to be nothing more than a glitch in your artistic future."

"And this is one of the many reasons I'm so into you, Adair Holliday."

The longer I hold Chorda, the lustier my high road gets. "Regardless, we're going to face people that accuse me of taking advantage. I want to build something solid with you the right way."

She rubs her nose against my jaw. "Don't you dare tell me what we were doing isn't right."

I stroke her thigh. "It's right with a capital R, but hear me out."

Chorda settles against me.

"As much as my hot balls want you right now, I'm determined to woo you first. Mesmerize you with my charm on a date before we cross the sweet line we nearly crossed tonight."

"Old-fashioned alert. We're both adults who've been working on the preliminaries of this relationship for a long time. Making love isn't a breach of etiquette."

"Call me a throwback. I need to slow my roll because it's you, Chor."

"Slow your roll?" She giggles. "We need to upgrade your phraseology, babe."

I give her hair a tug. "My point, Ms. Lear, is you deserve gallant. I want to be gallant for you even if it's hokey. I'm that guy." I draw circles on her back. "Will you allow me to savor your company in our new light before I savor your body? I want real, not a fall-immediately-into-bed situation."

Chorda runs a finger along my jaw. "Okay, my sweet fuddy duddy." She lays a gentle kiss on my lips. "Everything you say is what I want, too, Adair. This is real to me in a world where my reality is ninety percent construct and ten percent real."

I take her face in my hands and kiss her slowly, struggling to keep the heat at a manageable level and stay gallant. "Where shall we go on our first date?"

"Your pace, your pick."

"Hmm?" I dot her nose with a kiss. "I've heard tell witches love nature. Shall we start there?"

Chorda stares at our joined hands and must feel mine shaking. Her gaze shifts upwards until we're lost in each other's eyes. "Don't be afraid, Adair. This..." She fans her hand between us. "It's going to work."

I stroke her hair and smile. "I'm not afraid."

I'm terrified.

11

HASHTAG

I'M GOING ON A DATE WITH CHORDA LEAR, A DATE THAT VERY WELL may be the opening act of a life-changer. Gone are the days where I am required to nod, offer advice, and swallow my emotions while she spills her issues with some guy. Instead of resenting those sessions where I wished her affections would waft in my direction, I'm happy for the insight they've afforded me into how to please the woman who's put the skip in my step.

Anticipation is not the only thing contributing to my incredible lightness of being. I deleted every bit of secret footage I stole from Chorda. There are plenty of golden moments in the legit shots. When the time is right, I'll fess up about the spy cam. I'll tell her how beautiful and poetic she was in the illicit narrative, assure her those private confessions no longer exist, and pray she forgives me.

The fickle June evening skews cool, so I add a light jacket to my first date ensemble of jeans and plum colored long-sleeved tee. Anything in the purple family is Chorda's favorite color. As date prep, I scored a pair of small shears from one of the gardeners and went on a flower cutting spree. My handful of yellow hibiscuses, along with golden day and calla lilies, make quite the splash. In one of the Jane Austen movies Chorda chained me to the couch and made me watch multiple times, the ingenue is courted with fresh-picked wildflowers from a prospective beau instead of the hothouse flowers stodgy bachelor number one presented to her. Chor refers to the wildflower offering as a *the dude gets her* moment. I want to create that moment for her.

Flowers in hand, I skip up to the front door because now I'm a skipping kind of dude and ring the bell.

"Hot date on duty."

No one answers, so I give it a *ding-ding* double second push and glance at my watch. Yep, I'm right on time. When the door remains shut, I try a kicky patterned knock loud enough to echo inside before resuming my debonair stance as suitor. Bibs's grumbling spills out the open door.

"If you forget your key, go to the kitchen door instead of bothering me. I'm in the middle of a sensitive sauce."

I lay a hand to my heart. "Apologies, Madame. I'm here to pick up Ms. Lear for a date."

Bibs gives me the squinty sidewise once-over. "A date, is it? Does she know it's a date?" She eyes the flowers. "I see you spared no expense."

A flush of heat spikes up my neck as my cinematic gesture morphs into being ID'd as a flower-picking cheap ass. "The lady is well aware."

Bibs laughs. "I thought my hair would turn completely white before you finally came a courtin' that girl." She steps aside. "Do come in, sir. If we had one, I'd ask you to wait in the parlor. My date is with a bubbling sauce."

It takes willpower not to follow her and beg for a taste of said sauce, singing its herbtastic siren song. As Bibs disappears into the kitchen, Chorda calls from upstairs, shifting my culinary desires into more intimate musings.

"Adair?"

"None other."

"Sandals or sneakers?"

I happen to find Chorda's high-arched feet and brightly painted toes especially appealing, but natural terrain will be involved in our date. I'd hate for her to stub one of those adorable toes.

"Sneakers when we get there. Feel free to wear sandals in the car." There's a win-win.

"Gotcha."

Two minutes later, the most beautiful woman in the world descends the stairs. Her auburn hair is twisted into a messy bun that leans into a more carefree Chorda than the stress sandwich personified she's been of late. Bright green shorts show off a pair of legs I hope to become better acquainted with in the near future. Her green print, off-the-shoulder blouse makes our date already a success in my book. Green is *my* favorite color.

Chorda zeroes in on the bouquet, and her smile turns me to mush. It's freeing no longer having to hide my mushification with this woman.

"For you," I say and hand her the bouquet.

She takes a deep sniff and peeks at me over a hibiscus. "These are not from the hot house."

I pull down my fist in a victory pump. "Yes. Reference acknowledged."

Chorda hides behind the bouquet. "At least someone thinks me worthy of a golden gift."

I gently move two yellow calla lilies aside so I can kiss her cheek. "Midas will come around."

After a quick stop in the kitchen to taste Bibs's onion, basil, vodka sauce and add the flowers to the vase of still perky sunflowers, we hop in the Tesla and head east.

"Are you going to tell me where we're going, or is it a first date surprise?"

I tiptoe fingers across her shoulder and claim a loose strand of hair to twirl. "Your call."

"I want to guess. Give me a clue." She grabs my hand. "No, I'll ask you questions. Ten bucks says I'll figure it out in less than ten questions."

"You're on." Chorda loves her games.

She tucks her legs onto the seat. "Freeway, yay or nay?"

"Yay."

"Snacks involved?"

I scrunch my lips at my lack of snack forethought, especially after yesterday's alleged blood sugar fade. I've arranged our date to be an afterhours affair. The last thing I need is to be trailed by angry *Kickin' It With Midas* fans pissed at what went down at the failed choosing ceremony. "I will feed you if necessary."

Her hand snakes across the top of my thigh and continues until it rests dangerously close to my crotch. "You'd better."

I intend to say, "wooing here." My discomfiture results in "Whoo," and a groin pulsing along to the rhythm of the song on the radio. With triumphant giggles, she rests her wandering hand on her own knee as I execute a tricky freeway merge.

"Last night, you landed on nature. Are we going to park somewhere with a view in the Angeles National Forest and have sex in the car?"

"While that sounds romantic, I'd be worried the whole time a maniac would spring from the underbrush and attack us when my pants are off."

She slaps my shoulder. "Too many slasher movies. I'm cutting you off." Chorda hums to herself, thinking. "Are there more flowers involved in our date?"

"Ding, ding. We have a winner."

Chorda is silent for a long stretch, studying our route like a cartographer on a busman's holiday. "We're not heading into town."

"Is that your fifth question?"

"Not a question, merely an observation."

She claps her hands. "No food. More flowers, and—based on our trajectory—you're taking me to the Enchanted Garden."

"Damn, I'm out ten bucks."

Chorda strikes fast, dipping her hand into my back pocket to grab my wallet. She waves a twenty in front of my face. "Since I guessed in less than five, you owe me double."

"And this is why I stopped playing board games with you years ago. You're a rule-changing cheat."

She gives my earlobe a quick nip. "Changing the rules is fun."

I grab her hand and bring it to my lips. "I'm very okay with our recent rule change."

Last night, after I left Chorda in the gym, I tried to imagine our new reality. It was impossible to frame. She's not someone I need to get to know. She's Chorda, my best friend. What will Chorda and Adair be with delicious new layers?

"I love this place," Chorda chirps as we pull into the nearly empty parking lot of Enchanted Garden.

The name is misleading. The sprawling grounds are a mini wilderness divided up into sections with alluring names such as, Primeval Forest, Sacred Circle, Feast of Roses, and California Gold. Some portions of the park are manicured while others rock an untamed vibe. The gardens are the perfect metaphor for Chorda.

Once out of the car, Chorda grabs my hand, and we head for the main entrance. Her palm touching mine threatens new levels of mushification. Everything about our new beginning is enchanting.

The front gate is shut. As we approach, a tired-looking old-timer in a khaki Enchanted Garden shirt with a name tag that reads Mr. D, opens it a smidge and peers at us. "Are you Holliday?"

I hand off a hundred-dollar bill. "Yup. I appreciate you sticking around, Mr. D. is it?"

He snaps up the money and pockets it. "I can give you an hour."

"Perfect," I say, and he opens the gate wide enough to let us through.

Mr. D. gestures at a group of picnic benches near a wooden Café sign. "You're welcome to anything left in the grab-and-go case." With a wave, he slips into the gift shop.

I reclaim Chorda's hand, and we head for the grab and go. "Told you I'd feed you."

She nods at the gift shop. "If I'd known you had a man on the inside, we would have come here sooner."

We stuff a pair of basil, mozzarella, sun-dried tomato sandwiches and sodas from a vending machine into Chorda's bag and begin our trek into Primeval Forest. The sun dips behind the western hills to hand the forest over to shadow. Giant ferns nearly as tall as us line the dirt walkway.

Chorda drops my hand and darts over to a giant redwood tree. She leans in and inhales the bark. "Mmm, come smell."

I follow her through the underbrush and press my nose to bark.

"What do you smell, Adair?"

"Bark."

She swats my ass. "Close your eyes and take in its fragrance."

I obey and am rewarded with a deep, woody vanilla scent. "It's a vanilla shake."

Chorda embraces as much of the trunk as she can and whispers. "It's life. It's rebirth. It's ancient power."

As if Chorda called it, a strong breeze carrying a buffet of scents winds its way through bushes and between trees to find us. She leans her back against the redwood and shuts her eyes, absorbing the presence of the place.

I'm speechless. This woman belongs to the tree, to the breeze. She's more than a lover of nature, she is nature, a part of the force she summons with her adoration. I'm suddenly hungry to understand the part of her I've always kept at arm's length.

"Tell me about being a witch."

Her eyes open slowly, and I'm riveted. "Really?"

"I want to know it all. When did you first know? What does it mean to you?"

She throws herself into my arms. "I've wanted to share this part of me with you for so long."

I tilt her chin up. "I'm ready to share everything with you, Chor." I lower my lips to hers and slowly savor the kiss.

We wind our way through the Enchanted Garden as she shares what her craft means to her. How Chorda believes it's a gift and a responsibility passed through the O'Leary bloodline.

Chorda's knees suddenly buckle. If my arm hadn't already been around her, she'd be in a heap.

"That didn't feel like blood sugar. You crumpled."

"I tripped on a root."

I glance back at the path. No root in sight.

"Chor, are you sure you're okay?"

She waves me off. "I'm just strung out and tired. Let's sit. I have more to tell you." We settle on a bench in front of a waterfall high enough to block everything beyond it, encasing us in our own world.

"Our craft is a connection, Adair. My connection to my sisters, to my father, and to the natural power that infuses everything in the world we can and cannot see."

"Your gods and goddesses?"

Her smile is gentle. "Yes. They connect the past to the present and nurture the flow of life."

Staying one step removed from Chorda and her family's witchcraft has been my policy, but now, hearing her speak of it so lovingly and with unwavering devotion makes me question my skepticism. Chorda is honest about everything in her life. Why should her belief system be any different?

She drops her head to my shoulder. "What are you thinking, Adair?"

"I'm thinking I've been an ass to resist such a vital part of you."

Her hand plays with my knee. "Not a total ass, an annoying skeptic."

"Generous."

She kisses my jaw. "I'm patient. I knew you'd come around." Chorda pulls away to study me. "Have you come around?"

"I'm trying. The way you speak about your..." I press my lips together. "What do you want me to call it?"

"My craft."

I nod. "Your craft is like your songs, deep and soulful." An idea blasts into my head. I kick out a foot and disturb a turtle on the edge of the little stream spilling out of the waterfall. It snaps at my shoe before sliding into the water. "Will you say this again to camera?"

Chorda drops her head back and huffs a stream of air into the branches above us. "Is everything about the show?"

Damn. She's right. I'm blowing it. We're on a date, not a shoot. "No, of course not. You carry me away, Chor, and my wheels spin."

She plays with the hair above my ear. "How is it we never noticed before how good we can be together?"

I want to shout I've noticed it my whole life but conjured every excuse to deny it. I've been loyal to a figurative rule book, full of entries to prevent Chorda and I from stumbling into happiness.

I take a fortifying breath. "Fear, and most recently, dread of professional flak and potential fallout."

"If we go with your idea of making me an exec producer, don't we kill that?"

"Hopefully. You never know how fans or even our fathers will react." I grab a quick kiss when she flinches at the word *fathers.* "The P.R. flak could be ugly. I hate the thought of you being hurt."

"I can handle fan shade. Rubata and Glissanda deal with it all the time. They'll help me."

Doubt ricochets around my insides like a pinball. I can't picture the elder Lear sisters truly being supportive of Chorda given how, offscreen, they minimalize and pick on her. It frightens me that she chalks their friction up to a sisterly dynamic when there are dark edges she doesn't see. I pull her closer. "I'm going to be blunt. You've always been the darling of the show. Fan pushback from the choosing ceremony is new ground for you. Adding me to the mix could make it worse."

Chorda perches on my lap and slides her hands around my neck. "You're already in the mix, so shut up." She does an excellent job of shutting me up with a dash of her tongue over mine that shifts to an enticing exploration of my ear. Her voice is husky. "Define fallout."

Her ass against my cock makes striving for clarity of thought a challenge. If our hour wasn't nearly up, I'd delay the entire conversation with forest foreplay. "Fallout if we don't work. Fallout, fall apart... See where I'm going?"

Chorda is on her feet, hands on hips. "Why are you so obsessed with a doomsday scenario? Try assuming we'll be a brilliant couple."

When I reach for her hands, she pulls away. "Chor, you and me together is heaven, but I'm a practical guy. You could break my heart." When she opens her mouth to argue, I raise a hand. "Or I could break yours."

She clenches her hands.

I close my fingers around her fists. "I want to deny that possibility too. Shit happens." A wave of guilt for the spy cam shots I stole from her washes over me. My vandal footage is legit fodder for a heartbreak. "We're complicated. Our lives are tied up together. There's risk taking us to a new level. We could decimate a lifelong friendship."

She relaxes a bit and plops down next to me on the garden bench, staring at the waterfall. With a musical chirp, she whips around to face me. "Okay, my practical rule lover, let's spell it out right now." She runs the toe of her sneaker around the edge of a rock. "If we break up..." She shakes her head. "I can't believe there's even a need to say this." She fills her cheeks with air and blows. "If we break up, we agree to give each other a month of space to be pissed or mourn or whatever. After that, we grab cables and jumpstart the friendship."

I'm surprised jumper cables exist in Chorda's awareness. "You're proposing a dead battery scenario?"

"Blunt, but yes, one month to get over a breakup, no matter who initiates, then we hit replay to rebuild what we were before you saw me naked. Problem solved. If leaving the friend zone blows up in our faces, you won't lose me, and I won't lose you."

I've never discussed a breakup before a relationship got off the ground. Granted, I've never shifted gears from friends to seeing each other naked before. My need to diffuse the intensity of this topic rises to the surface. "Do you discuss naked with all your first dates?"

A sly smile sneaks across Chorda's plump lips. "Just this one."

"As much as I enjoy naked talk, I appreciate you indulging my practical side.

She slides a finger up my neck and tugs at my ear. "I get there's nothing simple about redefining us." Her gaze falls on a lavender rose bush growing behind the bench. She reaches to pluck off a bloom. "There's nothing simple about the pattern of these rose petals, swirling out from the center. They overlap and work together to make an exquisite design."

As Chorda pets the rose, the golden streak in her hair glows. I want so badly to touch the radiant strands and discover if there's warmth to its light. In my gut, I know such a touch would be more intimate than the way I touched her in the gym last night. Stroking her personal gold would be touching her essence. Such a step requires invitation.

Chorda's eyes drift shut as she inhales the rose's scent. "A rose is more than a rose. It's nature's expression of complexity and elegance." Chorda rubs the rose petals against my cheek the same way she dusted me with the sunflower after the ritual. "We're a rose, Adair. Let us be a rose."

It's killing me not to capture this beat of eloquence for the show. Chorda weaves her point into a graceful outpouring of imagery and emotion.

I burn to take her in my arms and promise we are her rose. I do believe we have a chance. I want to build an exquisite design with her.

Before I voice my intention, an overloud throat clearing rises from the path. *Curse you, Mr. D.*. Our hour is up.

I call out. "On our way." My fingers twine through Chorda's. "This is very heavy first date stuff."

"Did you expect anything less?"

Our lips meet in a smile, and we saunter out of paradise. The second we step through the exit, a small cluster of paparazzi descend to shout questions.

"Are you and Midas talking yet?"

Before Chorda answers, I give her upper arm a squeeze and shake my head to keep her from speaking.

"How does it feel to fall from grace?"

Chorda's brow furrows. She stays silent as lights flash at us.

"Are you here shooting *Kickin' It*?"

"Ms. Lear and I are scouting locations for future episodes." I nearly blurt her new executive producer status to quell any hint of impropriety at the two of us being caught after dark in a deserted garden. My wiser internal editor takes over. With *Kickin' It* in flux, such an announcement could deepen the shit storm instead of calming it.

We almost make it to the car when the bomb drops. "What's it like being the viral hashtag *Dischorda*?"

"Pardon me?" says Chorda.

We've power walked to my car. I throw open the passenger door and nudge Chorda inside. Faces press to her window as I round the car to the driver's side.

"Give us something, Dischorda."

I face the small crowd. "Ms. Lear has no comment on recent events except to say family is and always will be the center point of her life." After a door slam, I honk and ease into reverse. It's enough to put a period at the end of this unfortunate sentence.

Chorda grabs her phone from her bag, knocking our unopened grab-and-go sandwich boxes to the floor.

"Wait until we get home, Chor. We'll look at it together." She ignores me, so I pull over to see her cell screen.

It's all kinds of ugly.

The three trending hashtags: #dischorda, #chortruths, and #falseprincess are the least of the poison. Character attacks and accusations of Chorda finally showing her true colors fill social media. I'm astounded her truthfulness at the choosing ceremony spawned such hate. It's tragically out of proportion.

Tears stream down Chorda's face as she swipes at her screen. Rubata's voice fills the car.

"*Our sissy turned pissy and missied her chance to praise Da. Dischorda is foolish and mulish to turn total ghoulish on us. If you want to avoid the ghoul in you, grab my new palette of 'kiss kiss sweet' eye shadows.*"

Chorda taps her cell, and Glissanda's voice slides up and down the scale.

"*Doses of Ashwagandha would be a perf adaptogen to mellow the raging bear inside our little sis. The right tea tea for Chor Chor might mellow her dark side if she even wants to find the light. My new line of whisper fleece robes is guaranteed to shift anger into harmony. If you're listening, slide one on, Sister.*"

Un-flippin'-believable! Rubata and Glissanda turned full influencer bottom-feeder to hawk their wares while whipping up vitriol against Chorda. No wonder the fandom is skewing anti-Chorda.

I pull the phone from her hand and slip it into my pocket. "Enough for now."

She digs fingernails into my arm. "I have to respond."

"Don't dignify attacks."

"If my sisters can use their influencer status as a weapon, why can't I use mine as a shield?"

I must convince her to tread lightly. One wrong note could screw up things even more for the show. "Something's off, Chor. We need to understand what's going on before you lash out, or you'll wear the vandal hat." Leaning over, I kiss the wet spots on her cheeks.

She touches her forehead to mine, and we breathe together until her tears stop.

Chorda sits up and grips the dash. "The press, the fans, act like they own anything Lear." Her head drops against the headrest. "I get it's the price of fame. If you want one, you deal with the other. I've always felt one step removed since I don't put myself out there to the extent Glissanda and Rubata do." Her laugh holds no joy. "I thought distance would protect me. I sing a fool's song."

"You're no one's fool, Chor."

She retrieves her phone and shakes it. "Clearly, I am." The phone goes flying across the dash. "Where's my spontaneity of being? I do what I feel is right, and I'm a vandal."

"It's a nasty media surge. We'll squelch it," I say, catching her phone as it falls through the steering wheel.

Chorda grabs the phone again and jabs her fingernail against the screen, reading more trash. "Now everything about me is wrong, my body, my voice, my loyalty." A strangled sound escapes her beautiful mouth. "They're telling people to boycott my next tour."

"Please stop looking." I wrap fingers around her wrist. "We'll consult P.R. and plan a level-headed counterattack."

"When did my life become a war?" She holds the cell out to me. "Don't let me look."

I slip her blinged out phone into my pocket and wrap my arms around her. She rests her head against my collarbone. "It's a moment in time, Chor. Bad moments end to make way for better ones." I stroke her hair, being careful to avoid the gold strands that lost their sheen with her distress. When she starts to fidget, I reach down and retrieve our plastic sandwich boxes. "Dinner?"

Chorda smiles and produces the two sodas from her bag. We

eat in silence. I swallow down a sandwich into a stomach plotting mutiny. She only frees a single chunk of mozzarella and basil leaf from the bread and nibbles. If Chorda is facing this level of flak from the live broadcast, how much higher will it escalate if our relationship is outed? Accusations of sleeping with the boss can only hurt her.

I take a long swig of soda to find the courage to say the words I owe Chorda. "This is the shit I was talking about. If you don't want to compound the garbage by adding me into the mix, I respect that."

Chorda slaps the dashboard. "Stop it, Adair. I don't want an out. I want you." She grabs my hair and yanks me in, crushing her lips to mine. We lose each other in a cola and basil kiss, one that nearly erases the shitty ambush that ended our first date.

I brush a finger across her swollen lips. "I will always be there for you, Chorda. Always." I mean what I say. What I don't say is being there for her might not involve naked. I must be clear-headed as to what's the best course of action for Chorda, staying friends or changing our game. Any decision I make will be in her best interest, even if I break my own heart.

Despite the caffeine level of our dinner beverage, an emotionally drained Chorda is asleep as soon as the car hits the steady glide of freeway.

There's heaviness in my chest I can't shake. Tonight should have been giddy and playful as we explored this new phase of Adair and Chorda. My head is a muddle except for a single clear thought. I'm going to hunt down the traitorous Mr. D., who clearly tipped off the press, and get my hundred back.

12

LISTEN

I LONG FOR THE DAYS OF A LANDLINE HANDSET TO SLAM DOWN AND hang up on Desmond.

"Have you ever tried to control those bitches, Adair?"

"Do-not-ever-call-them-that! On my watch, no matter what goes down between you, Rubata, and Glissanda, you'll show respect." At the moment, I'm ready to launch both older Lear sisters and Desmond out to sea in a paper boat.

"Apologies. Allow a rephrase. I can't control those ladies."

"Don't placate me, Desmond. Be my man on the ground at the studio until I can return Chorda to the fold. I depend on you to support a reconciliation scenario, not make things worse." Despite the cool evening breeze trickling through my bungalow, a line of sweat drips down my spine.

Chorda sleepwalked into the house after our date ended in a dumpster fire. I haven't seen her all day while I've been negotiating with Rubata and Glissanda to take down and tone down Chorda hater posts on social. In the plus column, Dad's network cronies are good to go with the reconciliation scenario, including Chorda footage after I convinced them Hamilton is in the process of bringing Midas onboard. This will be a solid case of ask forgiveness not permission.

I brush hair out of my eyes. "Where are we on Midas approving your footage of the filler segments? I can't get him on the phone."

"Bad news, little brother. His last words on the subject were: 'Cobbled together tripe.'"

"He spoke to you?" Why the hell is Midas speaking to Desmond and not me?

"Not to me, to Rubata. She says he thinks the segments are too soft on Chorda."

"Rubata is not the poster gal of reliable."

Desmond's breath gusts through the phone. "I don't get the sense she's lying, Adair. Maybe I hit the emotional notes too hard and flipped Midas out. He's not exactly in an objective frame of mind."

The invisible tension rope around my head tightens. "I'm coming in for a face-to-face with Midas."

"He hasn't left his rooms since the broadcast, and Rubata is the only person he allows in."

The rope slides down around my middle and squeezes. "Who else has seen him? Do we have confirmation he's okay?"

"Molly, his chef, swears he's eating."

Well, that's something. I don't want Chorda to know how bad it is with Midas. She'll take full blame when Lear's monstrous ego is the true cause of his pity party. Part of me wants to let Dad know Midas is cloistering, but that would not bode well for confidence in my new leadership.

I take a deep breath. "Des, I've got the go ahead for the segments from the other network higher-ups. Since Midas has gone to ground, we're going to include Chorda's footage in the narrative without his okay."

"Hamilton is cool with that?"

"Yep." *Kickin' It With Midas* is past tense in my father's life, and Midas is blowing me off. I'm going with my gut. "In fact, I want to start airing the new episodes tomorrow night instead of waiting. The faster we put this situation in the rear view, the sooner we jump into next season's rebrand."

A choking noise comes through the phone. "Tomorrow night?"

"Why not? Both our segments are good to go. I reviewed the latest cuts today on episode one, they're ready."

"Adair, please give me time to rework my piece. Midas's 'cobbled together tripe' comment really bothered me. I'd like to add a few strokes to up the ante and pluck heartstrings."

I drop my head. Disappointment at any delay to revive Chorda's image and present the love letter of truth and beauty to her father drags me down. I defy social media to continue slinging mud after they hear her side. The sooner Midas gets off his ass and listens to what she has to say, the better. Every day the separation continues, Chorda's petals droop a little more. I swear this whole cluster fuck is making her sick.

I have a smidge of leeway to give Desmond a little time to finesse his Rubata/Glissanda segments, but I don't want a huge overhaul. "Describe strokes."

"I want to shoot scenes with Rubata and Glissanda commenting on the social media garbage.

I sputter and douse my screen with droplets. "That'll fan the flames."

"Imagine how effective it will be if their mea culpas are just as public as the negativity. Their remorse will lean beautifully into your spin of resurrecting Chorda's reputation. Imagine a silhouette shot of the two elder Lears weepy as they gaze at baby sister's empty room."

I swipe a sleeve across my spotty screen and ponder. With heartfelt testimonials and sensitive editing, Des might be on to something. A boost from the prickly sisters might be the ticket to tip Midas's scales in Chorda's direction.

"Okay, you've got twenty-four hours, Des."

"I'll make it happen."

A shading in his tone unnerves me. I write it off as a by-product of my own tension. I almost sign off but decide to get all unfinished business between my brother and I out in the open. "Des, before you go, I want to loop you in." I want him to understand that, under my leadership, he is an insider, not the fringe player Dad treated him as. "I'm naming Chorda executive producer alongside me for the *Kickin It* franchise."

Ice cold, dead nothing from his end of the line.

"It sounds out of left field, but you'll understand my reasoning soon. For now, think of it as giving her a *thing*. Rubata's got cosmetics and Glissanda her fashion. Chorda will claim producing."

Desmond's voice is low and strained. "Isn't writing music her *thing*?"

"Yes, but producing is an add-on she needs."

"Chorda Lear will be my boss?"

I borrow Chorda's reasoning from our gym workout. "The Lears have always been our bosses. An official title won't alter that."

Desmond grunts.

"Des, when we're past this, you and I will sketch out plans for your future with new Golden Pipes properties."

"Whatever you say, Little Brother. I've got work to do." He ends the call.

Damn. The last bone I tossed was too little, too late. Bad move to bring up Chorda's new title before we start actively planning next season. The intention was to make Des feel involved. Instead, I alienated him.

After a shower to wash off trepidation and sweat, I pull on shorts, a Golden Pipes Records logo tee, and flip flops with the intention of enticing Chorda into a second date of walking along a moonlit beach. I hope said plan will hit the right notes of nature and me. If she's still in a funk over the social media attack, which she has every right to be, tonight will be about ice cream and self-pity.

She didn't reach out to me today. Fear buzzes in my stomach at the thought Chorda spent the day deciding something new with me is in fact, a bad idea.

I grind knuckles against my chest where my heart has taken off running. If that's what works for her, I'll go back to being the absolute best friend a guy with a crushed heart can be.

In the kitchen, Bibs greets me with hands on hips. "My famous mud pie is in the freezer. Do not raise a spoon to it unless Chorda is with you. Understand?"

Ah, so Bibs anticipates ice cream and tears.

"Cross my heart."

"There's zucchini quiche in the fridge. That, you may eat alone, but I'd prefer if you'd slide some of it down Chorda's gullet as well. She's picking at food, not eating it."

"Bibs, do you think Chorda is okay, health wise? She seems to be..." I search for the right word. "Shaky?"

She smacks a wooden spoon against the counter. "Her fool of a father sent a storm cloud after her. Chorda is feeling its weight. Let her have her fade. It'll pass."

I lean elbows on the island and smile at Bibs to counter the scold. "Zucchini quiche, my fave. Don't feel obligated to cook for me too."

She flicks a wrist. "I've cooked for you your whole life. Why should I stop now?"

I round the island and pull her into a side hug. "I hope you know how much I appreciate you."

Bibs wiggles out of my grasp. "You'd better."

"Where's Chorda?"

She nods toward the beach. When she catches me glancing at the wine fridge, she swats my arm and comes as close to giggling as I've ever heard. "You behave, Adair."

"Yes, ma'am." I flash my best sweet face. "I'd behave better if I could bring Chorda her favorite non-mudpie snack to slide down her gullet."

Bibs shakes a finger at me and then proceeds to pack up brie and crackers while I grab a bottle of Zin.

"You'll earn more points with the Pinot Noir."

I feign shock. "Why Bibs, if I didn't know better, I'd think you were rooting for me."

She tucks a bottle of Pinot Noir in the cooler and zips the bag with a flourish. "Goodnight, Adair."

I kiss her cheek. "Goodnight, Bibs."

On my way out the glass patio door, I grab a woolen throw of O'Leary tartan off a chair in the dolphin room and toss it over my shoulder. A bit of cashmere under our bums will be a nice touch for a moonlight picnic after a romantic stroll at water's edge.

My dreamy-eyed fantasy takes a sour turn. Chorda's face from the press attack at Enchanted Garden wavers in my mind like a reflection in a pond. She was deeply cut. Here I am going full throttle into romance when our pairing might well add more slashes.

Not only will we have to field insinuations of impropriety on my part, but in lieu of her rejection of Midas at the choosing ceremony, she could be accused of hooking up with me to preserve her status on the show. No one will buy the truth of us.

What is that truth? My truth is being over the freakin' moon to quit hiding my feelings for Chorda. To take her actions at face value, she's all in. Is face value worth trusting, or am I a safe harbor, a wind break for the ugly gales ripping through her skies since her rift with Midas? Is Chorda's one month to get over a broken heart insurance I'll still be around when she stops needing the shield of our romance to lift her up?

I hate the direction of these thoughts. My tendency to make everybody happy could bite me in the ass. I need to know. I'd rather cut my tongue out, but I've got to ask Chorda about her vision of our longevity.

"Crimaney," I grumble to the moon. I'm going to initiate the "where are we" talk with Chorda after one date. Apparently, I left my balls in the bungalow.

Chorda isn't on the beach behind the house or at the tide pools. I breathe through the nervous clutch in my chest. Most likely, she's taking her own moonlight walk. I'm about to plot an intercept course when the sound of a guitar rises from the opposite side of the tide pools near the rock wall defining the edge of Lear property.

I make my way in the direction of the notes. Chorda sits cross-legged at the edge of the rising tide. I fear she'll be swept out to sea by an ambitious wave. Setting the picnic and tartan on the sand, I creep along the edge of the rock wall toward the water.

She's centered in a pool of cool moonlight that contrasts the toasty glow of her golden strand. Her face is bathed in warm light as she sings. Chorda hums a phrase and then adds words, changing notes, trading phrases as the song takes shape. She's writing. Oh, thank heavens, she's writing.

I get as close as I dare so as not to interrupt and lean against the rocks. The grace of her creative process transfixes me. Chorda is moonglow wrapped in a song of sea breeze. My entire being fills with a rush of love.

It takes me a moment to realize silence returned to the beach. I squeeze my eyes shut and send up a plea to the stars for her to keep singing. Sometimes when you ask, you receive. Chorda's voice soars to charm the night.

"Moon rises full in a deep blackened sky.
Waves cast curved shadows to swallow the stars.
Sing to the night of love yearning to fly.
Into the arms of the one who stays far.

Listen for heart play of what we can be.
Listen for currents of love's harmony.
Listen to spirits who sing of our days.
Listen to winds twisting round to our way.

Listen, my love, oh please listen.

Hear my sweet love call sound deep in your heart.
Can we not banish what stands in-between?
Crush deepest fears keeping lovers apart.
Come to me now shedding fortune's cruel sheen.

Listen to everything heart songs tell true.
Listen as whispers speak only of you.
Listen for beauty of risks worth the take.
Listen to promises never to break.

Listen, my love, oh please listen.

Lyrics are currency I sing to tell.
Of secrets not shared with anyone new.
My love is too grand for mere words to sell.
Through measures and notes, I reach out to you.

Listen to messages wrapped in my song.
Listen to melodies lasting ere long.
Listen for feelings too shy to reveal.
Listen for love my heart cannot conceal.

Listen, my love, oh please listen."

A whisper near my ear makes me jump sideways.

"Might you be the shitiot who isn't listening to her, Adair?"

I turn to face Justin Time, co-president of Rampion Records with Zeli and the biggest burr in Midas Lear's ass. They've taken up residence at Gothel's former beach compound adjacent to the Lear property. Personally, I like Justin. We chat fairly often. Midas would hang me if he knew the newly minted Rampion prez came to me for advice on producing reality TV and I indulge in mentoring him.

He's a creative dude and gave me solid ideas on how to shake up *Kickin' It* next season. In fact, the two of us are brewing joint Zeli/Chorda appearances to benefit both labels.

I keep my voice low, careful not to disturb Chorda. "Jeez, Time. Sneak around much?"

He matches my volume. "I made no effort at stealth. You, my friend, were in a trance." He claps my shoulder. Justin's eyes drift half closed as he listens to Chorda. His hand taps out the beat on his leg. When she pauses to work on a rough bit, he zeroes in on me. "Care to share why you're not listening to the moon sprite spouting hearts and flowers over you?"

I jerk my head up the beach to lead him away from Chorda. "She's not singing about me."

Justin coughs "jacklick" into his fist, and then laughs. "Don't even go there. Bibs let it slip you two are an item."

So much for staying under the radar. "Didn't realize you and Bibs were tight?"

"Your Bibs and my man, Rand, are a thing. Pillow talk."

Bibs and Rand Diggs, who woulda thunk Bibs goes for the bad-boy-biker type? Worry quickly trumps surprise. "I'd appreciate it if the pillow talk doesn't go further than you."

"And Zeli."

I sigh. "And Zeli."

He nods at Chorda. "For her sake, I hope you've got it as bad for her as she does for you."

My gaze returns to the woman on the beach and sticks there. "When you saved Zeli from the Rampion Tower—"

Justin whips his head around as if making sure we're alone and slashes a hand across his throat. "Saved is not a word we use when referring to the situation. Escape is where we land."

"Did you love her?"

Justin gets a gauzy expression on his face, mirroring my own. "I was a goner the first time I heard her sing away from the spotlight."

"Heard who sing?" says Zeli, materializing out of the dark.

I jump and grab my chest as my heart thuds like a brick falling from a two-story building.

Justin pulls her into a quick kiss. "You, Mrs. Rapunzel MacKenzie."

I scan the small cliff that tapers down to the water's edge. "Where are you people coming from?"

Justin spins Zeli, pulling her against his chest, and rests his chin on her shoulder. I envy the ease of their PDA.

"And I fell for him the first time he sang to me while dangling in a zip line rig over the Rampion Plaza." Zeli nuzzles Justin's neck.

"Well, I'm screwed," I say. "I can't sing."

"No, but you can listen," says Zeli.

Boy, am I listening now as Chorda's voice rises above the sound of waves.

Zeli lays a hand on my arm. "She sounds sad."

"Did you catch the choosing ceremony? It wrecked her."

"That shit was real?" says Justin. "I'd swear Midas drummed up a fake betrayal to pad his numbers."

"That would be a helluva lot easier to fix," I say, watching Chorda.

"Now I dig why the old vandal isn't returning my calls," says Justin, chewing his lip. "Dude usually enjoys ripping into me."

I turn to face him. "Not returning your calls?"

"We've been sparring over the rights to a Golden Pipe's song I want. All I get now is 'Mr. Lear is currently unavailable.'"

Midas jumps at every opportunity to clash with Rampion Records, even though I suspect he secretly appreciates Justin's brash and unapologetic ways so like his own.

Justin's further confirmation regarding Midas's radio silence coupled with Desmond's intel about the Golden Pipes president basically hiding out in his room cranks my concerns about Lear up another notch. I do need to see if I can force a face-to-face with him.

Zeli gestures at Chorda. "We popped over to confirm my gig

with Chorda on the night of Midas's induction into the Rockin' and Rollin' Pantheon. She said she has the perfect song."

It must be the song Chorda wrote for her father. If it debuts on *Kickin' It With Midas* and gets more airtime at the Pantheon gig, that could go a long way to mending Chorda's P.R. bruises. I'd been prepared to cancel the live performance, but this could be the public olive branch to reset everything.

I look beyond the couple. "You came over? How did you show up out of nowhere?"

Justin waves a hand toward a shadow in the rock wall. "You've never been in the caves between your property and ours?"

I stare where he points. "What? Caves? No."

"You should check them out," says Zeli, waggling her eyebrows at me. "Come on, hon. Adair has *listening* to do. Tell Chorda to call me." She blows me a kiss and drags Justin into the rocks.

They disappear. Justin's waving hand is last to vanish. I follow to discover an opening in the rock cleft leading into the caves. How is it I don't know about this secret entrance between the Rampion compound and Lear land? Then it comes to me. The iron fence surrounding the property used to stretch all the way to the water, blocking the rock wall, until the year a storm brutalized the cliffs and took out the fence down here.

Everything changed that year. Grant Gothel bought the compound next door to the Lear property to taunt Midas. We lost Aunt Deedee, and Midas grew the surly shell he wears. Glissanda and Rubata handled grief by cultivating burgeoning adolescent snark into their social media influencer personas. The rift between the two older sisters and Chorda began. When the storm swept the fence away and flooded the Malibu house, the grounds closed for the better part of a year. None of us ever bothered to explore the territory of the fallen fence.

The carefree childhood days I spent out here with Chorda ended.

A sustained note of pure loveliness pulls my attention to the water's edge. Chills run through me as Chorda begins her song again. It's different this time, as if her spirit joins her voice. The golden streak of her hair increases to the light of a hundred candles. As she sings, cross-legged at water's edge, the sand around her begins to lift in a swirling, silken curtain. Tiny particles in the sand cyclone twinkle, echoes of starlight. Their counterparts above pulse with the rhythm of Chorda's song.

The sense of awe I experienced during the sisters' ritual behind the Waterfall Palace returns. The elegance in which Chorda works her craft with the music is beyond the comprehension of my mind, but not my heart.

I envy the passion between Justin and Zeli and long for the same with Chorda. Bravery is not my default, but I swear, I will find the courage to destroy obstacles, both Adair-generated and real, to be with Chorda. If she'll have me, I am hers with no caveats or back out plans.

She sings.

I listen.

13

PINOT NOIR

CHORDA SETS HER GUITAR ON THE SAND AND RISES TO HER FEET inside the sparkling whirlwind. She reaches toward the moon, crossing her wrists above her head as she spins. Ruffles of her silky, yellow dress flutter around her in a shining blur as she finishes her song. "Listen, my love, oh please listen."

She settles onto the beach. Her funnel of sand and twinkles float to the earth a beat later. The only movement is strands of her hair dancing in the sea breeze.

I've moved close. "Singing about anyone I know?"

Chorda hugs her guitar and slowly turns to me. "You heard?"

"I listened."

Her lips curl up. "Touché."

"May I join you?" When she nods, I shake out the tartan throw and spread it on the sand a couple of yards farther from the water. After a quick unzip of the cooler, I free the wine and a pair of glasses.

Chorda brings her guitar and settles in next to me. She doesn't touch me as I uncork the bottle and pour. Our fingers brush when I hand her a glass.

I lift my own to clink with hers. "To listening."

We sip, never taking our gaze from one another.

I raise my drink again. "To your beautiful song."

She stares at me as if my words make no sense, a haze dimming the light in her eyes.

I nod at the guitar. "The one you were just singing."

As quickly as fog drifted into her eyes, it clears. I'm about to ask about the fade when she perks up. "You like?"

"I do." We clink again and sip. A niggle of worry twitches in my brain. I've never known Chorda to be spacey like that.

She screws the bottom of her wine glass into the sand so it doesn't tip. Fingers as warm as candle flame rest on my bare knee. "The song is about you." I lay my hand over hers as she continues. "I ached to write about you, about us. You gave me back the need to make music." Her gaze sails out over the waves. "I worried the song I wrote for my father would be the last time I could find the notes, the words. It was a struggle to write. That song was an ending. On the night of the ritual, I prayed to Bríg for the Golden Guitar to pass onto Glissanda or Rubata so I wouldn't waste its gift with my creative barrenness."

I run a finger up the smooth skin of her arm. "And this song?"

"A beginning, Adair. As we shot new footage for the show and you asked me questions about creating the music, it reminded me music is joy." Her eyes shine with tears. "You are my joy. I could sing about you forever."

My hand slides over her bare shoulder and around to the back of her neck. I pull her lips to mine and kiss the artist. Sucking her bottom lip, I savor the pinot noir clinging to it. "Please sing about me forever."

I pour refills. Chorda touches the rim of her glass to my lips, coaxing me to drain every drop. She repeats the action with mine.

"Ms. Lear, are you attempting to get me drunk?"

"If it guarantees you'll relax and not back off with excuses about doing things the right way. This is the right way."

She drinks straight from the bottle. My gaze is riveted on her slender throat. A single red drop trickles from the side of her lips, falling off her chin to drip into her cleavage. It's the sexiest thing I've ever seen.

I ease the bottle from her grasp and dip my head between her breasts to lick the drop. I taste my way up her beautiful throat until I can slide my tongue between her pinot noir coated lips. She arches, moaning. I'm as hard as the freakin' cliff wall.

Her voice is husky. "I would have settled for relaxed."

I grab her ass, encouraging her to straddle my lap.

"Oh," she sings. "This is so much better than relaxed."

She lays back onto the tartan, crossing her arms behind her head, and wraps her legs around me. I perch above her, breathless at the way her pale skin reflects moonlight. There's trust in her position, making me question my own worth to deserve it. If I hadn't already erased the secret footage, I would excuse myself to do it now.

As if I could walk away from the vision lying before me.

My fingers slide along the skin of her thighs and raise her hem to reveal the edge of skimpy lace panties. I walk my fingers up the sides of her dress, reveling in the sensation of silk beneath my touch. She shivers as I graze the sides of her breasts. With a crook of fingers, I slide the spaghetti straps of the dress off her shoulders and bunch every ruffle of her dress beneath those delightfully freckled, braless breasts.

"Pull it off," whispers Chorda.

"Oh, I will."

I dip a finger into the small puddle of wine at the bottom of my glass and paint each nipple with red liquid. Chorda closes her eyes. Faraway moonlight catches the red in her auburn lashes like sparks. She purrs and pushes her hips into mine as I swirl my fingers faster and faster to bring the tips of her pinot-noir-colored breasts to higher peaks. When purrs shift to growls, I suckle wine off her breasts until her nails sink into my shoulders.

I lean on my arms above her. "What else do you like, Chorda?"

She threads her hands in my hair to pull my mouth a breath away from hers. Instead of a kiss, the tip of her tongue tastes my lips. "Find what I like, my sweet Adair."

"You like..." I circle the tips of her breasts with my tongue. She hums with pleasure. I use my teeth to pull at each nipple, raising squeaks from Chorda. "I'm two for two."

Chorda's breasts rise and fall with deepening breaths. I grasp her in my palms and gently squeeze in a steady rhythm. Suddenly, she bucks against me, sliding the curves inside her lace panties across my arousal. I let loose a moan of my own.

When she tries to shed her dress, I capture her hands and press them above her head into the blanket. "You invited me to lead this dance."

I sweep my tongue inside her mouth, probing deeper and deeper as she reciprocates. It's a kiss to get lost in, slippery and wonderful. As soon as I've got her writhing, I take the bunched ruffles of her dress in my teeth, crawling backward away from her, my nose brushing against her skin until I work the fabric past her red painted toes. She draws her knees up, opening herself to me.

"Feel free to speed things up, Adair." Chorda sings to me in a husky tone. "I want you."

Grasping her hips, I flip her over. "You have me." I kiss and nip my way up the back of each gorgeous leg, leaving a saucy bite at the edge of her panties. "How's this?"

"Keep going." Chorda lifts her perfectly rounded bottom, egging me on. I cup a hand over the front of her panties to hold her steady as I kiss the elegant curve of her arched back. My palm is damp and hot with her readiness. I begin to move my hand up and down over the lace fabric. She quivers. A sustained note punctuates each stroke.

I rise to my knees, shifting my hands to her hips, and lift her to her feet, spinning her to face me. She wobbles. I hold her steady.

"I can't stay on my feet," she whispers.

"I've got you."

Leaning in, I tip her over my shoulder, relishing the roundness of breasts brushing against my back. I strip off her thin shield of lace and set her on her feet, still supporting her languid frame. A tangle of dark red curls draws me in. I kiss her there, melting into the pulse of her want against my lips. My tongue delves deeper to find the tight spot that starts her singing again. I suckle and savor until her knees finally do give way. She cries out and crumples onto the blanket.

The melody of her pleasure brings me to the brink of my own release. I've got to hold back. There are more mysteries to uncover in Chorda's challenge to find what she likes before I give in.

"Why are you still dressed, Adair?"

Before I stop her, Chorda crawls over to me and slides her hand up inside the leg of my shorts to stroke my cock. "I like this," she says, staring into my eyes.

"As do I." I let her work buttons and zipper to rid me of my outer layer, then she discards my boxers. I'm fully out for any passing dolphin or seagull to see. On our knees, we face one another. She rips off my T-shirt.

"I especially like this," she whispers, running her palms over my chest. Her tongue flicks across my nipples as her bare stomach presses against my cock. I can't tell if it's the roar of the surf or the hum of my own blood that deafens me. My body is a single raw nerve pounding and pulsing with need as Chorda caresses my length, her pace quickening and then slowing to keep me guessing.

We fall together onto the blanket and attack places on each other until we groan in harmony. I reach for my shorts on the sand to grab the condom from the pocket. Chorda steals the packet from me and shoves me onto my back. She takes me in her mouth for a long slow taste, nearly stealing my consciousness before she rolls the condom on.

When I try to flip our positions, she smacks my chest. "This is what I like," she says, and climbing on top, lowers herself onto me, taking in every inch with a slow glide until our bodies fuse together.

We rock to the sound of the waves, over and over. I raise my hips against her with one, then two thrusts to finish my dance. Her hand finds mine and guides me to attend to the place that allows her to take a final bow with me.

She drops onto my chest, and I wrap my arms around her. Waves slap the shore, spraying us with a fine mist. Droplets sizzle as they meet skin.

Chorda starts to speak, and I stop her mouth with kisses that last until the edge of a wave tickles my toes. "We've got to move," I say, rolling her to my side.

"Do we?" she says with a wink.

It's a hot night, and not only because a naked woman with curves to knock a man senseless lies next to me.

She slides up my body, offering a breast to my lips. I accept the gift to pay it and its partner the attention they deserve as the water soaks the edge of the blanket.

Chorda jumps to her feet and holds out her hands to me. "Dance with me, Adair." I'm anything but light on my feet as I join her. She twirls under my arm and pulls me against her. We sway in a slow dance that melts into a grind.

The water is halfway up the tartan and dangerously near our clothes. I can't let my shorts and the foil wrapped necessities inside the pocket be sucked into high tide. The wine bottle is about to set sail out to sea without a message. I'd love to pop a tiny scroll inside the Pinot Noir with the encouraging words: *Love rewards a patient heart.* It's a tad on the fortune cookie side, but without suggested lottery numbers underneath, it might be interpreted as wisdom.

We kick our things up to sandy safety as we continue our dance. She runs into the surf to twirl. The strand of gold in her hair shimmers. I'm overwhelmed with a need to feel her light between my fingers. The thought of touching it makes me begin to stiffen again.

I slowly follow Chorda into the water.

Her eyes fall to my growing readiness. "What do you like, Adair?"

"You, Chor. Everything about you." I slide my hands around to her ass and yank her against me. "This, of course." I drop a line of kisses up and down the side of her neck. "But most of all, this." I rest my hand over her heart. "You know I love you?"

She covers her hand with mine. "You know I love you too?" Her lips find my Adam's apple. "I've loved you for so long, Adair. Every time I blathered to you about boyfriends, I wanted to hear 'Screw them all, Chorda. I'm the one for you'." She kisses the cleft in my chin and then jumps into my arms, wrapping her legs around my waist.

"Screw them Chorda, I'm the one for you." We kiss as the water tries to knock us off balance.

We're too coated with sea spray to hold the position. She slides down my body until she's standing. Her hands cup my face. "And I'm the one for you," she says. "I want you. I trust you. I love you."

I rest my hands on the shoulders of the friend who's become a lover more precious to me than any hope I ever dared to dream. "I promise you the same." This beautiful soul gifts me with trust and love. Did I already break the promise of trust with my damned stolen footage?

"This is it..." She trails off and gives her head a quick shake. Confusion tightens her features.

"Chor?"

"I lost my train of thought."

I nuzzle her neck. "I've been losing mine all night."

She laughs and finds her focus. "What I want to say is, this is it. You and me."

"You and me," I echo. My gaze falls to her golden strand. It radiates light. "May I touch it?"

Chorda takes my hand and places it on her treasure.

It's smooth with a metallic texture. I slide a pinky from its top to end, afraid to cause damage. She coos at my touch. I pinch gently to measure the delicate weight of the tress. Her breathing grows ragged. When I dare to twirl the mystical hair around a finger, the entire strand heats and a corona of light surrounds my hand.

"It's exquisite."

"I've never let anyone touch it." Her expression turns shy. "I think I've been waiting for you to be the first."

"Did your gold streak make the swirly sparkle bubble when you sang?"

She laughs. "Not a bubble. You saw the manifestation of my connection to nature's energy, to my goddess, to my spirit."

A shudder runs though me as the realm of the unseen bleeds into my reality.

Chorda twines her fingers through mine. "Don't be afraid, my love. You're learning what I am. That's important to me."

"To me too." I capture her lips and imagine the sensation of joining Chorda inside her glimmering, golden energy bubble. She guides us to where the edge of the surf kisses the sand. We make love atop the cool blanket of the sea.

14

THE CUT

Thank heavens it's Bibs's night off. She'd have our heads on a platter if she discovered the sea-soaked heirloom blanket. Chorda dealt with the washing/drying of the tartan after we shared a very athletic shower followed by more rounds of discovering what we both like.

My naked body curves around Chorda in her giant bed as we both come down from the latest in a series of delicious pinnacles. This bed is a cloud. Ah, the soft mattresses of the rich and famous. My lips brush and kiss the nape of her neck while my hand strokes her golden streak. Her entire body gives off a low-level vibration when I touch her hair. It's mind-blowing.

"Painting me with wine," sighs Chorda. "Who knew you'd be so good at improvising."

I trail fingertips across her delightfully round bottom, thinking about the cooler full of cheese and crackers stolen by the tide. "You should see what I can do with brie."

She rolls to face me and throws a leg over my hip. "I'll take a cheese check." Her body is warm against mine as she relaxes toward sleep.

"A what?"

She answers with giggle purr. "A rain check, with cheese."

I nuzzle her neck. "I promise you an impressively improvised cheese check." Nipping the soft shell of her ear, I scoot to the edge of the bed. "I should go, Chor. Bibs gets up with the chickens. There are subtler ways to tell her we're together than being caught naked in your bed."

Chorda pulls at my arm, urging me to the center of the mattress so she can *mmm* and snuggle against me. Her hand reaches around to lightly spank me. "We're big ass grown-ups. She won't care."

I run a hand across her shoulder and down an arm. "Let's not test that theory. Sleep, my love. I'll see you soon."

She grabs a handful of my hair to pull me into a lazy smooch. "Don't go. I feel okay when you're touching me. Nothing hurts." Her eyes never open, and her breathing drifts into a sleepy rhythm.

Nothing hurts? I want to ask her what is hurting, but I won't wreck the calm she floats within.

I smile and dot her temple with a kiss. Soon, I won't have to leave her bed. With the rest of her life in a tangle, I've got to make sure we announce ourselves as a couple in the right way. We must appear genuine, the real deal, not a scandal or a publicity ploy.

What witty shipper blend will fans saddle us with? Chordair? That sounds like a vintage car. Adorda? Ugh, there's a piece of assemble-it-yourself furniture. Maybe we can sell the world on *Adorahh*.

I whisper, "I adorahh you. You adorahh me." Everyone is right, my default is pure sap.

I pull on sandy clothes never taking my eyes off Chorda. Her brow furrows, and a groan escapes her beautiful lips. I'm tempted to slip back in bed and hold her to chase away whatever troubling dreams dare to disturb my love.

As fast as the cloud dimming the light of her sleepy peace, serenity returns. Her breathing resumes its melodic cadence. Soft, almost imperceptible notes sneak through the song of her slumber. As impossible as it is to leave her, she needs rest. The stress of

Midas's buffoonery is wearing her thin, literally, and dulling the sharp edges of her mind. Nourishing sleep without me as a distraction is the right move.

I hum Chorda's sleep music as I make my way to the bungalow. Inside my impromptu studio, adrenaline from our fantastic night jolts me a thousand percent awake, and still a little turned on. I look down at the tidy bulge in my shorts. Making love with the right person cranks my sexual stamina to a whole new level. Not too shabby for Adair Holliday.

A light across the room catches my eye as a new email message brightens my cell screen. The phone sits on the edge of the editing console where I left it before my night with Chorda.

I check the call icon. Empty. It's still the hour of jammies and pre-daylight denial. Since I put the brakes on airing the first filler episode of *Kickin' It* to give Desmond time to polish, messages from work can chill for a few hours. If it's a dire family or Midas emergency, I'd get a call, not a text or email.

I drop onto my bed and picture Chorda embracing her own peaceful and, if I'm not mistaken, sexually sated dawn sleep. I do consider myself qualified to judge since I'm all too familiar with an unsated partner. Chorda's sexual fearlessness sparks a level of untapped daring in me I'm eager to explore further.

I gaze at the house and wish I could slip back into Chorda's bed to hide from the rest of the world. Nope, a quick cat nap is all I can afford before I don my showrunner hat for the day and become a responsible adult. I'll lie on my bed and bask in afterglow while I thank the last of the western stars hanging over the dark ocean for our incredible night. I chuckle. Maybe I'm turning part witch if I'm inclined to send thanks to the cosmos for finally allowing me to love Chorda Lear.

THE INCESSANT VIBRATION OF MY CELL AGAINST THE CONSOLE PIERCES my dreams of brie and wine dripping between Chorda's breasts. I only managed to thank a single star before my adrenaline crashed. I may have overrated the aftereffects of my newfound sexual stamina.

I roll out of bed and stumble over to my phone, yawning and scratching at misbehaving strands of hair as a new call comes in. In the sky, ruby red flares twisting through zig zags of burnt orange above the western horizon shoot a stream of panic through me. It's sunset. I've been out the whole damn day. My new habit of sleeping while the sun shines needs to end. Chorda's probably calling to make sure my heart didn't give out after our marathon last night and this morning. A doofy smile on my lips tingles in anticipation of a new round of Chorda nips and kisses.

It's my assistant, Gabs. I'm too slow to grab the call. A flotilla of messages from Gabs—and more troubling, an entire collection of missed texts from Golden Pipes Record and network exec names—fills my screen. I quick tap to get up to speed. There's a common theme: *What the hell is Chorda doing?*

I backtrack and carefully read through a series of flaming Chorda bashes. It's not merely social media toxicity or ongoing fan reaction to the choosing ceremony. Mucky mucks at the record label, our P.R. department, and the television division are seething about Chorda. I strain my brain to recall if we said anything at the Enchanted Garden press tangle to spark such a mess. It's the final message from the show's director that drops me smack dab into the middle of the disaster.

Hamilton would never let something this inflammatory on the air.

"The hell?" What inflamed the airways?

I grab the remote and snap on the wall-mounted television. It doesn't take many clickety clicks to get to the Golden Pipes channel. My stomach twists into tight spirals as I select *Kickin' It With Midas.*

"No!" Sure enough, a new episode of the show stares me in the face. Did someone screw up and put the first filler episode on air before Desmond added his tweaks? Even if they did, there was nothing incendiary enough in the last version I saw to provoke such upheaval. Maybe some noses are still out of joint about Chorda not singing for Lear, but not enough to raise the tower of WTF sitting on my phone.

I take a couple of steadying breaths and give myself a pep talk. "Chorda fans will understand." A paper sack for possible hyperventilation would be handy right now. I can't fathom how phase one of Chorda's narrative can be received so horribly. Shit, did Midas see it and put a hit out on me for including Chorda without his express permission?

I start the episode. At first, it plays out as expected, which calms me. Our chosen narrative dances through the beginning of the story of an estranged daughter longing to repair the rift with her Da. About three quarters of the way, shit hits the fan. It's my footage without sound. Instead, there's a voiceover posing as Chorda. It isn't her. I'm the one to order ADR on the segment, and I did no such thing.

The *I need to drop my head between my legs to keep from fainting* sensation dumps me in a chair.

The imitation Chorda voiceover is brutal.

"*Midas Lear is an over-the-hill bully who hasn't written a decent song in a decade. Why would I lower myself to sing his praises when I'm a natural talent and twice the musician he is?*"

Glissanda is first to chime in with a weepy countenance. "*How dare Chorda slander our father?*"

Rubata's commentary comes roaring in right behind Glissanda's. "*Our youngest sister would be nothing without the love and support Da has given her all her life. What does she do? Spit in his face on live television.*" She flaps an arm at the camera. "*Chorda, a natural talent? That's a hard no. She's the product of mix boards and Auto-Tune.*" Rubata wrinkles her lips, which look even larger on camera as she twitches each shoulder in turn. "*Ain't nothing authentic in my itty-bitty sissy.*"

I snap out of my stupor to seethe. Chorda is the last person on the planet who needs an autotune processor to shape the notes of her music. The woman has perfect pitch. I can't tell if it's Glissanda or Rubata, but one of the sisters is the narrator. Curse the family vocal genes for making the sisters sound so much alike.

Fake "Chorda" continues a bitchy tirade at Midas. Glissanda and Rubata infuse bitter digs guaranteed to turn Chorda's bad press into a bonfire. They officially christen her Dischorda, riffing on the offensive hashtag.

The onscreen Chorda is a self-serving, petulant favorite fallen from grace. The poetry of reconciliation we wrote together is robbed of its meter and rhyme. The false portrait of Chorda is the video version of drawing a beard and mustache on the Mona Lisa.

The boiling pot is further stirred with snippets of Midas in potty-mouthed glory caught after we cut the live feed on the choosing ceremony. I cringe as he roars onscreen, *"This is my fucking kingdom, you shitiots and jacklicks. You are not worth the dust which the rude wind blows in your face."* Lear grabs the director by the front of his shirt and shoves him. *"Do not dare accuse me of crossing a line. I'm the victim here. I am a man more sinned against than sinning."*

A scythe hollows out my insides. Reality show rule number one: Cameras are always rolling. Of course, the ugly was documented. Midas's post-Chorda spewfest is now cemented in the zeitgeist.

Infamy is still fame.

"This is the worst." I bite my tongue. Whenever I've labeled something *the worst,"* fate tends to throw something much worse my way.

There's a backbiter on the loose. It kills me to admit it, but I gave Desmond an opening to ignite this media slur with permission to recut his footage. He wouldn't dare. My brother is trying to win approval, not damn himself by screwing up everything we've carefully planned out. Behind painful suspicion, I harbor a teeny dust mote of hope he isn't the one behind this. It sickens me to think Midas's rage at Chorda drove him to create this piece of vindictive theater.

I call Desmond. It goes straight to voice mail. "Call me the fuck right now."

For a half second, I consider hailing my father. Running to him would be a colossal admission of failure. I call Gabs instead.

She's a mess. "Adair, where have you been. I've been calling you since the episode dropped. How fast can you get here?" Her voice breaks, and I know she's crying. I'm a royal ass for putting her in a position to field the shitstorm while I slept off my sexhaustion.

"Pronto, I promise. Who the hell authorized that episode to air?"

Gabs hiccups. "What? You did. I forwarded the email per your instructions and pushed the episode through."

I nearly break the glass on my screen getting to my email *sent* folder. There it is. My instructions to air this version of *filler episode one* last night. Some evil-for-brains hacked my email. Desmond and Midas both splash through the acid bath in my stomach.

I force my voice to hide the rage setting my blood on fire. Gabs does not need to take more shit for me. "Track down Desmond, and chain him to a chair until I get to the studio."

"I haven't seen him today."

My dust mote of hope Desmond isn't behind everything flits out the window. Desmond is the producer on site. At the very least, he should have blocked the episode or taken it down. He did neither. "I'm sorry you had to field crap, Gabs. Get me deets on where Desmond and the Lear sisters are right now, then you're off duty."

Her voice shakes. "Okay."

I make the calls to wipe the episode off the air. It's too little, too late. Even if that slice of tripe is off the Golden Pipes Network, the horror will be all over the internet in endless sound bites and quick clips. The only thing keeping me from sprinting to my car and confronting Desmond is ass-clenching fear Chorda saw the episode. She was adamant about refusing to watch the show until she's reconciled with Midas, but what if someone tips her off? This will destroy her.

As if summoned, her ringtone lights up my cell. I swallow the lump expanding behind my Adam's apple. *Stay cool.* "Hi, Babe."

"Hey, loooover," she coos into the phone. "Your improvising from last night knocked me out until now. Bibs is off to the movies with her fine hunk of Rand. I'm calling in my cheese check."

I nearly howl at the sunset in relief. She hasn't seen the show. I ache to warn her not to go anywhere near a television. If I do, she'll fly straight to the remote and watch the damn thing. By not cluing her in, I'm tightrope walking over the Grand Canyon in a monsoon.

"I've got a quick face-to-face in town. Can you wait?"

"How long?"

As long as it takes to grab a fleeing Desmond by the ankle to keep him from escaping to get to the bottom of this. "Couple of hours, tops."

"I'm wearing a pouty face." She laughs. "It's actually perf. Tonight's luscious sunset pushes me to write. Hopefully, getting creative will kick this damn headache I've been fighting for hours." Her sigh is a symphony. "I thought I'd never feel so motivated again. I shouldn't waste the inspiration of a glorious sky, even for you."

"You shouldn't waste inspiration for anyone." Despite the clot of anger and dread choking me, I'm jazzed Chorda will be writing. The return of her gift is more important than whatever I've got to clean up in town. "Go chase that sky, sweetheart."

"I will." She makes kissy noises. "See you for dessert." With a loud smack, she ends the call. I hope that means she'll be eating dinner.

Too late, her words sink in. *This headache I've been fighting.* Worry bites my ass. Chorda's stress is taking quite a toll on her. I shake it off. She's depressed. It's natural there are physical side effects. Assuming our budding relationship would counteract the grief over her father's rejection is damn selfish.

If the burden of all this continues to beat her down, I'm going to broach the subject of her health. That's a conversation I'm looking forward to even less than the one I'm about to have with Desmond.

I unearth enough pieces of clean clothing for business casual. Thank goodness, Chorda won't be anywhere near a screen tonight. When she gets in the zone, the rest of the world becomes a blur.

With the magic of speaker phone, I talk the list of ranting execs off the ledge. They are double dip pissed Midas is ghosting them. I'm grateful to the old ruffian. At least Lear's self-induced solitary confinement puts him out of the mix for now. Confinement I pray keeps his hands off a TV remote if he isn't the instigator of this nightmare. He's an even bigger bastard than I thought if he orchestrated this episode and then slunk back into hiding.

Once in my car, I dash off a call to I.T. to ID the hacker.

I can't wrap my head around Desmond dipping a toe in sabotage. He's too smart to put himself in a precarious position. He knows Hamilton would flame torch his balls for such a stunt.

I'm on the road, halfway to the Waterfall Palace when Gabs calls. "Desmond's assistant says he planned to go to movie night at the End of Scene Cemetery in Hollywood with Rubata. I messaged him with an urgent flag to call you."

"Well done, you, Gabs."

"There's more, Adair."

"Do I absolutely need to know?"

"The ratings for the episode are skyrocketing. The network ignored your instructions and kept it on air. We're beating Rampion's *Weekly Number One* for the first time this season. The choosing ceremony episode is also gaining rewatch traction."

A vise crushes my heart. Chorda's decline is killing it for numbers. That is so many flavors of wrong.

Gabs lingers on the phone. I pinch the bridge of my nose. "You're not finished, are you?"

"Midas called for a cease-and-desist order to prevent Chorda from singing any song in the Golden Pipes catalog."

I swerve into the oncoming lane. My Tesla corrects my death trajectory as I shout. "What!"

"Since she's under contract, anything new she writes is also property of Golden Pipes and can't be sung."

My volume may permanently damage Gabby's hearing. "This is utter crap. I'm hanging up, Gabs, before I plough into a wall."

"You're scaring me."

"I'm scaring me. I'll call you later."

All this ugly jacks up my ability to drive. I pull over and drop my forehead onto the steering wheel. Chorda can't sing her own freakin' hits?

A ball of ice grows in my stomach. Midas did see my Chorda segments and turned them into a weapon. The ugly cut is revenge for going behind his back.

Damn Desmond. He must have leaked Chorda's involvement in the filler episodes to Rubata. As soon as Ms. Jealous found out, I suspect she ran crying to Daddy, who stuck the metaphoric sock in Chorda's mouth and made his own version of our first episode.

My determination to get the rest of Chorda's segments on the air untampered with increases exponentially. Midas will not silence her on my watch. If I have to axe my way through his bedroom door to get him to listen to me, I will.

Double damn Desmond for further complicating dynamics by carelessly cozying up to Rubata in the wild. Will they go public as a couple? Such a reveal jacks up the possibility of Chorda and I doing the same any time soon. Holliday brothers with matching Lear girlfriends reads as a plastic-coated P.R. ruse.

I collect myself the best I can and enter the End of Scene Cemetery into my nav. I'll seal Desmond in a crypt until he coughs up answers.

15

BROTHER VS. BROTHER

GOSSIP IS A BAD GAME OF TELEPHONE. SO AND SO SAID THIS ABOUT blah blah. By the end of the line, it's a miracle if the original story maintains a speck of truth. The first filler episode of *Kickin' It With Midas* is the worst game of telephone ever.

I shuffle into the End of Scene Cemetery with the classic movie night crowd, a parade of peeps toting lawn chairs, coolers, and blankets to spread across the grounds. According to the website's map, flow is restricted to a single path in and out to avoid tromping on the final resting places of tinsel town's beloved icons. I'll bet celebrity ghosts can be a bitch if they're ripped out of eternal sleep by a pair of trendy gladiator sandals on *Spartacus* night.

Ahead of me in the cemetery is a massive white structure bordered with columns fit for the temple of a Greek god. Its smooth center span is a perfect movie screen. A semicircle of postcard-worthy L.A. palm trees enfolds the temple. As if floating on top of the farthest trees, the Hollywood Sign shines white against an onyx sky.

According to my deep dive, the V.I.P. section is up front to the right. Around me, wine bottles uncork with percussive pops as I make my way down the center aisle of groups staking their claims with low beach chairs and blankets. The movie tonight is a 1950's gem, starring a dashing heartthrob falling for a future princess. Many women in the crowd cosplay as the star with hair wrapped in silk scarves and sunglasses.

In the hope of not confronting Desmond openly or drawing attention to Rubata, I attempt one more call. It rings, then dumps into voicemail with the rest of my attempts. The number of rings suggests Des saw caller ID and declined to pick up.

"I'm here with you at the cemetery. 911, Des. Meet me at the blanket rental kiosk next to Dusty the Wonderdog's statue."

I spot the pair the moment I end the message. Desmond pulls Rubata to her feet. She's wrapped in her own scarf and sunglasses cosplay and towers above him in her circus stilt high heels. They push their way in the opposite direction of Dusty the Wonderdog. I curse my own shitiocy. Why did I tip off the guy who's been avoiding me? The two head toward the exit gate behind the movie temple.

To cut Desmond off, I hop and dodge my way through the crowd to the opposite side of the white marble structure, knocking over a wine bottle or two in my wake. The escape attempt does not bode well for his innocence. My regime of grueling Hollywood Hills' runs pays off as I whip around the back corner and nail my intercept course.

I launch at Desmond, pinning him against a fluted column. Before he can duck away, I press my forearm against his throat. He digs hands into my sleeve to loosen the pressure.

"The fuck, Adair," he chokes out.

I slide him around the column away from the exit path's sightline. "You should return my calls."

Des works his arms beneath mine and shoves me backward. I coil, ready to spring at him again if he tries to run.

He rubs his throat and glares. "Some of us worked all day instead of ogling Chorda Lear in a bikini."

I hope the up light from the fixtures in the marble floor hides my flush at the mention of Chorda in a bikini. "I'm working in Malibu, not ogling."

Desmond straightens his shiny dress shirt, appraising me as if I'm in the wrong. "I assume this assault is about the episode."

My hands ball into fists. I want to punch the smug look off his face. "What did you hope to gain, allowing that bullshit on the air behind my back?"

Des looks puzzled. "Behind your back? You and Hamilton greenlit it. In fact, you pushed up the schedule with your email."

I smack a fist into my palm. "Yes, behind my back. I never okayed a Chorda voiceover slam and the vitriol Rubata and Glissanda dumped on her." I press fingers to my temples to prevent anger from giving me a stroke.

This is his moment to tell me the episode isn't his. The silence narrows my suspects from two to one. New fury pulses through my veins. It is Desmond.

"How could you paint Chorda as such a monster? And what in the holy hell did you hope to accomplish with shots of Midas raving like a sawed-off lunatic?"

"Exactly what happened. Our ratings hit freakin' Mars." He catches my wrist as I cock my arm into a strike position. "You wrote a valentine, Adair. I crafted it into what it needed to be, an incendiary device."

"You admit the episode was your cut?"

Desmond keeps hold of my arm. "A rough cut. I tested a sharper edge. I was under the impression I had another day to show you the new angle and convince you to go with it. You pulled the trigger to air. I assume it worked for you."

"You thought turning Chorda into a self-centered, raving bitch would work for me?"

He cocks his head to the side. "Ah, I see how it is."

I pull my arm free. "What do you think you see?"

"Someone is being ultra-protective."

I face him down. "I'm ultra-protective of every Lear sister."

"It's done, Adair. I'm not going to apologize for spicing things up. We're in meteoric drama territory now, which translates to high ratings, which translates to bigger ticket sponsors."

"It's my show, Desmond. My show! I'll court sponsors my way."

I jump back when he gets in my face. "It's not news Midas is a foul-mouthed bully boy. If you'd get some perspective, you'd see villainizing him works in Chorda's favor. His reaction when the live broadcast crashed and burned was megalomaniacal gold."

His words hit me full in the sternum. Our story does need a villain who isn't Chorda.

Desmond points a finger at me. "You see it." He jerks his chin. "What? I don't even get a 'By Jingo, well-played, Desmond' from you, Little Brother?"

My face heats. "Cut the fucking little brother crap, and I don't say 'By Jingo.'"

"Think like a showrunner, Adair, not a lovesick puppy trailing after Chorda Lear. Yes, I intended for you to see the edgy episode first. I never suspected you'd greenlight it without giving me feedback. Yes, the episode tore Chorda down. Do you really think her daddy sass and mic drop from the choosing ceremony throws her in a deep enough pit? We want our girl to rise from the ashes of fan hate. To do that, she needs to look as dark as possible. Then her epiphany of how she wronged Lear, and her quest to make up with him will have fans raising golden Chorda statues." He grabs my forearms. "That's what I intended with my test version."

Shit. Shit. Shit. I don't know what to think. Desmond tried something that got hacked. I don't want to admit it, but there's storytelling merit in Desmond's narrative. I'm not ready to let him off the hook. "And how do you see that redemption arc play out when she can't sing until Midas drops his ridiculous cease-and-desist order." Midas didn't author the episode, but he still found a way to lash out at Chorda.

Desmond's flinch might as well be a neon *guilty* sign flashing above his head.

I speak through a growl. "Telling Rubata about Chorda's segments was sabotage."

He holds hands up in surrender. "I know. That was a really bad move. I feel truly awful and totally own the screw up. Ruby overheard me talking to you. I tried to backpedal and throw her off, but she got to Midas."

I step closer and pitch my voice low, hoping I sound menacing. "Make it clear to Rubata and Glissanda that Chorda is not out of the picture. Be stingy with specific details. Midas's ridiculous power play to render her mute will not cripple my segments. Chorda will sing."

He takes a step back. "I agree, the cease-and-desist is a cheap shot, but I'm sure it's a whim. Midas Lear will come out of his hole to get his ass kissed at the Rockin' and Rollin' Pantheon induction and welcome his estranged daughter to sing his praises."

I poke a finger into his chest. "Make it clear to Rubata it's her job to undo her dirty work and convince Midas to rescind the order."

Desmond shakes his head. "Don't you think the cease-and-desist is perfect dramatic fodder that works in Chorda's favor? Midas's bottom line has always been to boast the richest treasure vault of wealth and talent in the music biz. He'll see high stakes family shit in *Kickin' It With Midas* instead of the usual reality show fluff as dollar signs. When he pictures the lucrative *forgive Chorda* merch we can generate, he'll beg her to sing on the show."

"Midas doesn't put wealth before family."

Desmond snorts. "You seriously believe that?"

I lean against the column to give my brain a chance to reframe the purpose of the painful episode. I don't know what I believe.

"Since we're stuck with the aired episode, here's what I suggest," says Desmond. "Shoot Chorda's reaction to the content. Let her defend herself and refute the hashtag Dischorda campaign."

I rub my lips together and nod. "Since your *experimental cut* made it to air, you create content to counteract the poison words you put in Chorda's mouth. Shoot scenes of Rubata and Glissanda working toward empathy for their sister's situation. I'll come in with my piece of getting to know the real Chorda. We'll blend the halves to reverse fan opinion and open the door for support of a reconciliation.

"I promise I'll do whatever I can to help you fix this," he says.

The creative gears in my brain whir to life. "We'll craft Midas a spectacular exit from the show to avoid devolving the narrative into a drawn-out pissy fight with Chorda. That may lure him back on board and soften his attitude toward her."

"Choosing ceremony part two, The Do-Over." Desmond flashes his fingers in the air as if he's reading a theater marquis.

"Schedule a shoot for the second choosing ceremony finale a day or two after Midas's induction. You will get Midas to kill the cease-and-desist so Chorda can sing her tribute song on air."

"On it."

Suspicion caps the geyser of my creative juices. I narrow my eyes at Desmond. "There's still the issue of my email hack greenlighting your unapproved version of the first filler episode."

He looks genuinely surprised. "You think I did that?"

"You reworked the tone of the episode without consulting me. A next logical step is rushing it to air before I had a shot to nix it."

"Why would I ask for more time"—he pushes hair out of his eyes—"and go straight to air?"

"For the same reason you sent Dad your stuff before I reviewed it—to best me."

Desmond looks down. "That was a shit thing to do to score points with Hamilton." He meets my gaze. "I swear to you, brother, I never intended my experimental cut to bypass you."

I want to believe he is in earnest, but we've sung this tune together before. He oversteps, and I forgive. My single option is to give him enough rope to prove his loyalty or hang himself.

From my vantage point, the Hollywood Sign sits on Desmond's shoulder like a pet bird. Hollywood, the land of fame and fantasy.

My brother asked for a place at the table, and our father made him crawl for it.

I make a split-second decision to be clear withDesmond where he lands in the new pecking order. "You need to score points with me. Dad officially passed the baton. He's name only. From now on, I pull the *Kickin' It* strings." I close my eyes for a long moment to center myself before I look at him. "It's in my power to fire you."

A look of panic seeps across Desmond's face. "Hamilton's out?"

I seize the upper hand. "We've not officially announced, but yes. Regardless of your intention, you muddled the agreed upon narrative. If you'd proposed your version to me before creating it, we could have found common ground instead of me having to hunt you down."

Desmond's voice is strained. "Don't fire me, Adair. Without your backing, I'm as good as done in the business."

In my brother's face, I see a son yearning for a father's approval that never came. I'm torn with how I should handle this. "I've got serious trust issues with you, Des."

He nods. "I deserve that."

"Damn straight you do. I'm not the gullible shitiot you seem to think I am." Des knows he's on shaky ground. I've got the edge. "One whiff of further shenanigans, and you're out."

Desmond covers his mouth, stifling a laugh.

"Shenanigans is a perfectly fine word." I bust out a steely stare. "If I find out you had anything to do with that email, I'll shove your hand into the body of the Golden Guitar and turn you into a freakin' statue."

His eyebrow quirks up. "I see Chorda's got you buying in to the Lear mythical bullshit?"

I don't dignify his fishing expedition with an answer. "Addendum—whatever you're up to with Rubata better not blow into a social media scandal. If it's the real deal with her, own it."

"She's a Lear, Adair. There's nothing real about us. I'm a convenient escort, not a bedmate."

Is that a dribble of disappointment I hear in his voice? If Desmond is lying to me or wrong about Rubata's lack of feelings, he's playing with redheaded fire. My gaze darts around the rows of columns. "Where'd you stash her?"

"I didn't *stash* anyone." I've managed to jostle my brother's cool veneer. He jerks his chin at me. "Stop sounding like a preachy clone of Hamilton."

My own composure stretches wafer thin. "I sound like your boss, whose primary concern is the health of the *Kickin' It With Midas* franchise."

Desmond sheds his prickles and resumes a look of contrition. "I swear to you, I'm all about the team effort."

"You've got one last chance, Desmond. Meet with the writers and beat out a script for the second choosing ceremony finale. I'm putting you as lead on the reshoot; however, final approval on everything is a hundred percent me. Are we clear?"

"I won't let you down, Adair." He holds out his hand for me to shake.

I wait for confirmation I've done the right thing to wash over me. Instead, nagging suspicion that, once again, I am in gullible shitiot territory wins out.

"Make it happen." Without taking his hand, I walk toward the exit. Using the curve of the path as cover, I duck behind a monument topped with a bronzed statue of a swashbuckling Hollywood legend brandishing a pirate sword. Peeking around the far corner, I watch Desmond study the path until he's satisfied I'm history. He motions to the shadows. Freakishly tall, in platform heels in the shape of a gold cursive L, Rubata struts over to him. The backlight from the temple through her sheer harem pants illuminates long legs and a jeweled thong.

Heads together, Rubata and Des engage in a heated convo with negative body language and waving limbs. Has my brother come to his senses and set Rubata straight on the potential hornet's nest of public canoodling?

My misguided optimism is short-lived. A bomb goes off in my stomach when Des snatches Rubata in a pelvis-to-pelvis slam followed by a near pornographic kiss topped off with mutual ass grabbing. Dammit, anyone with a cell phone could round the corner of the temple and catch them. Desmond obviously gives zero shits about my warnings.

Rubata backs Des up against a column and hitches her leg around his hip. When he yanks her head back to better service her mouth, the scarf flutters to the ground.

I clamp molars to keep from crying out in shock. Freed from the scarf, the strawberry blond tresses of Glissanda Lear, not Rubata, thread between Desmond's grasping fingers.

16

COWARD

MY ASS IS GLUED TO THE SEAT OF MY TESLA. IF I STAY PARKED HERE on the final curve before reaching Garinish's front roundabout to enjoy the vista of a nighttime sea, I don't have to face Chorda. I don't have to break the news both her sisters are involved with Desmond. I don't have to tell her hashtag Dischorda is the tip of a Titanic level P.R. iceberg. I don't have to reveal Midas is holed up in his room and has communicated solely via Rubata since the night of the choosing ceremony. I don't have to fess up about the cease-and-desist order. I don't have to let it slip my gut tells me Desmond is up to something so I've given him enough rope to hang himself. I don't have to confess I stole scenes from Chorda with my button cam even though they're now cyber ash.

Except, I do. Every single *I don't have to* on my list is a massive *I have to*.

Chorda and I are beginning something beautiful, something important. If I don't come clean about the garbage piling up around us, I'll ruin everything. She trusts me. Trust deserves truths, even if they are wart-on-the-nose ugly. Chorda Lear has a right to know her Hollywood Hills are on fire.

As I round the final curve, my shroud of doom lessens. Chorda is intelligent and inventive. She'll help me sort through these burdens and move forward. That's what partners do, share the load.

My brain and car screech simultaneously to a halt when a familiar vintage red Ferrari 360 Modena comes into view smack dab in front of the house. How in holy hell did Desmond beat me here?

Not bothering to knock, I use my key and blast into the house. Voices rise from the kitchen. Female voices.

"How about...line the lip to add some zip his eyes will slip to Cupid's bow to dip a kiss of sizzle bliss." Rubata taps her bottom lip with a finger. "Or...it ain't hip if the lip don't zip."

"Everything doesn't have to be a rap, Ruby."

Rubata's here. The perfect setup for Desmond to dally with Glissanda behind her back. A flash of Rubata strapping a brick to the Ferrari's accelerator and sending it over the cliff races through my mind.

"Hello."

The sisters' heads snap up in unison. Chorda's eyes twinkle while Rubata's darken.

I wear my friendliest smile. "This is a surprise."

"Just to you," snaps Rubata.

Chorda makes a move in my direction but stops herself. It appears their sisterly chat didn't include mention of the new status between Chorda and me.

"Ruby came to check on me and bring me white willow powder for my headaches." She runs a hand up Rubata's arm. "I'm helping her with a jingle for a lip-liner tutorial," says Chorda.

I nod. "You saved me a call, Rubata. How's your father?"

"Wallowing."

Chorda's twinkle fades.

I rub my chin. "Wallowing that includes only you answering his phone?"

Rubata flicks her wrist. "As I explain to Chor Chor every time she tries to call Da, he needs his space."

There's one thing off my list. Chorda knows about Rubata commandeering Midas's phone.

I glance back into the living room. "Where's Desmond?"

Rubata's eyes narrow. "Not here."

I feign shock. "He let you drive his baby?"

Chorda shoots me a *stop poking* look. What I really want to ask is why Rubata came all the way out to Malibu. Is she amping up her game to keep Chorda away from Midas? The bigger the rift, the better odds for Rubata to get her mitts on the Golden Guitar. I wonder if Midas softened toward Chorda, and Rubata is spooked. The second choosing ceremony bait I dangled in front of Desmond may bring more than one ignoble agenda to the surface.

Rubata huffs. "Time to drive the baby out of here. End of dischush."

Chorda lays a hand on her sister's arm. "Stay, Ruby."

As much as I want to boot Rubata over the cliffs, Chorda's joy at connecting to someone in the family shines in her eyes.

"Not gonna happen. I promised fans I'd post my tutorial tonight. All my props and wardrobe are at the Waterfall Palace." Rubata grazes duck lips across Chorda's cheek. "Honey, you're fab to hang here. I'll chirp if Da cools off."

Chorda flinches at Rubata's *if*.

Rubata raises her palm to Chorda, and they clasp hands, matchy matchy rings clicking together. They chant, "Lear, Lear, Lear. Sister, sister, sister. Always, always, always." The sisters stroll arm in arm out the front door. Rubata shoots me a backward glance laden with nasty. Middle sis is pricklier than usual tonight. Did my car observation hit a nerve or is Desmond in general a sore subject? Does Rubata suspect Glissanda is stepping out with her man?

Scents of garlic and creamy culinary magic from the stove distract me and kick off a huge stomach gurgle. How much has this sisterly pop-by messed with Chorda's frame of mind, especially after Rubata's *if Da cools off* comment? The headache issue concerns me too. Is Chor hurting so badly her sister had to schlep out here with magic powder?

The front door creaks open and shut. In a tame-for-her sleeveless dress covered in a sunflower print, Chorda returns to the kitchen and stumbles just before falling into my arms.

It's only fair to let her enjoy whatever heavenly meal is in the offing and a little distance from her sister's visit before I lay all my heavy on her.

She pulls me into a kiss that says, "*I missed you. You're where you belong.*" After a thorough lip-plumping hello, Chorda pulls back to look into my eyes. "Welcome home, love."

Her words undo me. I'm home, home with Chorda. The sense of joy makes me believe I could float. If she's put a spell on me, I want it. This is so right. We are so right. An all-consuming sense of rightness is heady stuff.

Chorda takes my hand and leads me to a stool at the kitchen island. "Sit."

I dutifully obey as she sets a tall glass of something iced and amber with a lime wedge on the rim in front of me.

"I made it from Da's secret whiskey stash. Try it." She leans her elbows on the island to watch me drink. "Ruby says she thinks Da's thawing."

Questions over Rubata's motives for giving Chorda hope and then slapping her with the big *if* clench my throat. Cool ginger whiskey eases the tightness. "Delish."

Chorda claps her hands. "Good. I want my man to be happy."

"You accomplished that mission the moment I saw you." I tug on the front of her dress to bring her in for a kiss.

She indulges me for a few beats before ending the connection with a loud lip smack. "I have news." With a flourish, she grabs a fancy linen envelope with gold lettering and waves it through the air. "Special delivery from Prospero Tempesta. I've been invited to perform at the opening of *Stalk*."

My worries over negative repercussions from Rubata's visit disappear with Chorda's news. The words *cease and desist* race through my mind in a stock market scroll. I cut them off. The *Stalk* venue is slated to be under construction for another two years. This vile C and D order will be long gone by its opening.

The elite night club will crown a new mega tower in Hollywood. Prospero Tempesta of Tempest Records is one of the key investors. Why is he sniffing around a Golden Pipes artist? "I'm surprised Tempesta offered an opening night slot to talent outside his label."

A personal tempest clouds my thoughts. With Midas off the rails, is Prospero making a move to lure Chorda to his label? Over my cold, dead body. Is thievery how these moguls define success? Success is a worthy goal. One I subscribe to wholeheartedly. Grant Gothel, Midas Lear, and Prospero Tempesta claim to be about success. In truth, power and control are their mistresses.

"*Benedict and The Boulevard Three* are headlining from Tempest Records." She studies the invite and purses her lips. "I can't imagine that group without Beatrice." She taps a finger on the envelope. "Zeli is on the list from Rampion and *The Mermaids* from Miaqua Music. Seems as if Prospero wants to keep *Stalk's* entertainment booking options fluid."

"Makes sense."

Chorda's gaze drifts into the ether. "Maybe Beatrice had the right idea walking away from this circus."

I wave the invite to waylay the subject of walking away. "Wow, the opening night gig is two years out."

Chorda twists into a peppy dance move. "*Stalk* is going to be the hottest ticket in town. I want in."

I relegate *Stalk* to a brain back burner. Whatever Prospero's agenda might be, the offer put zing in Chorda's step. There's color back in her cheeks. She deserves this nod to her talent.

My beautiful woman turns her attention to a bubbling concoction on the stove. She scrapes noodles and shrimp into thick, pearly sauce.

"Homecooked dinner. Very domestic of you, Chor."

She giggles. "Right? Truth—Bibs made it. Reheating is the extent of my culinary talents. I do plan to apprentice with our resident master chef so I can cook for my man someday." She plates the pasta for both of us.

"You'd better make sure Bibs is sitting down when you tell her." I taste the pasta and moan. "If you pull off any dish this yummy, I'm yours forever."

I down more of Lear's prize whiskey. I notice she isn't eating.

She leans on one elbow to face me. "I'm blown away at how much I love this. Waiting for you to come home. Running to meet you at the door. Having dinner ready. It is domestic. It's settled and calm. No one's nagging me to get into hair and makeup or holding me to a specific call time."

I slide a hand to the small of her back. "I'm loving my part in our scene."

"It's not a scene. It's life. A version of the life I think I want, with you, a simple life without stressing out about the show or fans or fame every day. A gig here and there after my tour could strike a decent balance." She runs fingers through my hair. "I couldn't even consider a commitment before you opened yourself up to understand my craft and what a vital part of life it is for me. Now that you accept everything I am..." She lays her hand on the golden streak in her hair. "I realize how much I want to make a home, a future with goofy, wonderful you." Chorda spears a fat, cream-coated shrimp and feeds it to me.

Well, hell. How can I ruin this perfect moment for her with the volume of shit I should share when the woman I love is saying these perfect things? Her surety is a tad on the overwhelming side, but I'd be a colossal liar if I said I'd never fantasized about a life with her. Chorda's dreams are my dreams.

She's the artist, the one with the ability to express visions and emotions. I may not be an artist, but I believe in the one here in front of me.

"Too fast?" she says, checking me out in a sideways glance. "I mean, we've only been officially dating a few days, and I'm laying a lifetime at your feet."

I shake my head and trail a finger along her golden strand. "I think we've been dating our whole lives." I take a fortifying breath. "I'm asking you not to be so quick about distancing yourself from the show you've worked so hard at. Fame doesn't have to mean an oppressive spotlight. It's recognition and appreciation for your music. You don't chase popularity the way your sisters do. It comes to you honestly. It's a gift."

She shudders at my touch on her hair. "I will never chase it. If anything, I'd rather hide from it. Wouldn't it be bliss to stay out here away from Hollywood insanity most of the time, just the two of us, and make a life?"

Ripples of panic run along my spine at this latest mention of Chorda walking away from the show. I must find the balance between how much she's willing to give and the amount of Chorda presence her fans need to stay loyal. A balance to keep her on *Kickin' It*. Documenting the tour she so badly wants could be a compromise to start. As I told Desmond, the health of the show is now my responsibility. If Chor embraces an executive producer hat, we'd share that goal. Hiding out at the beach sounds dreamy, but I love my job as much as she loves making music. Cliché as it is, the show must go on.

Chorda steals the fork from my hand and sets it on my plate. "What's freaking you out, Adair? Talk to me."

I'll start a slow leak of information and gauge how far to go. "It's Glissanda. I mean, Rubata."

Alarm pales her cheeks. I miss the pink. "Is it about them and Da?"

I squeeze her shoulder. Great, now I've pulled her into the

vortex of my freak out. "No. The two are, ah, involved with Desmond."

She grabs my hand. "Both! I knew Ruby had a thing for him, but Gliss too? How do you know?"

"I witnessed Des and Glissanda wrapped around each other."

"Glissanda not Rubata? At the Waterfall Palace? OMG, if Ruby catches them, she'll lose it." She grabs the front of my shirt. "This could be bad."

Chorda knows Desmond and Rubata are a thing? There's a little jab she didn't share that with me. Damn sister code of silence. If she asks me again where I saw Glissanda and Desmond, I'll have to spill the scene at the cemetery. Engage deflection. "Maybe they're sharing."

She slaps my arm. "They'd never..."

Even though I don't mirror her high opinion of the sisters, I am a crapdog for using their romantic hijinks to cover up my own chickenshittedness of not coming clean about everything I should tell her. Chorda's talk of defection from the show, my confrontation with Des at the cemetery, and Rubata's visit make me spazzy. Now I've got her worked up.

"What are we going to do, Adair?"

I spin her barstool toward me. "We're going to stay out of it. They're big girls."

She storms over to bay windows overlooking a night garden of gold and pale-yellow flowers. "What is happening to my family?"

Sliding up behind, I pull her to my chest. "All families experience rough spots." I rub my nose against her temple. "Oft times, said spots bring people closer."

Her laugh rumbles between us. "Oft times?"

"Mayhaps."

She faces me to clasp her hands behind my neck. Thank God, the Adair Holliday signature nerdiness diffuses her tension.

"You adorable throwback," she says and gently sinks teeth into my bottom lip. Sensation zips straight down between my legs.

I whisper against her mouth. "I think we'd better turn the stove off." I need to douse the sizzle coursing between us and tell her the laundry list of shit she deserves to know, but doesn't she also deserve passion? It's not an either/or, merely a lovely pause before we hit play on reality.

Chorda pushes off me and, with an ass-swishing vixen stroll, kills the flame under the shrimp alfredo. The last vestiges of slack in the crotch of my pants disappears.

"I'd like to see you repeat that walk while Bibs teaches you how to cook."

She shoots a sultry glance over her shoulder, backs away from the stove, and leans down in version two of turning off the stove which points a magnificently round bottom straight at me. Her dress scoots high enough to flash a yellow thong. "Maybe she'd prefer this."

My hard-on sets a new personal best record. "Doubtful. Were I your master chef, such cooking posture would be encouraged."

In one swift movement, I tuck in behind her, grinding my record-setting need against that magnificent round bottom. Chorda grabs the edge of the granite counter next to the stove to push against me. Riding the rhythm, she sings sweet notes of pleasure I've come to adore.

My upper brain maintains just enough blood and awareness to realize the bay windows could provide quite a show for a passing security guard. I grab Chorda around the waist and swing her to face the living room archway. Setting her on her feet, I smack her ass. "Shall we continue domestic bliss in your bedroom?"

The woman is fast. She snaps off the lights with one hand and cups me with the other. "You really want to go all the way upstairs?"

I drop my head back and groan as she strokes me. "I really want to go all the way."

She literally leads me by the cock into the living room, where she snaps off another bank of motion sensor lights.

My voice is strained. "Sweetheart, in about thirty seconds, I'm not going to be able to stand."

Chorda walks her fingers up and down the outside of my fly. "Hard day at the office, dear?"

There are words in my head, and there they stay.

She steps away to cup her breasts and unleash a sexy grumble. "My dress is constricting." Slowly, she undoes one button at a time, widening the gap to reveal a sunshine yellow bra skimpy enough so she spills over its top. This may be my first erection to literally bust the seam of my pants, and these are my favorite pair of work slacks.

Chorda wiggles out of the dress. I fall onto the couch with a groan.

"Oh no, you don't," she says, pulling me to my feet. Her eyes fall to my crotch. "Someone else is constricted."

I grab for my belt, and she slaps my hands away. With motions so slow it's all I can do to keep from crying out, Chorda undoes my belt and then carefully eases the zipper down, quite an achievement given the current state of my bulge. My slacks drop to my ankles. Light from the garden spills into the room, etching every one of Chorda's curves in a golden glow. I step free of my pants and clutch her hips. When I try to press against her, she holds a hand up to stop me.

"Take off your shirt."

I'm tempted to do the cliché and rip open my shirt to send buttons flying.

She waggles a finger. "One at a time, please."

I breathe deeply and pace myself as not to end the party before it begins. Our gazes lock on one another. As I free each button, she circles her palm over the newly exposed skin of my chest, always pausing over my heart. After the last button, Chorda leans against me to shrug off my shirt.

She takes both my hands in hers, and we hold each other at arm's length, bodies bathed in amber glow through the windows.

Chorda sighs, and the enchanted strand of her hair brightens. Our skin reflects its dazzling metallic sheen.

"You are the only gold I need," she whispers, then to my surprise, begins to sing.

Walk with me love, within natures night glow
Ignite simple blooms with passions power
Savor sweet breaths mingling ever so slow
Rise oh sensations to fill the hours

Float with me, join with me, never to cease
Fill me with light and the promise of peace
Float with me, join with me, through every sigh
Fill me with joy as together we fly

Lie with me love, in the depth of the dark
Silence my lips with your kisses that woo
Worship our bodies to raise sacred sparks
Our touches sing songs of hearts paired so true

Float with me, join with me, give me your light
Fill me with hope as we lovers take flight
Float with me, join with me, living a dream
Fill me with grace under Bríg's bless'd beam

Eyes closed, Chorda sways to the melody she creates. Pinpoint bursts flare around her. These fragments, akin to the first smatterings of a light rain, sparkle like diamond chips. The delicate sphere expands, capturing me in its twinkling sheath. Is this Pan's famed pixie dust that allows a person to fly? I am ready to leave the confines of Earth and float skyward within the energy of Chorda's voice.

The urgency of my blinding lust isn't quenched, but it pauses in a kind of stasis, allowing Chorda's song to slide over my shoulders and chest, satin across bare skin. If this is her witchcraft, I long to be part of it. Every heartbeat quickens my pulse. When I shut my eyes, I imagine life blood as a molten, golden river carrying energy to every ounce of my soul. I am alight with Chorda's song. No longer a skeptic, I believe in her power with everything that I am. I vow to protect her and the magic she weaves around us.

Chorda folds into my arms, resting her ear against my heart. "Bríg sings through me because of your faith in every aspect of who I am. The goddess senses you in my light. She approves of our love. If she had seen doubt in your heart, my song would wither. Instead, you, my love, reawaken my gift. Music once again joins with me."

I tighten my arms around her as the weight of responsibility tightens around me. Pressure much, Bríg? "Did you summon your goddess friend the way you did the night of the ritual?"

"I felt her watching from afar and invited her here."

I fight the urge to scan the room for otherworldly voyeur goddess activity.

"I'll help you discover the god or goddess you'll connect to the way I do with Bríg. Now that you believe, you're ready to seek."

I bury my nose in her hair, filled with the scent of marshmallow melting over a campfire. "I'm not Irish."

Her breath warms my neck. "You're as much nature's child as I am. You will be welcomed by the right energy."

Chorda's lips against my neck wear away the last fragments of the floaty bubble of calm that surrounded me during her song and deity debrief. Urgency to join with her in body, spirit, and light is more powerful, more overwhelming than my body can contain. My dizziness is beyond lust or the desire for fulfillment, it's a need to bond, to promise. My drive to be consumed and surrounded by Chorda's flesh erupts from me in a roar. If this is a goddess thing, sign me up. A force hovering just beyond my comprehension overtakes me.

"Chor," I rasp. "I need you right now."

Slender, guitar-playing fingers jerk my boxer briefs to my

ankles. "I know," she pants. "I can't wait either. It has to be now." She flings her bra and thong through the air.

In a frenzy, I grab her up into my arms. Growling, I crush my mouth to hers. Tongues join our dance of lost restraint. Her legs wrap around my waist as she rocks into me. We fall to the couch. Chorda's legs part, insisting I get on with it.

"Can't...be...gentle." I brace myself above her body and slide my fingers inside her, making sure she is ready for the onslaught I'm about to unleash.

She moans and smacks my hand away. "Now, Adair, now."

Lightning-fast fingers grasp my girth. Its beating pulse pushes against Chor's palm as she guides me in. With my first thrust, I bury deep within her burning pathway. She grinds her hips to capture any fragment of me not already embedded.

Float with me, join with me, through every sigh
Fill me with joy as together we fly

I move to the memory of her song as I sink into her with blinding speed. I'm already falling over the edge, so I slip a hand between us to awaken the place to bring her flying with me. The more pressure I give, the more she writhes, enhancing my efforts. We both pant words with no clear beginnings or ends. I arch and cry her name, filling her with a release more abundant than I've ever experienced. With matching howls, we join completely.

Chorda's hot breath slides across my neck and down my chest as she gasps for air. Still joined, I ease us onto our sides, so I don't crush her. My hands tangle in her hair as I gulp my own breaths.

"Did I hurt you?" I wheeze.

She rubs her nose against the underside of my jaw. "Did I hurt you?"

A laugh rolls through my chest as I fit her against me. "I'm still in one piece." My body hums with reluctance to disconnect so I stay inside her. "Chor, what's happening? This intensity..."

"Think of it as a benefit that comes with a goddess's stamp of approval."

A flush runs up my neck as I slide gently in and out of her. "It's a whole new level for me."

She squeezes around me. "It's super spesh for me, too, Adair. I don't want to simply make love to you. I want to seduce you and drive you to want me more each time than you did the time before. I feel adventurous with you." To illustrate, she slowly circles her hips, and I harden inside her.

I run my tongue over the shell of her ear. "Every time with you fragments me. I have to reassemble my atoms."

Her hand travels lightly over my ass and then around to my balls. She caresses with an amount of pressure to explode several neurons. I immediately grow to fill her. This may prove to be a faster encore than our previous record setting evening.

"How do I thank your goddess?" I tease her nipple with my tongue while keeping up my rhythmic slide.

"Appreciate it, Adair." She gasps into my hair as I jolt my hips to drive deep. "Appreciate it all."

I thoroughly appreciate my new favorite goddess's approval rating in a much more languid fashion than our first dance. Afterwards, we both drift into sweet sleep.

A blast of AC covers my body in goose bumps, and I jerk awake. Chorda is mashed between me and the back of the couch. Her melodic snores disappear into the cushions. It's probably a projection of my own feeling of fatigue, but she looks more delicate, breakable than she did during our lovemaking. Before the arctic chill reaches her, I grab a fuzzy blue and white throw off the couch. Regretfully, I cover the naked body I could write my own songs about.

Sitting, I smooth my hair and stare out the window at a nocturnal critter running up the trunk of a palm. The sensation of a drunk buzz wearing off washes through me to let in an avalanche of guilt.

I grab my shorts and pull them on as if not being naked will make things better. It doesn't. I'm a vandal. Instead of coming clean

with Chorda about machinations behind the curtain, I indulged my
prick. Holy shit, I didn't even use a condom. What the hell is wrong
with me? How am I any better than Desmond with his Lear sister
double-dipping?

A warm hand rests on my back. I turn to see Chorda's sleepy
smile.

"Hi," she says.

"Hi." I lean down and press a gentle kiss to her lips. "Chor, I am
so sorry I got carried away. I hold up two fingers. "Twice." We
should have gone up to your room so I could grab a…"

Her finger rests on my lips to silence me. "We're covered,
sweetheart." She mimes popping a pill.

I kiss her finger. "Still, I should check with you before I plunge.
I promise, I'm clean as a whistle." I whistle, aiming my stream of
musical air at Chorda's lips. She whistles a single note before my
tune is stolen with a quick kiss.

"Adair, I plan to spend the rest of my life making love to you.
Think of our lack of caution tonight as a new first." Her head
nudges into my shoulder before settling. "We're on the same page,
right?"

I stroke her hair. "Absolutely." I should speak with more *oomph*,
but my half-truths half-strangle my answer. I do mean it. This
woman will be my life, unless I fuck everything up and continue to
keep things from her.

"Something else," she says, tracing the line of hair down my
stomach to the top of my pants.

My thermometer-busting level of guilt prevents the gesture
from revving me back up.

"Adair, I think I'm ready to start working on the new episodes
with you."

Oh, shit! She'll see the tripe that already fouled the airways.

Come, clean, Adair.

"Chor, there's a bit of an issue with the show." She stiffens next
to me. "I'm an insufferable coward for not already telling you about

it." It was a huge leap for her to even think about reengaging with the show, and I present her with a nightmare. I thread an arm around her. "Know it can be fixed, but I don't think you're ready to see what's aired."

"Something's already aired?"

I proceed to describe the toxic episode and reveal the email hack. I explain Desmond's angle about tearing her down and then rebuilding her image. She listens, contributing a single tear that meanders down her cheek before it slides beneath her jaw.

"We need to shoot disclaimer footage to counter Desmond's misguided go at high drama. I swear the rest of the episodes I'm working on are bridge builders. I'm eager for you to see where I'm going with your story. Keep an open mind, okay?"

The loving looks from her I've been privy to since I walked in the door fade to unreadable.

The pitch of my voice rises, and I click into my signature Adair Holliday tap dance around an uncomfortable issue. "I know you don't want to give in to your Da's bullying and flatter him, but he's not playing fair. He took out a cease-and-desist order to prevent you from singing any Golden Pipes songs."

She clutches her stomach.

I barrel ahead. "I believe my spins on the filler episodes show your song is an authentic love letter between father and daughter and will make him kill the cease-and-desist."

I wish she'd open a line of dialogue, so I know where her mind is at. No such luck. She fixates on the window and pulls the blanket tighter around her.

"Chor, if you hate what I've got so far, we'll torch every frame and start from scratch."

Chorda jumps to her feet.

"I don't need protecting or sheltering, Adair. Confusing my compassion for weakness is a no-go for me." She grabs her chest and gasps.

"What is it, Chor."

"My heart is going nuts thanks to you."

I hang my hands between my knees and stare at my feet as if breaking eye contact will slow her heartbeats. "I blew it." I raise my gaze to meet hers. "I know you're not weak. I've watched you spit fire our whole lives. With everything happening between us, I lost perspective and kept things from you." My shoulder quirks up and down. "Misplaced protective instinct is as alpha male as I'm capable of."

A hint of a smile fades across her lips. "I find you extremely capable of alpha male-ing." She opens her blanket, inviting me in. I slip my arms around her as she wraps us up. "If you truly want me to produce *Kickin' It* with you, no more keeping tough stuff from me."

I kiss the top of her head. "You're letting me off too easily."

"I am aware, but it's my choice."

Here's my opening to fess up about the spy cam footage. Do I add further blows to what she's trying to digest? Every unsanctioned moment I shot with the button cam is history. I trashed it. It doesn't exist anymore.

"I am sorry for being a shitiot, Chor." A shitiot whose integrity is in question. If I can't live up to being the person she needs, I should back off. A lump swells in my throat, making it hard to swallow. How in the world can I back off after a goddess's thumbs up?

I should be floating in ecstasy that this amazing woman chose me to define her future happiness. Guilt keeps my feet on the carpet.

"You know how badly the mess with Da has me spinning." She rises on tiptoe to kiss me. "I get you were trying to save me from more hurt." Her cheek is soft against my chest. "I trust you, Adair."

When she says trust, a drop of self-loathing scorches my tongue.

I fully intend to spend the night spooning Chorda in her bed, but my lies of omission squeeze my balls, not in a good way. After an hour of thrashing our blankets into a burrito, I kiss a groggy Chorda goodnight.

"White willow," she whispers and points to the metal water bottle on her nightstand.

I sit next to her on the bed while she drinks. "Another headache?" I catch the bottle as it slips through her fingers. She sinks back onto the pillows and is asleep before answering me. I trudge back to the bungalow awash in my own brew of guilt and concern over Chorda's damn headaches and develop a whopper of my own.

17

TAPPING OUT

ONLY A JACKLICK BELIEVES A GOOD HOT SHOWER WILL SLUICE AWAY layers of deception. In this morning's light, I am such a jacklick. My less than hundred percent honesty level with Chorda makes me more fidgety and nauseous with every passing minute. After my new co-executive producer and I watch my cuts of her segments, I'll spill the last of my withholding, the button cam footage.

With a towel wrapped around my waist, I tidy up the bungalow. Chorda will be here in less than an hour. I've got no choice but to lead with Desmond's *tear down Chorda* episode. She deserves to know what's out there. My part is to illustrate how that sour note can be a baseline to launch into the narratives I've built to spark reconciliation between Midas and her.

My towel slips to the ground. I kick it hard enough to send it flying against the window, leaving a damp smudge on the glass. What if she hates what I've done? My intentions are heartfelt. While I didn't purposefully pander to fans, as showrunner, I must consider audience impact when telling the story. I want the world to love Chorda as much as I do.

I'm a teenage girl dressing for a first date as I blow through three outfits before settling on beige chinos and a striped button-down. I hear Chorda singing her way to the bungalow. My lips sneak into a smile. She's writing something new even as she strolls down the path. I'm damn delighted her gift is flowing.

"Ah-dare, Ah-dare," sings Chorda. I throw open the door, and she checks me out. "When are you going to let me take you shopping?" She trails a finger over my bicep as she comes inside.

"I fear what you'll make me wear." There's such a lovely midday breeze, I leave the door open and roll a chair up to the large monitor in the middle of my editing set up. "Ready?"

She pushes me onto the chair and snugs herself on my lap. As sensual as Chorda can be, our current position also settles into familiar comfort. I crave this surety between us as much as our passion.

Her finger taps the edge of the console. "What am I looking at, partner?"

"Does this mean you're a definite go for the co-producer plan?"

Her answer is a quick kiss to the underside of my jaw. "Let's see if your mad editing skills impress me enough to keep you on the payroll."

I fiddle with controls and hope the shaking in my fingers born of fear isn't obvious.

"Do you want to see the episode that aired?"

Fingernails dig into my thigh. "Do I?"

"It's harsh, Chor. It tears you down. Your call."

She chews her pinkie nail. "Let me see your new stuff first."

"Deal." I kiss her shoulder. "Here's the next episode to air after we spiff it up with you addressing last night's unpleasantness."

She tenses for a beat, but then snuggles against my chest. "Got it."

The terror at showing this to Chorda begins to subside as she giggles at the daddy/daughter history in the episode. At the end, she's a little teary.

"It works," she says. "Next."

My *Chorda the Artist* episode earns a curt, emotionless head bob that starts my heart thumping an anxious beat.

During episode three, where Chorda gets candid about refusing to sing her praise song to Lear, she abandons my lap to pace the room. I hit pause. "We can tweak anything you want, Chor."

She flips her hand for me to continue. Before the fourth episode, which was supposed to be my heartrending love letter from Chorda to Lear, ends, she's sitting on the bed, arms crossed with a frown that scares the piss out of me. I swear spikes of heat—and not the good kind—surge from her body, attempting to roast me.

I tense. "Let me have it."

Chorda springs to her feet, arms flailing. False starts spill from her lips. Even though she covers her face with her hands, I see her skin blanch.

I am so dead.

"I'm calling my father." She bolts out the door.

"Chor, wait." Even though I'm half a second behind her, she's already got the phone to her ear. Of the reactions I played in my head, calling Midas was not on the list. What prompted her urgency? I linger on the small slab of a porch, waiting for permission to approach.

"Rubata?" Chorda checks the phone screen. "Why are you still answering Da's cell? Let me talk to him."

If Lear has rejoined the living and is deflecting Chorda's call, he's a bigger ass than I took him for.

"Put me on speaker. Da. Da! Please talk to me."

Her shoulders rise until they nearly touch her ears. Chorda folds in half like she took a sucker punch. Shit, her hand presses flat over her heart. Is she developing panic attacks and migraines thanks to her family?

I rush to her and lay a hand across her back. There's sharpness to her shoulder blades I swear wasn't there last night. We're definitely going to have a chat about her health.

With a soul-crushing cry, she straightens and heaves the phone into a planter of yellow canna lilies. "He won't talk to me." Chorda marches in a circle, unleashing a string of curses as vile as any Midas tirade. Fisted hands punch at the clouds. After a long, angry squeal, she turns to me, twisting the ring with the green and black stone as she bellows. "Rubata said Da forbids me to go to his induction ceremony, and he's cancelled my live duet with Zeli."

Damn Lear and his pride. No doubt, the mad fool's edict is born of paranoia Chorda might steal a fraction of his limelight. She's the only Lear sister who committed to join him at the Rockin' and Rollin' Pantheon celebration in the first place. Glissanda and Rubata tapped me to schedule *Kickin' It* camera crews to cover their separate Hollywood A-lister watch parties on Lear's big night. Events intended to boost their own self-aggrandizing P.R., not their Da's.

The level of my anger rises to meet Chorda's. "That's messed up, Chor."

Lear deliberately tortures her by continuing to shut her out. She's a butterfly under the magnifying glass he aims at the sun. How did he slink so low? His hissy fit after the choosing ceremony is in character for him, but I fully expected him to soften by now. This is Chorda, his favorite, his baby. Their bond has always been sweetness and light. That's why her sisters toss snark and diss her. I truly believe they love her, but competition for daddy cracks the Lear family foundation.

Desmond, Glissanda, and Rubata share more in common than I realized. Hamilton makes Des feel second best the way Midas makes his two older daughters feel when held up to Chorda. Still, Chor and I do not deserve to be punished because our fathers play favorites.

"And you!" Chorda snaps at me, bringing my head back into the scene. "Why didn't you tell me right away how bad things were?"

I take a step closer. "I didn't want to add to the crap you're already dealing with. It's wearing you down. The headaches, you're not eating."

"And..." She yells loud enough to jostle birds perched in a nearby palm to take flight. "You planned to air these episodes even if I never approved them."

I sputter. What she says is true. Whether Chorda agreed to preview these segments or not, I was going greenlight them all. She's right to be furious with me.

"All your promises of co-creative control were bullshit. I thought I was going to see rough ideas, cobbled together edits. These are polished episodes. You told my story without me." Her humorless laugh could crack glass. "You've made your priority clear —the show, not me."

I lay a hand over my heart. "I truly thought my narrative was in your best interest."

She rushes me and stabs a finger into the center of my chest. "I'll be the judge of my best interest."

I raise my hands. "Please consider my perspective. You've been making noises to stop engaging with the show, and a deadline was biting me in the ass. Will you give me credit for prepping this to play out to your benefit?"

She spins to face the sea. The ends of her hair begin to rise. *Oh, shit.* Am I about to be smacked with serious witch anger?

Survival instinct tells me to give her space, but I'm a shitiot in love. Chorda is wrong, survival is not my priority, she is.

"Please believe the story I'm trying to tell with these episodes comes from a place of love. A place that wants you to patch things up with your father because being at war with him is tearing you apart." The gauntness of her face reminds me of the physical toll the estrangement is costing her. "Besides the headaches, you're losing your train of thought. That's not you, Chor."

Her personal cyclone blows her hair into a snarl around her head. She twists the ring on her finger. "I don't know what to believe. I need to process." She sprints down the path away from me toward the steps leading to the beach.

My thoughts jumble. Last night, Chorda said she saw us together for the rest of our lives, and I've already fucked up. I mentally flip through the pages of two playbooks. As showrunner, it was my duty to create episodes. As Chorda's partner, I should have sought her creative input from the first. I was so scared of her potential disconnect with the show, I ploughed forward instead of giving her artistic choices she deserved.

It's time to fix everything. I shove through the canna lily planter to scan the beach below. No sign of Chorda. She might want space to process, but I need to be present for her even if she starts throwing things. I'm terrified she'll crumple the way she did at the Enchanted Garden and knock her head on something.

Taking the wooden beach steps two at a time, I hit the sand. "Chorda?"

The afternoon sky settles into gray as the day cools. Mist rolls off the water to coat the beach with a sense of unease.

"Chorda?" I beeline it to the tide pools. All I hear is the smack of water against seaward rocks. As waves recede, skittering seabirds pick at tiny bubbling holes in the wet sand.

"Where are you?"

My gaze locks on the rocky wall separating the Lear and Rampion properties, the site where Chorda and I first made love. Heart clanging against my ribs, I charge along the cold sand near the boundary of Lear land and stop where the last of the boulders dip into the sea.

"Chor?"

Beyond the water line, a wave roars and slaps down as if telling me to get lost. In the stillness that follows the assault, I make out the gentle notes of someone crying. It's Chorda, but I can't see her. In the next lull between breakers, I hear sound from the cleft in the rocks where Justin and Zeli disappeared the other night.

I'm surprised at the width of the opening. The offset of the rocks makes the pass-through look deceptively narrow. Once inside the maze, the echo of Chorda's soft sobs is easy to follow. I move through a passageway that runs to the sea. A dozen steps in, the ceiling drops low enough to make crawling necessary.

Up ahead, a natural arch of stone lets in dim light. I wiggle through it into a cave. One side is open to the sea. A single sentinel rock guards the cave's seaside entrance. With each wave, twin streams of water break around the guardian to feed a miniature lagoon bordered by a narrow, semicircular rock ledge.

Shadows dance across the walls of the cave, shifting as each new wave blocks the light in a different pattern. This is a private place. My blood begins to hum the way it did the night I witnessed the sisters' ritual. Not just a private place, a sacred place, a place of magic. I shouldn't be here uninvited.

Chorda sits at the center of the rock ledge's curve, feet trailing in the water. I shiver in the cold and damp while she is calm as the sea laps against her shins. I'm pulled by opposites, one to approach and the other to allow her the solitary peace and perspective the cave surely offers.

Chorda makes the decision and speaks without looking at me. "Air your episodes, then I'm off the show."

I want so badly to approach her, but I'm rooted at the entrance. "May I join you?"

Chorda finally faces me and shrugs.

The rocky ledge digs into my bare feet as I pick my way over. I ease down next to her. Stalling the conversation, I roll my pants up to the knees. Freezing water batters my skin.

When she speaks, it's the ocean and not me that earns her gaze. "If I stay on the show, our relationship is not going to work, Adair. *Kickin' It With Midas* can be your thing. It's not mine. It's drained both my emotional and creative wells. I'm finished."

I can't support this. Chorda's presence on the show is the reason it can go forward without Midas. I'm suspended over an alligator pit, hanging on a frayed piece of yarn. "I know everything is a hot mess right now. We can reshape the show together to feed your creativity, not batter it."

She drops chin to chest. "Have you heard anything I've been saying these last few days? I hate it all—the intrusion, the judgement. I just want to write songs and sing to people who genuinely care about my music." Bruises show through the fair skin beneath her eyes.

"Then that's what we make the show about. We'll spin off Rubata and Glissanda to feed the reality show audience and transform *Kickin' It* into an artistic outlet for you."

Chorda sits straighter and aims the full force of her scrutiny at me. "This is a sales pitch. Tell me, Adair, where is the line between your professional ambition and loyalty to me?"

I raise a mist-damp hand. It glistens in the scant light pouring in. "I deserve that. Be angry with me. I should have included you in shaping your narrative. I stupidly thought I was being transparent about my vision while we created your footage. It's not the same as building the segments with you." I shake my head. "It was wrong not to tell you about the horrible first episode as soon as I found out. It's my screw up."

To my surprise, she twines equally slippery fingers through mine. "Yes, to all, but it doesn't change my mind. Adair, I want you. I want us. *Kickin' It* intrudes in our lives. I need separation."

The icy water is nothing compared to the fortress of ice rising around my heart. Chorda wants to kill the show, my show, our show. I one hundred percent believe we can be together and make a show together. Survival means bringing her over to my side.

Chorda runs her thumb over the peaks and valleys of my knuckles. "Ruining the choosing ceremony was the right thing to do. If I'd given the Golden Guitar a chance to choose me, it would have blurred my double existence of real life and reality show even more than it already is."

It's hard to breathe. Chorda is escaping from my visions of a new *Kickin' It*. "Do you see yourself on any show for Golden Pipes?" I clench everything possible waiting for an answer.

She releases my hand and clasps her own together, leaning forward as the water driving against the rock ledge sprinkles her face. "Maybe. I'm drawn to the vibe of Rampion's *Weekly Number One*. A show about loving music and new talent might work for me."

Relief turns my muscles to oatmeal, and I nearly slip off the ledge. "Do you see us producing that vehicle together?"

The corner of her mouth curls up, then presses back into a line. "Only if you stop keeping things from me. I demand full transparency and honesty. I need you to partner in every sense, not gatekeep and parcel out the bits of truth you assume I can handle."

"I will be that partner, Chor, in the art we make together, in love, in life."

I move in slowly, testing every inch of progress to her lips. If she flinches or backs away, I'll stop. I press my mouth to hers gently, tentatively, the same way she almost kissed me at the tide pools. Unlike that night, she opens to me and slides her tongue over mine, hot breath momentarily chasing away the chill of my panic. The deep and lingering kiss I crave never blooms. In its place, Chorda's passion downgrades into a test, a question, and doubt. Our kiss becomes a bubble, destroyed by too rough a touch. A kiss that feels as if I might lose her.

She's first to break away. "Can you truly live up to your promise?"

Her hopeful smile gives me the courage to take the final step to complete truth. "Yes. So, there's one last piece I need to share."

Her smile dies. She pushes me away. "Damn you, Adair."

I need to touch her, to know she's with me. I need to earn that. "I swear this is the last of it." My hand circles in the air. "It's really bad, but I already fixed it. I'm all in with transparency and honesty."

Chorda huffs. "Stop stalling."

Fear makes me lightheaded. Truth is the price for moving forward with Chorda. "I wore a button camera when we shot your scenes."

She gives a crisp shake of her head, not understanding. "A what?"

Every breath hurts. I point to my chest. "A hidden camera. I recorded the night at the tide pools and every moment of our sessions, not just the obvious shots."

Realization dawns. Her already too pale skin loses the last of its color.

"I'm an ass, Chor. I thought catching candid moments would tell your story at a gut level."

She stands, backing away with a glare. My heart stops when she nearly loses her footing on the slick rocks. I've never seen her so unsteady. Fingers press into her temples and circle. "Moments you didn't trust me to give willingly."

I rise too quickly, and I'm the one to slip off the edge, ending up waist deep in the tide. "It's gone, I swear, every second of footage. You saw it wasn't in the episodes." It's not the time to share how beautifully raw and perfect she was in those stolen shots.

Chorda glowers above me on the ledge. "You couldn't stop yourself from a ratings grab."

A tangle of seaweed wraps around my calf. "I felt compelled to show your story in the most authentic way. It was always my intention to show you the footage and give you final say whether or not to use it." I peel the slimy string off my leg. "Once I watched it, I knew it was too personal, and no one had the right to such private moments."

Her voice bounces off the walls of the cave. "No one but you, the bastard who stole them from me."

It takes a couple of tries to scrabble up the slick rock face to slide my ass onto the ledge. "Most of the button cam material duplicated shots you knew I grabbed."

"Most of it. Not all of it. That's the issue here, Adair." She slaps her hands against the rocks and then lets out a cry of pain. "I'm volcanically pissed at you."

"I'm pissed at me. The hidden cam was a total dick move."

Chorda is at me so fast I swear she flew the distance between us. She looms above me and crushes a handful of my wet shirt. I feel her shaking.

"Do you swear on Bríg there is nothing else you're keeping from me, Adair Holliday?" Her gold streak flares, threatening to burn.

I dig deep for anything I've left out and find nothing. "I swear, Chorda. I'm begging you to accept my apology and my promise I will never screw up so badly again. From this second on, we go forward together on everything from what you want for breakfast to whatever you choose your professional future to be." I bury my face against her stomach. "I love you, Chorda. Forgive me."

I can't tell if the salt stinging my eyes is from my own tears or the spray of seawater. Gently, Chorda disengages.

A half-truth is a full lie. My lies of omission may have done us irreparable damage. When you've wanted someone for so long and then it happens, your reason clouds and you do desperate things to risk not losing what you've found.

"Go, Adair. Air everything you showed me tonight as the end of my involvement on *Kickin' It With Midas*. Once those episodes are history, you and I will see if there's anything to salvage between us." She turns her back on me, deflated. I'd prefer spent-fuse, angry fireworks.

I slink out of the cave, grateful for the barest flicker of hope Chorda's *if* lights in my vandal heart.

18

UNCUT

I SNAP THE LID SHUT ON THE LAST EQUIPMENT CASE, PUTTING MY bungalow studio out of business. Too many potential endings hover in the air around me: the end of *Kickin' It With Midas* without Chorda, the end of my rise at the Golden Pipes channel if Midas as much as flicks a finger of disapproval in my direction for trying to reconcile Chorda and him on air, the chance at a decent relationship with my brother, and worst of all, the death of my dream future with Chorda.

Every one of these ends traces back to me and different choices I might have made. I feel hollowed out, hopeless. Oh, to return and paint the past with golden strokes.

After I left Chorda in the cave two nights ago, I cut Desmond's segments into my Chorda narrative. Thank whatever goddess may not be shooting flaming arrows at me, Desmond was able to reign in Rubata and Glissanda to supply sweet sister moments. A shot of the pair gazing dewy-eyed into Chorda's empty bedroom even got to me. Thanks to fans clamoring for the next chapter of the Midas/Chorda drama, there was no opposition in greenlighting the filler episodes to play as a two-hour special last night.

Chorda agreed without much enthusiam to allow me to join

her, Bibs, and Rand to watch Midas's Rockin' and Rollin' Pantheon induction up at the house this evening. It's a first step. At least, I hope it's a first step to repair our relationship. My dread is, tonight she'll invoke her dead battery plan and return us to *friends only* status. She's going to be vulnerable having to watch Midas receive his honor without being a part of the celebration. I've rehearsed multiple groveling scenarios.

My ringtone, the *Kickin' It With Midas* opening credits, interrupts my descent into stress and fear. I see it's Bibs and hit the speaker icon. "Hey Bibs, be there in a few."

Her panicked voice blasts from the phone and scares the bejeepers out of me. "Adair, come quick. All hell is breaking loose."

"What—"

She cuts me off. "I've called for extra security on the grounds, but the crowd at the gate is keeping everyone busy. It's a madhouse."

"Bibs, what's happened?"

"A witch hunt."

Fear injects pain in every heartbeat. "I don't understand."

"It's the modern version of pitchforks and flaming torches, boy. Chorda is being attacked in the media and blamed for Midas's no-show at his Rockin' and Rollin' Pantheon induction."

My body becomes ice crystals threatening to shatter as I grasp Bibs's meaning. "Attacked? By whom?"

"By everyone. Her sisters are screaming that she cursed the Golden Guitar."

Anger pounds in my chest. Never have the Lears discussed their witchcraft as anything more than their connection to nature. Talk of spells or rituals is private territory. How dare Rubata and Glissanda out the possibility of curses to hurt Chorda. Curse them!

Bibs wails into the phone. "An angry mob is at the gate for Chorda. That fool Midas contributes to the madness with his invisibility act."

"On my way." I stuff the cell into my pocket and sprint out the door along the path to the house, trying to make sense of witch hunts and no-shows. Every security light on the property blasts across lawns and gardens. Out on the water, searchlights crisscross the beach. A huge black SUV from the security detail skids into the roundabout drive at the front of the house to join two of its brethren.

Rand Diggs opens the front door with a glare strong enough to singe eyelashes as I pass a pair of security guards stationed on the porch. His gray caterpillar mustache twitches as he speaks. "What the hell have you done, boy?"

A shriek cuts through the house from the dolphin room. It's Chorda. I push past Rand and jump down the three stairs. She stands in front of a flat panel mounted to the wall. Both hands cover her mouth, but a flurry of screams escape.

The sight of her stops my heart. I swear she's lost ten pounds in the last two days.

She catches my reflection in the glass wall and spins toward me, fury in her eyes. I rush to her, despite the warning in my head.

"Tell me wha..." Words shrivel. Splashed across the screen is my dead spy cam footage. Gone are the scenes of Chorda's love letter to Midas or her beautiful philosophies of music and creativity. It's pure hate. Shots of her splashing through the tide pools shriek of a woman with dark intentions. She looks like a witch summoning curses from starlight. Even Chorda's tongue in cheek comment telling Lear to fuck off is onscreen, shaped into an attack.

Chorda slaps both hands to my chest and shoves. "This horror show is the secret footage you swore you destroyed, isn't it?" She thrusts a finger at the screen. "I never said the horrible things coming out of that Chorda's mouth." Her breath hitches. "I never would."

I watch in shock as the beautiful moments I surreptitiously caught of Chorda become the bonfire of her destruction. It's a thousand shades of nasty. On-screen, Chorda is every bit the fiend the witch hunters accuse her of, a daughter out to destroy a father.

Bile rises in my throat as more reaction shots and comments from her venomous sisters call Chorda out on her hate and misuse of their craft to further blacken her name. The on-screen Chorda claims her talent alone keeps the Lears in the spotlight. More voiceover reveals that her refusal to sing to Lear at the choosing ceremony was to unveil the real dynamic of the Lear family. The personification of Dischorda insists Glissanda and Rubata leach off their younger sister's musical gift since they are incapable of writing a single note. She also claims to be the creative force behind Rubata's cosmetics and Glissanda's clothing lines, downgrading her sisters to mere figureheads to serve Chorda's grand vision.

The dark presence on-screen is everything the real Chorda is not.

"I swear, Chor. I deleted every frame."

She yells at a vocal cord popping level. "Then what the fuck is this?"

How in the holy hell did someone get a hold of my footage? What I interpreted as classy noir shots of an artist are misshapen into confessions of a bitter witch. My Chorda, an amazing, kind, and genuine woman, comes across as the basest of villains.

Chorda disintegrates into a chair. Hands cover her face as she sobs. I slowly move next to her and lay a hand on her shoulder. My love is in pain.

She smacks me away and leaps to her feet. Tear-dampened cheeks catch flickering light from the screen. "The moment you strapped on a secret camera, you broke us, Adair."

My usual minimalist strategy to deal with her anger is woefully inadequate in the face of this disaster. I fight my own tears. "Please don't go there, Chorda. I love you. My whole world is about your happiness." My bones crumble. Years of friendship, of love, turn to dust, and I don't know how to reverse the destruction. "I stole those scenes to help you reconcile with your father."

"You have no right to make decisions about my life."

Her words feel like a door slam to the heart. "You let me make decisions about your life every time I edit your sequences. Have I ever hit a wrong note?"

The gold strand in Chorda's hair flares, but not as bright as it's been. "That's a show, Adair, a fiction. You've ruined the real life I saw for us, our forever. You were always the person I've loved and trusted most."

"Always? *Our* forever?" A toxic stew of emotions from her accusation and use of past tense pulls every muscle as tight as a bowstring. "What extra sense was I supposed to possess to know you imagined us together until a few days ago?" I'm breathing so rapidly, it's hard to speak. "For years, you forced me to endure the minutiae of every relationship you had in search of the illusive *one* with no hint I was in the running. It was torture."

"Adair, I've admitted you are my illusive *one*." Her gaze bores into me. "All those years, I waited for you to see me as more than your friend, but you never gave me any hint you wanted that too."

The hollowness of her cheeks and the way she presses the heels of her hands against her heart set my brain screaming. *Shut up, Adair.* Chorda is upset and clearly battling crap health. She deserves nurture not a raving ass. My own volatile mixture of guilt for my part in our struggle, frustration Chorda is pushing me away, and panic drive words out of my mouth before my rational mind takes over.

"I've given it to you now." I lay both palms against the cool glass window, meeting her stare in the reflection. "Please don't put a noose around my neck because a shitiot stole my footage."

"Footage you stole behind my back." She slaps the window near my hand, her sister ring colliding with the glass in a metallic bang. "Which Adair are you, the man who claims to love me or the one whose purpose in life is to chase ratings? Defending yourself when this"—she jabs a finger at the TV—"trash is a result of your lies makes it clear which one you are."

Her sting is venomous.

"We'll find the asshole responsible and deal." Heart beats are pain as the probability of Desmond's guilt washes over me.

Chorda reads devastation on my face as only she can. Her lips press together so tight they lose their natural plum color. "There's always more than one lie, isn't there, Adair? You do know who did this."

I barely get the words out. "I'm afraid it's Desmond."

"All you Hollidays can go to the devil. Get out, Adair. Get out of my house. Get off my property. Get out of my life."

Chorda storms past me into the living room. The emotional blow of her mistrust knocks me into a chair. This is how it ends when you are given the unbelievable fortune to be in love with your dream girl, your best friend, the person you might be able to make a family with, and you lie to her.

I leave through the door to the beach steps and circle like a condemned man back to the bungalow. The last thing I ever wanted was to be part of the problems in Chorda's life, and I've becoming her biggest one. I doubt she'll even honor the dead battery pact we made at the Enchanted Garden. Our bridge back to friendship is in flames.

My chest cinches tight with the knowledge that this additional strain might send Chorda's waning health into a danger zone. Bibs surely has noticed by now Chorda needs more than whatever white willow shit Rubata brought her. As soon I wrap my head around this, I'll call Bibs and have her get Chorda to a doctor. If she's talking to me.

I squeeze my eyes shut. At this point, I'm to blame more than anyone else for the strain on Chorda. I promised her love and trust, but my fuckups gave her headaches and panic attacks.

I snap on the TV in the bungalow. I'd better know the extent of the damage I'm going to answer for. I become aware of steady vibrations from the phone in my pocket. I don't bother reading the mountain of messages and call Gabs.

Devoid of greeting or warmth, she snaps at me. "I will not talk to you, Adair. Read my text."

My mouth drops open as she ends the call. Gabs hung up on me. She's never hung up on me. I flick to her text.

Adair, I can't work for someone I've lost respect for. How could you hurt Chorda?

Shit, who else thinks I'm behind this? Is Desmond putting the word out I'm the author of tonight's hate fest? I call him. No answer, of course. He's probably gone into the witness protection program to avoid what he knows I'll do when I catch him.

I call Rubata, Glissanda, and even Midas. Then I call their assistants. I call the director, our editor, and stage manager. No one picks up. Am I blackballed? As a last ditch, I call my father. The call goes directly to voice mail with a message stating he will not return calls until after next week.

I've got to get my ass to Hollywood.

As I grab my keys, the scene on TV abruptly shifts from replays of poison Chorda to a shot of Midas. He's dressed only in boxers as he splashes through the stream in front of the Waterfall Palace. Even though the scene is dim, moonlight picks up a multitude of gray streaks in his coppery hair. He yanks at flowers, crushing petals in his hands and letting the broken bits rain into the stream. Face tilted to the sky, he howls and raises his arms at the moon.

"What the hell?" I turn up the volume.

"*I am a king. My subjects tremble when I roar.*"

He comes off as a complete nutjob. The footage of Midas's rant after the choosing ceremony follows, adding more damning strokes to his portrait of madness.

The next cutaway shot digs a knifepoint into my spinal cord. A jamb of reporters gathers outside the Rockin' and Rollin' Induction event for Midas in San Francisco. Speculation after speculation of why the honoree didn't show dip and roll across the screen.

Bibs is right. Lear ditched his own induction ceremony. Why?

They cut back to Chorda's damning diatribe. Every channel I

flip to covers the nightmare. Incendiary commentary pours off screen. I've seen enough. As I'm about to snap off the Golden Pipes channel, the screen flashes with a news crawl. The season finale of *Kickin' It With Midas*, a second choosing ceremony, will air directly after this update on the family feud.

What the fuck to the power of ten? How can there be a second choosing ceremony about to happen? I put the brakes on scheduling the new finale shoot until after we hear if Midas references the Golden Guitar at tonight's induction. Did Daddy Lear blow in from his isolation like a storm to retake the helm of his show and insist on a reshoot of the choosing ceremony? In a last-ditch effort, I call the sound stage phone. The recorded *shooting in progress* message plays.

The pieces of a nasty puzzle begin to fall into place. Here's a classic Adair blunder. I gave Desmond creative control of the second choosing ceremony. The asshole took my offering as permission to bypass me. He's orchestrated a second choosing ceremony so one of his Lear daughters can step into the center stage spotlight. The daughters whose segments he produces.

My stomach sloshes to the floor. Chorda is surely trying to solve the same puzzle. Why did I leave her? I should have insisted on staying by her side as friend or lover to help her navigate this end of days reality.

I sprint to the house, texting Chorda as I go. Security guards that usually greet me with friendly smiles stare me down. "Sorry, Mr. Holliday, we're instructed to see that you vacate the property."

Never in my life have I been unwelcome on Lear land. It's a blow to the solar plexus. I start to ask for Chorda. Based on the hard-assed looks aimed at me, that'll be a no-go. "Please ask Bibs Delany, the housekeeper, if she'll speak to me."

The guards look skeptical. Thank goodness my—up 'til now—good guy track record prevails. One guard heads into the house and is back in a flash.

"Ms. Delany says to meet her at the kitchen door. Five minutes and then you leave, Mr. Holliday."

I give a curt nod and dart around the side of the house. Bibs is waiting for me at the kitchen door. She dabs watery eyes in a red, puffy face.

"Tell me this wasn't your doing, Adair."

I grab her in a hug. "No, Bibs, I had no part putting such rot on air, but I'm not blameless. I will explain everything soon, I swear. Please let me see Chorda."

"She's gone."

Dread squishes my chest. "Gone? Her car is in the roundabout."

"She said she needed to get to her Da straight away. Rand took her to the Waterfall Palace on his bike."

Dread morphs to terror as I picture Chorda racing into town on the back of Rand's motorcycle past people ready to burn her at the stake. If she's recognized, they might swarm the bike.

I can't get lost in wild imaginings. It's time to act.

"They took fire roads to avoid chaos at the main gate. Go after her, Adair. She shouldn't face this fecking mess without you."

I kiss her cheek. "I'll find her, Bibs. I promise."

19

MISSING

THE DREAM YOU'VE HAD ALL YOUR LIFE CAN DISINTEGRATE IN A heartbeat because of stupidity. Chorda is right. The moment I pushed record on my cursed spy cam, I compromised our future. She was willing to give me anything I needed to make the art to reconnect her with her father. I didn't trust it would be enough.

I will never doubt Chorda Lear again.

I will make things right. If she rejects me once this ungodly snarl in our lives is past tense, I'll respect her wishes.

The slow going on bumpy fire roads kills me. L.A. traffic kills me more. Hairs on the back of my neck stand up, needles digging into skin. A thick cloud of disaster descends on two things I hold dear, Chorda and *Kickin' It With Midas*. I can't get to the studio fast enough.

Will Midas be sitting on his throne overseeing the second ceremony? I can't fathom the mogul passing up his induction to hand off the Golden Guitar to Rubata or Glissanda.

All week, I've let my fantasies about a future with Chorda take priority, and it's come to bite me in the ass.

A name from the news on the radio snags my attention: Grant Gothel.

All that remains of the West Sector Minimum Security Facility is a hill of charred remains. The fire started in the dead of night, trapping many inmates in their cells. The few survivors came from isolation cells in the heightened security wing for high profile prisoners where the fire originated. Due to the intensity of the blaze, identification of remains will take time. Rampion Records has yet to release a statement about the demise of its former president, Grant Gothel, who was being held for his lengthy list of crimes.

"Because no one is sorry to see that villainous son of a bitch fried."

Villainous.

Desmond's name flares red in my thoughts. Any doubt I had about my brother weaseling his way around my authority dies. Des gave me the final push to follow Chorda out to Malibu. He played into my soft spot for him as a brother and feelings he suspected I had for Chor to get me out of the picture. Once he was the ranking Holliday at the studio, his machinations with the other two Lear sisters could proceed unchecked.

I've been played, and my careless trust let it happen. My foot jerks on the gas. If not for the Tesla's built-in safeguards, I would rear-end the car in front of me.

Traffic slows to an even more maddening crawl to gawk at the rising structure of *Stalk* behind chain link. It's skeletal for now, but I've seen renderings where steel transforms into the elegant, twisting spiral of a beanstalk boasting every imaginable shade of green. The tower already dwarfs the surrounding buildings.

The distraction is short-lived, and misery returns with a vengeance. I pound the steering wheel for my arrogance in stealing the button cam footage. Desmond found it before I hit delete. The bastard squirreled it away until he could use it against me. Who else would even be looking in my files? He reworked the shots and added voiceover to harpoon Chorda. His sabotage forwards the agenda of the other two Lear sisters, his prizes.

Angry tears prick my eyes. What a jacklick I am to believe the

Holliday brothers could be a team. Desmond's been biding his time to best me and stick it to our father. What better way than to destroy the very thing about to set me above him, *Kickin' It With Midas?*

Fully aware it's a long shot, I call Gabs. In what I'm sure will sound like a pitiful rant, I spill my suspicions about Desmond and his part in the Chorda smear campaign.

"If you believe me at all, Gabs, I've got a huge ask. Find my car at the studio. I'll leave my keys on top of the front right tire. Use them to get into Desmond's office. Find his laptop and grab it." After another round of apologizing, I end the call.

I've just asked my former-by-choice assistant to sneak into Desmond's office and commit burglary. At the rate I'm going, no one in the known universe will be speaking to me come dawn. Chorda never wants to see me again. Gabs will lose any residual respect she might still hold for me. I'll be a crushing disappointment to my parents. In Bibs's eyes, I'll be a failure if I can't help Chorda. Desmond's hatred if I manage to thwart his plan for the second choosing ceremony will be a gash between us that will never heal.

Half-brother or not, I plan to fire his traitorous ass.

My gaze finds the moon, one sliver from full, like Midas's mind if his stream wading antics are any indication. So much for his personal god protecting him. Sweat breaks out along my hairline at the thought of Chorda's goddess pissed off at me as well. Will she send my car careening into a pole as payback for my lies? If Bríg saw the honest love in my heart for Chorda before, I hope she still sees it shining bright enough not to destroy me.

I have no god or goddess to ask for help. If only I'd been open to Chorda's beliefs earlier, I might claim otherworldly backup tonight. What a fool I've been to discount the essence of what makes Chorda Chorda for all these years.

"I promise you, Chorda. I will meet your goddess and fall at her feet."

Chorda says I can connect with my own deity. If that spirit watches me now, I hope he or she knows how much I need their help. I remember a phrase the sisters spoke to the trees.

"Mighty hawthorn, I ask for your spiritual energy, protection, and hope to light my way." I doubt there's a hawthorn tree here on Hollywood Boulevard. Hopefully, the one in the Lears' garden has excellent hearing.

Above me, a building wrap for the new Rampion Records show, *Sing Me Your Tune,* blocks the stars. Sidewalks full of tourists and theater-goers mill around the Pantages. Hollywood Boulevard closes in on me. To keep myself from driving onto the sidewalk to skirt traffic, I scan Midas's social media on my phone to see if I can find any explanation for his absence at the induction ceremony. Every account is marked *suspended*. I flip over to Rubata and Glissanda's socials, which blast tandem "burn the dark witch" themes.

I'm at least three traffic signal cycles away from turning on Hollywood and Vine when the flash from a video billboard lights up my car. A twenty-foot tall *Kickin' It With Midas* video advertisement beckons the fandom not to miss tonight's second choosing ceremony. Under it, a mob congregates. They wave signs that turn my bones to jam.

Dischorda is Doomed

Ditch the Witch

I feel utterly useless and alone. There are no trees or goddesses to help this fool. I've got to find Chorda on my own and do my damnedest to stop the second choosing ceremony from putting the Golden Guitar into the wrong hands.

I skid through the first hint of a red light and race to the bottom of the winding road leading to the Waterfall Palace. Two steep hairpin turns up, I screech to a stop. The narrow street is jammed with news vans and more *out for blood* fans holding painted signs of Chorda slams that break my heart. I want to roll down my window, shriek, and remind every last person who Chorda Lear really is, to shame them for turning against a person based on rancid media hype.

I linger a beat too long, and a news team spots me. I hear my name shouted, and blazing light cuts through my windshield. A herd of reporters and paparazzi surge in my direction.

"Adair Holliday. Adair, Adair, fill us in on the live show. Is the new choosing ceremony why Midas ditched his induction ceremony? Is Dischorda involved?"

People jump away from my car like frogs on a skillet when I screech into a U-turn and blast down the curvy road. I'm a shitiot for not realizing the main entrance gate to the Waterfall Palace would be a press nightmare.

Every breath is pure agony as I race down the hill and around streets to the private service road behind the property. My maniacal fishtailing on the curves could land me over the edge of a cliff in these Hollywood Hills. Hyperventilating, I make it to the rear gate. After checking for press on my tail, I punch in the code.

"Chor-da. Chor-da." I repeat her name like a heartbeat as the iron gate slides out of my way.

Tucked between the bushes at the end of the rear drive to the house, I see a motorcycle. I pray it's Rand's. I pull into the family parking and rush up the steps to the rear of the Waterfall Palace, darting off a text to tell Gabs where the car is.

Grav, the security guard, is on duty at the back slider as usual.

"Grav, is Chorda here?"

He nods in the direction of the sound stage. "You just missed her. Big doin's at the studio tonight, huh?"

A surge of gratitude rushes through my chest, quickly chased by fear. I've found her, but she's heading into a tiger cage. "What about Midas? Did he go down to set?"

Grav shakes his head. "Haven't seen the boss lately. You know Midas prefers to make a splash at the front entrance on shooting nights."

I'm dying to quiz Grav on his last Midas encounter, but visions of Desmond or the sisters harming Chorda light my ass on fire. I fly down to the studio parking lot and duck behind a car when I see a line of security guards I don't recognize in front of the stage door. I can't risk being banned from the studio the way I was at the Garinish house.

Sticking to a path behind cars and in shadows, I make my way around to the office side of the building and punch in a code. The business end of the place is empty until I get near wardrobe and dressing rooms. Here, it's hopping, as wild as any performance night. I slink around until I get to the scenery dock and from there slip into the studio.

The throne room set is the same as the night of the first choosing ceremony with two heart-stopping exceptions. Chorda is not on stage with her sisters, and Lear's golden throne is blanketed with gold and white lilies. Flashes of Deedee Lear's funeral play through my mind. These are the same flowers that covered her casket, flowers of mourning and death.

My instinct is to burst out on stage and stop the morbid farce ruining my show. Cameras already roll. It takes me half a second on my cell to confirm my fear. The show is streaming live.

Onstage, Rubata and Glissanda repeat their praise songs. Midas's portrait is projected on the LED screen behind the throne with the year of his birth followed by the current year. It's a funeral. Desmond is telling the world Midas Lear is dead.

In a daze, I work my way around the backstage for a better look. How can he be dead without anyone telling me or Chorda or Bibs? Something foul this way stinks. And where in the name of sanity is Chorda?

I need to find her. Did they catch her and lock her away? Should I search while the enemy is distracted with their fantasy? If they have her, what are Desmond and her sisters planning to do with her? They know she'll whistle-blow. If this malevolent crew is demented enough to cook up one funeral, who says they won't be down for another?

Sharp keening draws my attention to center stage. The two Lear sister kneel before their father's throne and wail. The faux theatrics grind my gut. As one, the pair rise, support each other, and cross to the glass case holding the Golden Guitar.

Glissanda lays her hands atop the glass. "Our father's dearest desire was to pass his beautiful Golden Guitar on to one of his daughters so the Lear music legacy will live on." She looks straight to camera. "Until our youngest sister, Chorda, stole that wish from him."

Rubata lays her hand on Glissanda's. "Tonight, we shall fulfill Da's dream and claim his gift together. As sisters, we will raise our voices in song with our Lear family treasure. Not one daughter, but two, will honor the dreams of a father wronged."

When they grasp the lip of the cover, Chorda explodes from behind one of the set's turrets.

"You will not touch it."

The sisters shove the lid back down. It slams onto the base. I hold my breath, afraid it will shatter. Chorda shoves between the two eldest Lears and the case. Her features and diminished body stand out in sharp relief under the unforgiving stage lights. Curse me for not dragging her to the doctor at my first inkling something serious was going wrong with her.

Chorda's spirit hasn't diminished. She faces her sisters, battle ready.

"The guitar can only be accepted from the hands of the one it belongs to. It belongs to Midas Lear, not either of you."

Rubata steps up to Chorda. "Those beloved hands can't pass on the Golden Guitar anymore. You broke Da's heart and killed him."

Chorda wavers for a beat before regaining her power stance. She sweeps arms across the set. "This is a lie. My father is not dead."

Glissanda holds her arms toward Chorda. "Da is gone, and now our youngest sister slips into the same madness that took him." She gestures down the length of Chorda's body. "Look at her. She's wasting away."

Chorda doesn't back down, stretching her arms wide to flatten palms against the front of the case, a warrior defending that which she holds dearest. "I'm perfectly sane. You two lost your minds if you think you can touch the Golden Guitar."

I inch near, hiding behind the scenery closest to Chorda, ready to spring into action if she needs backup. Heat from stage lights send rivulets of sweat down the sides of my face. Behind me, on the far side of the faux stained glass shielding me from the control booth, I hear a familiar voice: Desmond.

"It's ratings gold. That crazy witch showing up will send the broadcast through the roof. Wait for my go before we remove her. Everything she says enhances our narrative and adds more dollar signs."

"You son of a bitch." I blast past scenery and wrap fingers around his throat.

Desmond's eyes stretch in shock as he tries to pry my hands off his jugular.

"What have you done?"

His voice squeaks past my grip. "Midas sent instructions for the ceremony to go on."

"Midas *sent*? You didn't meet with him?" I loosen my grip enough to give him air, not remove the threat.

"I didn't need to. Rubata brought the script Lear approved before he passed."

Rubata brought, not Midas. Something wicked festers in my gut. "You shitiot. Midas never saw a script. Rubata is playing you."

Desmond's face turns magenta. "That's not true. You hate the fact Rubata and I are saving the show. You and Chorda look down on the rest of us from your pedestals of privilege. The two of you possess no fucking idea how hard we unanointed work for the scraps we have."

Scraps? Rubata's never seen a scrap in her life. I reel from the depth of my brother's hatred. It's true our parents' clout gave Chorda and I a leg up on our dreams, but we work like dogs to deserve the advantage. Desmond's sense of being wronged blinds him to everything but his own trajectory. I'm rattled by how deep his damage goes. Now, he's been seduced by this opportunity and tainted by Rubata to knock us aside and claim what he perceives is his due.

This is no time for armchair therapy. I need answers. "What did Rubata promise if you unleashed your horrible attack episode? Where the hell is Midas?"

He swallows. I feel lies take shape beneath my fingers. I squeeze his throat again. "Let me be clear. Your jig is up. There's proof enough to bury you." I'm bluffing, but *I have hunches enough to bury you* is not an effective threat.

"Rubata promised me everything you and Hamilton deny me, respect, a purpose."

Desmond's duplicitousness born from years of resentment wring out my last hope of salvaging a relationship with my half-brother. He doesn't want to work with me, he wants to replace me.

"You're a fool, Desmond. Rubata is setting you up to take the fall when this farce to get her hands on the Golden Guitar goes south. And it will go south." I suspect their tidy cabal includes Glissanda as well. A double whammy of Lear sister influence gives the ugly scheme enough oomph to nearly succeed. "You're a convenient villain."

A flicker of dismay crosses Desmond's face. His gaze darts to the stage where light streams from the golden streak in Chorda's hair to form a pulsing sphere around the three sisters. The moment I loosen the grip on his throat, he breaks free. A fist flies at my gut.

I twist in time. The force of his punch sends him stumbling forward. He whirls around for a second attack, eyes narrowed to slits. "I will not let you take this from me, Adair."

As he lunges, Chorda's cry rends the studio. The distraction kills his momentum. I use the advantage to drive my fist into Desmond's jaw. He crumples onto the stage floor. My first ever face punch is a knuckle-cracking doozy.

Onstage, Rubata circles Chorda like a tigress poised to leap. "We've worn you down, Chorda." When she twists the sister ring on her finger, Chorda clutches her stomach. "You can't fight us."

Glissanda slides closer to the case while Chorda tracks Rubata. The three jockey for dominance. With the speed of a comet, Rubata lunges at the glass case and shoves the lid backward. The mechanism groans as the top flies off, crashing against the steps leading up to the throne. Shards of glass explode and lodge into scenery.

"No," screams Chorda, kicking to force her sisters away. It's too late. In the same beat, they both advance, sending a weakened Chorda to her knees. They reach past her into the case and grab for the Golden Guitar.

When Rubata's fingers touch the neck of the instrument, and Glissanda's its harp-shaped body, a flash of honey-colored light bursts from the case, engulfing the studio. I shield my eyes. When the blaze dies, two golden statues stand in the place where moments ago, Lear's daughters fought over his treasure.

Chorda wails and paws her way up the statues of her sisters, calling their names. She rests a hand on each of their cheeks and weeps. When they don't respond, she taps the green and black stone of her sister ring against Rubata's and then Glissanda's.

"Lear, Lear Lear. Sister, sister, sister. Always, always, always."

Nothing happens.

Gasps and muffled shrieks erupt in pockets around the studio as any doubt of the Golden Guitar's magic is wiped away.

Chorda wraps her arms around her gilded sisters, sobbing onto their metallic shoulders. "Ruby, Gliss, I can't lose you." She backs away from the gold effigies and spins to face the Golden Guitar. In a flash, she reaches inside the case.

I charge onstage, yelling her name, and catch Chorda around the waist as she grabs the guitar. When I pull her away, the guitar is in her arms—warm, human arms. We topple backward, and she rolls away from me.

"Don't touch it, Adair."

"How can you touch... Why aren't you..."

In answer, she slides a finger along the streak in her hair. It's true, the speculation about her gold strand. The guitar chose Chorda long before Lear ever cooked up the self-promoting choosing ceremony that ripped his family apart. If he isn't dead, we're going to have words.

I leap to my feet and grab Chorda's upper arm to help her stand. It's so delicate, I'm afraid I'll snap the bone beneath my fingers. As I guide her to her feet, I'm careful to avoid the cursed guitar. "Come on."

With mayhem breaking out behind us, we sprint for the rear stage door near the scenery dock. Back on his feet, a shaky Desmond bellows for cameras to keep rolling while the director's voice blasts through the P.A ordering a stop.

Rand materializes from behind a row of flats painted to look like vine covered stone. He scares the hell out of me with his *enraged aging rock-star ready to kick over an amp to prove he still can* vibe.

"Go," he whispers. "I'll hold them off."

"Meet us at your bike," hisses Chorda. I take her hand, careful not to touch the guitar now slung over her shoulder. We run.

At the end of the parking lot, there's a hidden break between hedges leading to the Lears' terraced gardens. Thank heavens Desmond never explored the Waterfall Palace grounds the way I did as a kid. Once we're through the opening, we move deeper into the garden until we stand before the dolmen, the entrance to the ritual ground.

Chorda braces herself against the massive stone portal. There's a frightening rattle to her breathing.

Still nervous around the forbidden stone, I move as close to Chorda as I dare. "Why did you risk touching that thing?" I jab a finger at the guitar. "If something had happened to you"—I clasp her hand—"my heart would turn to freaking gold right along with yours."

My heart does skitter, scared she'll pull her hand from mine.

"My father is not dead."

I give her hand a squeeze. "Agree."

"We've got to find him. He's not in his right mind. Did you see those shots of him in the water, howling?"

I bob my head. I'm so damn grateful she's speaking to me, touching me.

"I thought he'd still be in his room since he wasn't at the Pantheon induction." A sob of infinite sorrow, not her usual melodic cry, escapes her lips. "There was a packed suitcase, and his tux was in a garment bag. He meant to go." She shakes her head. "There's more, an empty glass by his bedside, and I swear..." She grips my arm, keeping her body between the guitar and me. "I held it up to the light and found greenish residue clinging to the bottom. I'm afraid it was dried malachite."

"I don't understand."

"Malachite can be poison. The crystal absorbs negative energies. If Da drank elixir with malachite..." A shiver wracks her too-thin frame.

My gut curdles. Did Midas fall so low that his rift with Chorda drove him to drink poison? Not in a thousand years. More likely, the old buzzard drank heavily enough not to notice someone was poisoning him.

Someone he trusted.

"Could malachite make him slowly lose his marbles before it did him in?"

A whine escapes Chorda's lips. "I'm afraid it could."

My hands begin to tremble. Rubata commandeered Midas's

phone. Did she impose herself as Lear's gatekeeper to harm her own father? I hate adding to my list of dark suspicions, but Desmond couldn't pull all the shit he's managed without high-level support. Lear sister support.

How involved is Glissanda? Her liaison with Desmond at the cemetery burns in my memory. Both sisters resent Chorda being the favorite and Lear for making her so. Taking their youngest sister and father out of the equation solves their problems. Chorda played right into their hands by refusing to sing her praise song to Midas.

Is Chorda's deterioration their doing?

My gut turns to lead as my head fills with curses and spells. Have they wreaked some supernatural foul play on Chorda?

I squeeze Chorda's hand. "I believe Desmond and your sisters are behind everything."

She pulls her hand from mine and turns away. If Chorda is finished with me, I'll be the Tin Man, a body without a heart.

"Tell me what you need to do, Chor. I'm with you. We'll go with your dead battery scenario after we find your father. Right now, I'm with you."

She leans the guitar lovingly against the dolmen as if the instrument is Midas himself. As soon as the guitar touches stone, the dolmen glows with a golden sheen. Chorda takes a step closer. "Do you believe any amount of time would be enough to get over you?"

I blink repeatedly to absorb what she's saying.

Chorda runs her hand gently over my eyes to still them. Her hand lingers on my cheek. "You being here for me now, in the middle of this colossal horror show, tells me which Adair you are. Can we rewind to the moment back at Garinish when you said, 'I love you. My whole world is about your happiness.'?"

I fit my body to hers and slide Chorda's golden strand between my fingers. "I do love you, and it is. My world will always be about your happiness, whether we're together or not. Everything you are, Chorda, is precious to me. I'm yours forever as a friend or in whatever capacity works for you."

Her words come out in a stuttering cadence. "I was devastated by what they painted me to be in that awful broadcast. I blamed you."

I trail fingers down the side of her face, along her neck, and down her side where I can feel every rib. "You're right to blame me. Those shots would never exist if I hadn't been a false friend and kept secrets from you."

She twists to face me. "I know who you are, Adair. The guy with a heart as big as the full moon who puts people before personal success. I do believe you intended the hidden camera to seek out uninhibited truth and beauty to tell the best version of my story for Da. A jacklick twisted something precious into a weapon."

It was me who handed Desmond the weapon. "Forgive me for providing the means and using deceit to benefit the show."

"The show we make together. The show that allows us both to lead the lives we choose." Her hand grips the back of my neck. "I blamed *Kickin' It With Midas* for all my pain. I vilified it and you when I've always been a willing participant." Chorda touches her forehead to mine. "By damning the show, I also damned your creative passion. I'm sorry."

"Boy, do we have communication issues to work on."

"I'll go first," says Chorda, pulling my mouth to hers. Passion and promises flow through the kiss like electricity obliterating a surge protector. I nearly weep. Broken pieces of us begin to find their way back together.

She ends the kiss quickly. "I love you, Adair, but my father is in danger. He needs the Golden Guitar. It's who he is. I know it will play for him and bring him back to me."

Damn, Chorda saw the footage of Midas off his rocker in the stream and knows her Da is unhinged. "Chor, Rubata is the only one who's talked to him in person the past few days. And we can't ask her where he is."

Chorda's eyes shine with tears. I kick myself for bringing up her gilded sister. She searches the ritual ground as if Midas might step out from behind the willow tree. "I know who we can ask." She grabs the guitar and my hand to pull me down the path.

"Wait. Are you up for this?"

She rests a palm against the side of her neck. "I have to be, even if my heart races or if breathing and even thinking are painful. It's for Da."

I'm an absolute shit. How much pain has our lovemaking caused her?

"Oh, Chor." I cup her face in my hands. "And I've hurt you when we—"

She covers one of my hands with hers. "No, never. Bríg means for us to be together. You never hurt me, Adair."

Chorda crushes my hand, yanking me down to the stone circle. "Focus on Da. I'll do whatever must be done to help him. Believe in me."

"Always." I believe in Chorda, but I'm terrified she overestimates her physical capability in handling any Midas rescue plan.

As soon as I'm in the middle of the stone circle, my own heart races. The energy running through the place threatens to short-circuit heart and mind. Chorda lays the Golden Guitar upon the small rock table in the center, then darts to the wooden chest in front of the rowan tree. Next, she carries an armful of candles and gemstones to place around the Lear family legacy.

"There's no time for a formal ritual. I'm going to try to call Bríg and pray she hears me. With arms raised to the rising moon, she sings, "Dearest Bríg, forgive reaching out to you in haste. I invite you to be with us under the moon. Help us fight the forces trying to hurt Da."

A gust of wind strong enough to knock over the tallest white candle ignites it instead.

"Take my hands, Adair." She reaches for me across the table. "Tell Bríg you believe and honor her. Promise her you're with us."

"I don't know how." The gravity of my next words renders me mute. What if I say the wrong thing? What if I make the candle go out?

Chorda's eyes are closed. "Say what you feel."

I shut my eyes. "Um, goddess, ma'am. Chorda believes you're real. So do I. Please, help us find Midas Lear. He is important to me. He is my family." I'm filled with a sense of certainty Bríg is real. I did sense her presence that night at Garinish. She was the power that blessed the union of Chorda and me.

The first night I saw the sisters summon the goddess, the ritual was organized. Tonight, we're scattered and desperate. Can this work?

A new gust knocks me off balance. My eyes snap open to find a second newly lit white candle glowing beside the first. At the base of each candle, a row of crystals catches the flicker of dual flames.

Chorda begins to sing to the tree at each compass point. Wind circles, growing in strength as she addresses each tree. This is happening. The previously skeptical Adair Holliday embraces Chorda's craft with no reservations, only hope.

When she addresses the hawthorn, I swear I hear the roar of waves pounding the shore as if the wind brought surf to the garden. I may be losing my mind, but the smell of salt clings to my nose.

"He's at the beach," says Chorda, and the wind calms.

"Did you hear waves?"

Her golden strands glows, but dimly. There's a pulse to the light as if it wants to brighten but lacks the energy to pull it off. "You heard the sea, too, Adair?" The expression of adoration on her face brings tears to my eyes. I'm such a lout for pooh-poohing Chorda's beliefs all these years.

Over Chorda's shoulder, the nearly full moon shines above the hawthorn tree. The sight of it jars me out of my mushy moment. I've seen that moon in the same quadrant of the sky. I grab my phone and bring up the scene of Lear howling in the stream in front of the Waterfall Palace. The same nearly full moon crests the top of the hawthorn.

"Chor, the moon." I flash the screen at her. "It's tonight's moon. Your father was here not long ago. Maybe he's farther downstream, not at the beach."

"No, I heard waves. I smelled salty air."

I nod.

"Chorda, Adair, you down there?" Rand's raspy voice sounds from the top of the path. The candles wink out.

"We're coming," says Chorda, and slings the Golden Guitar over her shoulder. We rush to join Rand.

Chorda passes through the dolmen and grabs Rand's forearm. "Da's near the sea."

Rand rubs his lips together, making his mustache dance. "The beach house? Garinish? Bibs would call."

Chorda sways. "Oh, Adair, what if he's near the sea cliffs?"

To the west, the sky brightens with a spike of lightning. The flash reveals a bank of gray, flat-bottomed clouds stretching across the horizon. Thunder wastes no time joining the party. A faint red ring flares around the moon. Chorda's skin is translucent.

Rand pokes at his phone screen. "The cliffs are closer to Justin and Zeli's place than Lear property. I'll call them."

Chorda's hand quivers in mine. I can't draw her to me without bumping into the blasted Golden Guitar. I'm no good to her as a statue.

"They're on it," says Rand, texting. "I'll have Bibs tell security. Come on, Chorda, we'll take the bike."

Chorda is the essence of misery. "I can't risk the guitar touching you, Rand. Connect with Justin and Zeli. Find Da. We'll be right behind you."

Doubt washes over his features, but he kisses her on the top of the head and sprints away.

I'm sick, thinking about how long it will take us to plow through traffic and get to Lear. If the Golden Guitar is Midas's way back into his head, we may be too late. "I'll break every law of physics to get you to the coast, Chor."

She points to the moon. "Do you see the red ring? It's a killing moon. We need a faster way."

20

HELLO GODS, IT'S ME, ADAIR

CHORDA GRIPS MY SHOULDERS. I JERK AWAY WHEN THE GOLDEN Guitar begins to slide around her body.

"Adair, if you still hold any doubts about my craft, my beliefs, step away now."

My insides glow with the warmth of sitting in front a campfire. Anything Chorda tells me is possible, is possible. I have no more uncertainty about the power and strength she draws from goddesses or trees, only wonderings of how I can share it more deeply with her.

"No stepping away."

We run back to the ritual circle. After placing the Golden Guitar on the stone table, Chorda gestures for me to follow. She winds her way around the circle of stones, chanting in Irish. Lightning forks in the western sky. Distant thunder rumbles through the soles of my feet.

Nestled against the hill facing the house, I catch sight of a huge stone Celtic cross I missed before. My gaze is drawn to the dolmen, the portal stone I always believed would whisk me away into another world. Carved on the dolmen's header stone is the name

O'Laoghaire, the Gaelic patronym for O'Leary I've seen on the coat
of arms in Midas's office.

What I believe to be ancient, deep-rooted energy crackles
through the air. It rises from stone, tree, cross, crystal, and candle.
Sacred power surrounds us and vibrates through my core. I swear
I'm expanding. I check my arm as reassurance I'm not actually
blowing up like a balloon.

Chorda shifts from chant to plea. "O, you kind gods, bring me to
my father so I might cure the breach in his abused nature."

We return to the table in the center of the circle. She gestures
for me to stand to one side as she runs to the chest in front of the
hawthorn to retrieve what appears to be a small stone bowl.
Chorda slips behind the tree and down a slight incline. She bends
and scoops water into the bowl from the narrow stream behind the
ritual ground.

Returning to the table, she settles the bowl next to the Golden
Guitar. Through the water, I see the shine of bluish crystals.

Chorda reaches over the table to take my hands. "Bríg, I join
hands with my heartsong to call for your grace and wisdom to
aid us."

Veins in the hawthorn's leaves begin to sparkle with faint
light. A sense I can only describe as the perfect blend of energy
and peace flows through me. Chorda's goddess has come. I know
it as certain as I am standing in a mystic garden with the witch I
love.

Chorda squeezes my hands. "Say everything I say."

I nod, and she closes her eyes. I do the same.

"Bríg, we seek safety for Midas Lear, a son blessed by the
Sidhe."

I repeat her words. My body grows warmer as if the sun
emerged from the clouds to soak my skin.

"Welcome, dear goddess."

"Welcome, dear goddess."

Chorda sings her next words with the resonance of a sacred

song sung thousands of times. The tune takes form, bending the air around us.

"Manannán Mac Lir, chosen god of my father, a son blessed by the Sidhe, join with us to bring justice to this night."

I've heard that name before, but I stumble over the pronunciation. I quickly swallow my lame ass attempt and force myself to reenter the rich blanket of wind, warmth, and light rising from the ground to encircle us. My voice gains strength as I repeat the rest of Chorda's words. We may call to an unfamiliar god, but I do know of the Sidhe, the otherworld to which the Lear family pledges their very existence.

The legends they believe, the stories they tell, my heart beats with certainty they are all real. The connection floats around me like gold mesh, forming to my body until it finds the shape of my spirit. Magic seeps into my soul. My flesh joins with this ancient Irish family, the O'Laoghaires, whose spirits surround my life. They are my life. I'm no longer an observer, the son shuffled between homes a continent apart, or a brother who is seen as a nemesis instead of a person to love. Here in a place that connects worlds, I am inside the forces Chorda embraces as her truth. I belong to her family. They are my truth, as is she.

An unfamiliar voice wavers through my head. "*Daughter of Bríg, you bring an untried seeker. He must meet the test I set before you, one of faith and truth. Rise waters. Blow ye winds. Allow the seeker to aid in the rescue of our ruined son from the betrayal of false children, of tigers who masquerade where daughters' love should reside, and the Sidhe shall see him.*"

I stumble backward and squeeze my eyes to keep them shut, terrified I'll screw up Chorda's spell if I attempt to see a form connected to the voice. A bead of water drips down the bridge of my nose and falls to my lips. It tastes of salt and sea.

Chorda's grip tightens. "Did you hear my father's god speak to you?"

I'll have a million questions when the world stops spinning. "I think, maybe." Chorda owes me a heck of a debrief when this is over.

She hums a soft, slow note and then speaks. "Beloved Bríg, I call upon your shield to bless our journey to where mighty Manannán Mac Lir sends us so we may save his ruined son."

My throat constricts with emotion, and I struggle to repeat her words. There's an Adair inside my skin and another outside it. Instead of feeling fractured, my consciousness intensifies. It's empowering and humbling, exhilarating and terrifying. From north, south, east, and west, energy swirls and bends through the air. Sensations like damp leaves brush my skin. Tiny beads of moisture from whatever touches my neck dip under my shirt to drip over my heart. The air smells clean, a forest after the rain mixed with scents of bark and loam.

The trees are touching me. They judge the person locked in the ritual with their Chorda. Wordless questions float in the air around me, questions these energies and I share. Am I worthy of the magic that joins its voice to Chorda? Will I fulfil the oaths of loyalty and love my heart swears to this woman? Reaching out with my spirit, I vow to spend this lifetime and any others the fates grant to prove my dedication to Chorda Lear.

Chorda gasps, and a new voice echoes through my thoughts. Its masculine timbre holds the same intensity as its predecessor with added undertones of sensitivity and easily given emotion.

"Son of the arts and teller of stories, the oaths of your spirit call to me. While I find you in Bríg's light, it is through I, Lugh, divine keeper of oaths, your pledges will find the garden in which to flourish."

I'm pulled to these words. Intention grows in my gut to reach out and speak to the new visitor. My heart knows, gaining his allegiance is key to saving Lear. "Mr. Lugh, will you accept my sincerity and protect the oaths of love I have for Chorda Lear so they may flourish?"

"What do you offer me in return, untried seeker?"

There's a tremor in Chorda's voice. "Adair, do you realize what you're doing? You're pledging to a god."

"It's okay, Chor." Every heartbeat ignites bursts of heat inside my chest. I imagine that heat turning into sparks flowing out of me to form a tiny swarm like the mystical bubble Chorda summoned when she sang on the beach. The ball of light finds its way into the shadow of a hand reaching down through the clouds as I speak. "I offer you the story of a foolish man who did not believe beyond the fragile shell of his reality until a sweet heartsong painted the path of new awakening."

"*And will such a man remain a fool?*"

My chest constricts, and I draw the shallowest of breath. My thoughts chat up a freaking god. Such convos may be a day-to-day thing for Chorda, but I fear my body may be turned inside out and hung from the hawthorn tree. Both head and heart know my next words will either convince this Lugh dude I'm team O'Laoghaire or send him packing with an immortal eye roll.

I clear my throat. "As foolish as all men remain, but this mortal requests the honor to accept your wisdom and guidance to someday become a learned fool."

Three voices blend in my head, two male and one female. "*To accept our aid, daughter of Bríg, you must denounce your bond to the phantom queen.*"

"I made no such bond," says Chorda, her indignation clear.

The trio of voices roar so violently, I swear a crack opens down the middle of my brain. "*Then a bond was thrust upon you.*"

My brain crack shifts to my heart as Chorda speaks. "I beg you to rid me of this bond." I hear deep sorrow embedded in her words. She knows who thrust the phantom queen's—whoever the hell that is—bond—whatever the hell that is—on her.

Chorda screams. My eyes snap open to find green flames surrounding her left hand. There's a loud snap, and her sister ring shatters into green dust for an instant before the wind steals it away.

The skin of her ringless finger pales in moonlight. She cradles the Golden Guitar against her body, gasping over and over. With each rise and fall of her chest, more color returns to her skin. I watch Chorda transform in live, mystical, time-lapse footage. She blossoms, a flower in starlight, as her body reclaims its rightful shape.

"Chor, you're...back."

She touches a hand to her temple, heart, over her body, and to the golden strand of hair that now shines as bright as a beacon for those lost in darkness. Her gaze meets mine. "I am."

I take her left hand. "Why did the voices zap your sister ring?"

Staring at her finger, she forces out words. "It was spelled to bind me to Mórrigán."

Mórrigán, the goddess I heard Rubata and Glissanda gush over. Before I unleash my own curse to condemn phantom queens, witch sisters, and spells, a deafening roar swallows the air around us. The liquid in the stone bowl begins to boil as a sparkling wall of water taller than the rowan tree rises from the stream behind the ritual ground.

I call out for Chorda as the shining wave circles us. We're encased in an iridescent sapphire tunnel of mist and spray. We reach for one another and manage to grasp hands as suction pulls up deeper into the watery tube. Tumbling through this bizarre portal is disorienting, but not unpleasant. Outside the sheen of the boundary, familiar scenes sweep by. We fly past the Waterfall Palace. Behind us, the letters of the Hollywood Sign shine bright, and in the distance, neon blue disks of the Rampion Records Tower rise beyond the streak of light that is Hollywood Boulevard.

Time and space blur and bend around us. We float as images waver on the outside of our supernatural highway. Windows in the cluster of Century City skyscrapers shine in escalating lines of golden rectangles. Their glow shimmers and sparkles like candy glass. These lights from manmade buildings attempt to compete with stars and fail.

All around us, faint voices crisscross. I strain to hear distinct words. Am I missing vital instructions as to my purpose in this waking dream? Is it only a dream that I fly above Los Angeles in a water cyclone with Chorda? The remnants of skepticism hiding in the corners of my mind seek each other and attempt to reform. I wave a hand to scatter doubt into disparate fractals.

I do believe this is real. I believe Chorda's goddess, Lear's god, and my new bestie, Lugh, are sending us down an enchanted highway to save Midas. It's then the whispered words become clear.

"*Breath of gods, send your beloveds on their journey.*"

I try to speak, to ask Chorda if she hears what I'm hearing. My lips move without voice. A vicious wind blasts through the mist encircling us. Chorda's hand is ripped from mine. I watch as she's sucked into a whirlwind of slate gray clouds shot through with spikes of lightning. My body convulses as thunder shakes the fabric of whatever holds me above the ground. Ahead, a roiling, black smear puckers with twisting circles of white—the Pacific.

Panic squeezes like I'm wrapped in a thousand bungie cords. These god folks better rock a fully operating GPS. Being dumped in a pissed off ocean in the middle of a thunderstorm is not my idea of a party. I holler for Chorda as the distance grows between us. She shrinks until all I see is the reflection of lightning in the body of the Golden Guitar.

I stroke my arms as if I could swim through the sides of the god tube. With a giant crack, the shroud holding me disappears, and I fall.

21

MY WITS BEGIN TO TURN

IN THE SKY AROUND ME, A STORM RAGES. I TUMBLE THE LAST FEW feet and smack into a patch of wildflowers. I duck as lightning sears the air far too close. My body aches like a funny bone slammed into a wall. Finding my feet, I shake off the pain. My head whips around to get my bearing. I'm at the trailhead near the path where I shot footage of Chorda only days ago.

"Adair!" The sound of my name rides the wind between thunderclaps.

Looking west toward the cliff's edge, two figures wave me on. Through the sheet of rain, I stumble across the rocky surface to join them, hyperaware of the deadly cliff ahead of me. Thunder shakes the ground beneath my feet, and I drop flat as a bolt of lightning takes out a clump of brush not two yards away. Flames shoot up from the dry patch but are doused into a line of white smoke by incessant rain.

Fingers clamp my bicep and yank me to my feet.

Justin Time shouts in my face. "Are you okay?"

I touch my chest and hips as if checking to make sure everything is still attached. "Yeah."

Zeli tugs at my sleeve. "Come quick. They're over here."

"What do you mean 'they'," I shout, but a brutal gust steals my words. I'm sick as the edge of the cliff seems to skitter in the flashes of lightning. Is Rand with Lear? Bibs? Security? And where in the name of her gods is Chorda?

The three of us pick our way toward the slap and roar of waves echoing against the cliff. Equilibrium and balance take a holiday as we try to navigate menacing winds and the onslaught of needle sharp rain. We walk like drunks on a moving sidewalk to the top of the path that leads to the overlook where Chorda and I shot her scene.

Justin pulls Zeli away from the edge. After the next thunderclap, I slowly approach to peer down. The sight below strips me of sanity. On a tiny ledge halfway down the switchbacks to the overlook are Midas and Chorda.

"We begged her to wait for Rand, but she freakin' ran down the death path," yells Justin.

Zeli smacks his shoulder.

Lear is dressed in tattered shorts and bare feet with clumps of wildflowers spilling out of his pockets. A necklace of seaweed hangs over his shoulders. Has he willingly donned these trappings of the seacoast, or did whoever dumped him here dress him like a lunatic?

He shakes fists at Chorda, and she shrinks back, holding the Golden Guitar up as a shield.

I nearly vomit, examining the steep path to the ledge below. There is no choice for me, crippling fear or not. I've got to get to Chorda before this decimated version of Lear goes full animal on her.

I take a shaky step onto the path. Justin and Zeli shriek at me to wait. I ignore them. Wind slams me against the rocks. I ass plant every third step, working my way down to my love and the man who's a second father to me. My chest heaves with sobs I can't hear above the wind.

"Let me get there in time," I repeat over and over, hoping our trio of deities, Bríg, Lugh, and Lear's sea god call in favors from comrades in the Irish god's registry.

When I reach the narrow shelf where father and daughter face off, Chorda holds up a hand to keep me in place. Ribbons of light leak from her golden strand but are stolen by the wind.

"Take my hand, Chor."

The bowed cliffside is an acoustic shell amplifying Lear's ranting. "Do not deny me a dramatic death." He slashes the air before him. "Your goddess, daughter, will see you to a brilliant afterlife. Midas Lear is tied to the fiery wheel of hell." He stabs a finger to his eye. "Even my tears burn like molten lead ready to run in the river below this world."

Chorda takes a step toward Lear. "I'm here, Da. It's going to be all right."

"Chorda, no!" I shake from bone-chilling cold and the thickness of approaching death in the air.

Lear stretches out an arm to point at Chorda's face. "Do not cry your false tears. I am finished with those who pretend to weep for me. If you've brought more poison for me like your sisters, I'll drink it now. It is the price of truth for three daughters devoid of love for their father."

"I love you, Da. I've brought your guitar. Play for me."

I step as far onto the shelf as I dare, terrified I'll provoke Lear into something drastic. My gaze darts over the edge to catch the flight of gulls seeking shelter from the storm in rocky ledges. They're so far below, they look like bees. Further down, surf claws at the rocks, looking for purchase to climb and sweep us into a grave of churning spit and foam. Dizziness presses against my temples, and I grapple to hold on to a shard of rock sticking out of the cliff.

"It will not play for me," shouts Lear, swiping hands through the air as if to erase the Golden Guitar from existence. "All that once knew me have forgotten who I am. Now, rains come to drench me. This thunder in my heart"—He thumps his chest as reddish-gray curls swirl around his head—"put there by the daughters who falsely cared for me, will kill me."

Did the malachite Rubata and Glissanda gave him make his chest thunder and his mind shred?

Chorda is close enough to grab Lear's hands. "Da, it's your Chorda. I will never hurt you."

He recoils from her touch and swipes hands on his shorts. "Let me wipe my hands, they stink of death. My world is worn to nothing save betrayal from false children."

Midas presses against the cliff. Here's my chance. If I strike quickly, I can pull him down and restrain him until Rand can bring reinforcements. I slide up behind Chorda. "On three, I want you to sit. I'm going to grab your father."

Instead of going with my plan, Chorda blocks my way. She positions the Golden Guitar against her chest and begins to strum. The music of the guitar comes alive as she sings the song she wrote for her beloved father.

"*Five droplets of gold break off from the sun*
As they touch the sweet earth, threads of family are spun."

His daughter's song hypnotizes Lear. Wonder spreads across his face. He slides down the rock wall until he's on his knees. Chorda ducks her head out of the guitar strap and holds the instrument to Midas. "Even though the Golden Guitar will play for me, it will never truly be mine until I take it from your hands, Da."

He stares at the instrument. "Memory of how I painted you false, dear one, fills me with shame."

Chorda sets the guitar on the ground in front of her father.

"Let it go, Da. I'm here. I love you. All is forgiven."

Chorda does not need a goddess assist. This woman, the essence of kindness and love, is her own benevolent force. I slowly approach until I'm able to wrap my arms around her to let her know I am with her in the quest to save her father. "We are both here for you, Midas," I say. "You are not alone. You never were."

Golden threads flow off the end of Chorda's strands and wrap around Lear's wrists. The magic strings pull his hands toward the guitar until he lifts the treasure into his arms.

Midas stares at the guitar. "My Chorda, with the Golden Guitar, the two of us will make music together. We will denounce the cage of fame that's driven us here. Our voices will rise in song, and we will laugh at the gilded butterflies who thrive on red carpets, social media hits, and the adoration of strangers."

Lear's words hit me like a spear through the chest. I believe that I value storytelling in the shows I make above success markers. The truth is I'm more gilded butterfly than I admit. The thrill of having a hit show, positive reactions from our fandom, revenue, finding the next big idea like my interactive app to make money, those things drive me as powerfully as the art. They linger in the outlines of my consciousness and motivate me to a degree I'm no longer comfortable with. If she'll have me, I will partner with Chorda to embrace the creation of art before money. Yes, those trappings are necessary evils, but I vow to shift my priorities.

A glimmer of Midas Lear, separate from this madman in the storm, begins to show.

I whisper in Chorda's ear. "There's your Da."

She tries to break free from my embrace. I hold fast as Midas leaps to his feet and strides to the edge, a sheer drop one misstep away.

He raises the Golden Guitar to the storm. "From the blood flowing through the veins of the family O'Leary, I bequeath the gift of songs yet to be discovered to my beloved daughter, Chorda."

From the heavens, a highway of lightning explodes into a thousand forks. The mightiest bolt strikes the Golden Guitar. Chorda and I are thrown onto our backs. I watch in horror as a surge of energy leeches a gilded stream from the guitar. A ribbon of gold undulates in front of the cliff, and with a deafening blast, the ribbon bursts into a curtain of golden metallic droplets. he next gust of wind pulls the shining sheet out past the breakers until its glow flutters down to the surface of the sea. The blanket of gold joins the path of moonlight that breaks through the clouds to dance on the water for the space of a breath before shimmering beauty sinks beneath the waves.

The gale dies. Rains disappears. Lightning and thunder return to the realm of the gods, and Midas Lear stands on a rock ledge holding a plain, wooden guitar in his hands. Tears stream down stubbly cheeks as he strums a series of notes.

"Oh, dear one, I have nothing to offer you but this humble instrument, stripped of its worth." His shoulders sag as he points to Chorda's glowing strand of hair. "Curse me for not granting you the legacy of your birth from the day it graced you with its golden touch."

Chorda scrambles over to Midas and throws her arms around him. "Your love is all the legacy I want, Da. My music will always come from truth, not the shimmer of gold."

Father and daughter settle into stillness, foreheads together. I try to subtly retreat up the path to give them a moment. Midas's call kills that plan.

"Adair." He beckons me with the crook of his thick index finger. "You fucking marvel, I heard your name on the wind, and it was not spoken by Manannán Mac Lir. Who invoked your spirit within the breath of the gods?"

This is it, my moment to go all in. I could deny my dancing with the gods experience or embrace a world where deities agree to take my calls. My brain rattles with Midas's insta-switch from off-his-nut to breath-of-the-gods tribe elder, but then I meet Chorda's eyes. The love and belonging that meets me seals the deal. Embracing her world of believing in entities larger than anything my heretofore narrow mind could fathom is the path I choose. This woman is my life.

I swipe a hand across my chin. "Well sir, I'm pretty darn sure I made a pinkie promise with a fellow named Lugh."

Midas narrows his eyes for a moment and then bursts out laughing. The lion that is Lear finds his roar as he wraps his beloved daughter and me into a rib-cracking hug. "You've got a shitload to learn, you son of a jacklick."

22

UNCOVERED

Justin's paramedic pal, Snapper Bakke, trusses Lear in blankets and whisks him off to the house with Bibs and Rand in tow. Chorda is torn between staying inside our shared blanket or following her da.

I rub my nose behind her ear and whisper. "I promise we'll be right behind him."

Chorda slips out of our cocoon and embraces Zeli. "Thank you for finding Da. If I hadn't gotten to him in time—" She breaks out in sobs as Zeli comforts her.

I ache to pull Chorda inside our blanket and promise her a lifetime of never facing this brand of near tragedy again.

Justin slaps me on the shoulder. "That was some shitiotic family drama, dude."

A figure picks its way across the clifftop and shouts my name. It's Gabs.

"Gabs!" I can't believe she's here. My message didn't disappear into the void. I toss the blanket to Justin and run to her. She's got not one, but three laptops cradled against her chest.

"I called the house when you didn't answer, and they told me where you'd gone," she says, out of breath. "Here." She thrusts the laptops at me.

"Three?" I catch her blush in the moonlight.

"After Desmond's office, I slipped past Grav into the Waterfall Palace while hell was breaking loose in the studio."

My gaze falls on a sparkling, ruby encrusted laptop cover. The one underneath it wears a case of gold with bejeweled Gs around its edges. "Where exactly did you slip?"

Gabs attempts to train a stray hair behind her ear. "Rubata and Glissanda's rooms." Her words spill over like one of the waterfalls at Midas's Hollywood palace. "When they turned into golden statues, I figured they wouldn't miss their laptops." She slaps a hand over her mouth. "I sound awful."

I peel her fingers away. "It's okay, Gabs. We're all in shock, but you're right. They don't need them anymore. Their files could have information to help me suss out everyone who's involved with all this shit that made it to air."

Gabs gives a tiny squeak. "You didn't hear?"

"What?"

"Rubata and Glissanda are okay. Lightning hit the studio and the power blinked out. When it came back on, they were lying on the floor screaming bloody murder." She bites a fingernail. "They're going to be pissed about the laptops."

The same bolt that robbed the Golden Guitar of its magic must have blasted the studio as well. I shiver, wondering which Lear family god was responsible for such myth-busting transformations. Whoever it was, I will be super polite if he or she ever shows up in my new reality.

"There's more." Gabs chews her lip. "I asked Robo Robbie from Rampion to do some light hack—investigating." She blushes. "We're seeing each other." Before I can reprimand or celebrate her audacity, she blurts out. "You're going to hate what he found."

I give a curt nod for her to continue.

"Robbie found a dummy trash icon in Desmond's files full of your private footage."

Instead of anger, sadness overwhelms me.

She shakes her head. "Desmond didn't hack you. Rubata sent the false emails as you."

I flash back to Rubata's gatekeeping, the deadly malachite residue Chorda found in Midas's glass, and a spelled ring.

Gabs winces. "I get if you have to fire me, but please, please don't get Robbie in trouble. He hacked to help Chorda."

"Fire you? Hell, I'm promoting you. What do you think about an associate producer spot on *Kickin' It With Chorda?*

Her eyes go wide, and a smile follows. "Seriously?"

"Cross my heart." I hand her the laptops. If there is a *Kickin' It With Chorda*. I'll find a vehicle for Gabs somewhere on the Golden Pipes Channel. Maybe she and Matty can spearhead the *Characters in Search of a Sitcom* project. "Your first duty is to not let these out of your sight and tell Robbie job well done."

She accepts the stack of criminal electronics.

"Thanks for not giving up on me, Gabs." I nod. "I'll call you with next steps."

Damned Desmond. He did dip into my material and copy it before I deleted it. I was sloppy, but he's a fiend. Tears sneak out the corners of my eyes. My brother betrayed me. I wanted to elevate and celebrate his talents, and all the time, he was waiting for an opening to backstab me. Our father will forever have a hard heart for Desmond.

Here's my chance to rise above the fragmented fallacy of the Holliday family and build a real one with Chorda. Not one where partners live thousands of miles away and only connect when it's convenient. Not one where children battle one another to be top dog with a parent. I'll fiercely love the family we make with a bond strong enough to please Bríg, Lugh, Manannán Mac Lir, and any other Irish legend who wants in. I swipe at teary eyes. We will be what the Lears were when Chorda's mom was alive.

As bold as the wind that brought Chorda and I from the Waterfall Palace to save Midas, I blow over to where Justin, Zeli, and the woman with the golden strand of hair linger uncomfortably near the edge of the sea cliff.

"Chorda Lear," I cry out, and three heads swivel in my direction. I snatch Chorda's hands in mine and drop to one knee. "I swear to your eavesdropping gods, you are more precious to me than any Golden Guitar. You are my magic. My heart beats to the music of your spirit. You have always been and always will be my dearest friend. Will you accept me into your life as the man who will never leave your side and will cherish your art and the beauty of your soul above everything else in this life and beyond?"

I stand and run a fingertip down the gold shining in her auburn hair. It brightens under my touch. "Will you marry me, my darling friend?"

Chorda jumps into my arms, wrapping her legs around me while she covers my face with kisses. "If you didn't ask, I was going to ask you," she says, laughing.

Zeli claps her hands. "'If you didn't ask, I was going to ask you.' That is totally a song," she says and throws herself into her husband's arms. They kiss.

Chorda and I follow their lead with kisses of our own. We fill what almost became a tragic night with love.

A sheer whirlwind of golden sparkles begins to rise around the four of us as Chorda's magic twinkles in the darkness. I swear the clouds sing their own melody to accompany my love's conjured light.

Suddenly, Chorda drops to her feet and cocks an ear toward the cliffs. "Do you hear that?"

Justin and Zeli break apart. We all listen. It wasn't clouds singing. A haunting, feminine voice rises above the surf. It calls with enough longing to break a heart.

We rush to the edge of the cliff until we pinpoint the sound of notes harmonizing with the sea. Down below, where sea foam frosts the sand, lies a man with his head cradled in the lap of the singer. Long strands of hair, glowing azure in the moonlight, stream around her face like waves to hide her features. The man looks as lifeless as the golden statue in front of the Waterfall Palace. The woman smooths hair off his face as she sings to him.

Chorda clutches my arm. Our decision to help is made via the mental shorthand we've always shared. I don't relish navigating the rocky path down the cliff for the second time tonight, but the scene below is bad news.

Our movement catches the woman's attention. Her face whips in our direction as clouds cover the moon to drop a veil over the night. When the veil lifts a moment later, the woman has vanished.

"You all saw a babe on the beach, right?" says Justin.

Chorda and I look at one another. Hand in hand, my fiancé and I head down the cliffs.

EPILOGUE

THICK BLACK EYELASHES DUSTED THE TOPS OF CHEEKBONES SET IN A broad face. His skin knew the touch of the sun. Only the sea-drenched shirt clinging to a well-defined chest separated the lifeline on Azure's palm from his heartbeats. When she spotted this man sinking like a stone beneath the waters of an angry sea, she thought him drowned. Her sole purpose was to deliver him to the beach so he might be found by a family who would surely mourn him.

Then his heart began to beat.

He lived. His chest rose and fell with the return of breath. In the light of the near-full moon, she traced his lips with the tip of her finger. Eyes the color of chocolate syrup opened to gaze at her in wonder.

"Are you a dream?" he asked.

She kissed him then, tasting the tang of the sea and the fire of life returning from the edge of nothingness. As his eyes drifted closed, now with the grace of exhaustion rather than death, she began to sing to him. He wore a sleepy smile as her voice floated over sand and surf. The beautiful man sang one single note, a harmony to the melody of her song. They both fell. He into a quiet from which he would awaken, and Azure into love.

A few months later...

Music from Adair and Chorda's wedding reception drifted up from the sound stage as Rubata Lear slunk out the massive oak main doors of the Waterfall Palace. Newly dyed cherry red hair matched the gloss on her pouty lips. She'd traded her bridesmaid gown for an all-black ensemble of leather, denim, and combat boots. After all, she was going to war.

Rubata stopped at the pedestal where a golden Irish chieftain once stood. A thin sheen of gold dust across the top of the marble base was all that remained of the statue since the Golden Guitar released its magic to the sea.

She peered into the shadows beneath the trees. The vandal better not stand her up. If she took another step to search him out, she'd set off her ankle monitor, the fashion scourge of her house arrest.

A tall man in an inky suit stepped out of the darkness and seemed to bring the shadows with him. He ran a finger along the top of the pedestal to gather shimmering metallic dust. His fingertip shone gold in the moonlight.

Rubata huffed. "You want a dustpan and broom to scoop up the rest?"

He held out a hand. "Ready to be free of Midas's tarnished gold to seek an opus of your own?"

Rubata kicked out her leg with the ankle monitor. "As soon as you pony up your part of the bargain."

She took his hand for balance and nearly let go. His fingers burned her skin. He laid his other hand on the monitor. Seconds later, the cuff melted into a black pool next to her foot. He reached into the congealed pile of plastic and plucked out a thumb-sized piece of metal holding a blinking light. With a smooth underhand throw, he chucked it into a golden urn next to the front door.

"We'll be off and away before the authorities learn Rubata Lear changed her destiny." He shot a look of disdain at the Waterfall Palace. "Welcome to the team."

"A team of two without Desmond."

A jovial sneer twisted the man's lips. "Dear Mr. Holliday's finest hour was his inability to convince a jury he was incapable of attempted murder." He lays a hand over his heart. "The way you cried 'blackmail,' dear Rubata, was an inspiration. You blindsided your Desmond."

Rubata snorted. "Ambition made him an easy mark." She smoothed her lipstick with a pinkie. "The jury loved me."

"And you had an excellent coach."

She dipped her head toward the man. "Many thanks." Her lips drew into a pout. "Our team needs recruits."

White teeth shone in the dark. "Oh, they're coming. A certain sea witch is eager to make the acquaintance of one bonded to the phantom queen, Mórrigán."

Rubata spun her ankle, relishing the absence of the monitor. "Sounds perf. Let's bounce. Mr. G."

His eyes lingered on her hand and the exposed skin of her wrist that glowed a faint shade of gold in the moonlight. "Call me Grant."

Thank you for reading! Did you enjoy? Please add your review because nothing helps an author more and encourages readers to take a chance on a book than a review.

And don't miss WILD AZURE WAVES, book three of the *Rockin'
Fairy Tales* series, available now. Turn the page for a sneak peek!

You can also sign up for the City Owl Press newsletter to receive
notice of all book releases!

SNEAK PEEK OF WILD AZURE WAVES

Each stroke of my oar cutting through the water sings.

Shuuush.

I'm alone in the channel between Lalale Island and the Santa Barbara, California mainland, writing a song with the sea as my co-composer. As I gift the ashes of my loved ones stolen by fire to the waves, I'll raise my voice in fresh notes of farewell.

A tap of the metal band around my wrist against the oar lock sounds a clear *ring.*

Shuuush, ring.

For percussion, I s*lap* the flat of the oar against the side of the canoe.

Shuuush, ring. Shuuush, slap.

The ocean adds notes of *hissssss* to soften our composition as my bow cleaves whitecaps. The water and I agree on momentary silence. Every song needs beats of silence to allow time for the music's energy to fill a soul.

Ring, ring, slap. Hissssss.

Silence.

The wind chimes in.

Oooooo-whip.

That's it, our song's missing bridge.

Shuuush, ring. Oooooo-whip. Shuuush, slap. Oooooo-whip.

I join my voice to the progression of notes.

"Time to fly. Farewell. You will soar. Farewell."

Silence.

"Beat, beat wings. Sailing. Seek Cloud's Path."

Silence.

"Farewell. Farewell."

As I near the mid-point of the channel, I'm still weighed down by the thick sorrow that hung in the air earlier when I crossed the sands of the island to the canoe. Members of the artist commune I'd lived with my entire twenty-five years watched me carry the four urns in my arms until I nestled the ashes of lost ones in the bow of my friend, Juan Luna Azul's, tomol. He's proud of this canoe he built with his grandfather, Juan Estrella Azul. The family learned the art of building tomols, the traditional plank canoes used for generations by the Chumash, from a boat builder who joined our artist commune on Lalale Island when my parents were kids. Neither Juan Luna nor I are Chumash, but he thought it fitting I use the traditional vessel for this burial at sea.

My parents, brother Piyo, and his fiancé, Tani, would hate any type of melancholy sendoff, so there'd never been an official memorial, but sadness is still etched on the faces of their friends nearly a year after the fire.

Whenever we lost friend or family, my parents said, "*Death is cool, Rai, a beginning for the next adventure.*" I smile. To them, everything was *bitchin'*, *boss*, or *cool* with the occasional *groovy* tossed in. The Lalale Island artist commune that birthed our family company, Cloudpath Music, will forever languish in a sixties time warp.

Only Emerson, Tani's father, walked all the way with me to where the sea lapped at the shadowed sands of the lagoon. Now, I look down on his thinning, gray hair. For many years, he was the one looking down on the once scrawny son of Lucas and Corinne Cloud.

"It'd be cool if you rowed out with me, Em," I'd offered.

The moon rose over his shoulder as he shook his head. "I've said good-bye to my Tanya. This fabricated ritual is something you cooked up for your own closure."

Perseverating on Emerson's dig ruins the rhythm of my stroke, and I stop singing. Tani hated being called Tanya. Damn Emerson for bumming my night. For years before he adopted his Mr.-Serious-Business-Dude persona, he bought into the laid-back vibe of what he now labels a *hippy dippy* island commune. The rest of the commune understands the respect I'm trying to show with my ritual. Emerson avoided disparaging my intentions in front of our friends, especially Tutu, Juan Luna's grandma. She'd string him up to the closest palm and throw rotten fruit at him.

I dismiss the negativity of his sendoff. My heart knows my family would welcome a joyful song of farewell as I steer the tomol toward the deepest part of the channel.

The urns rattle in the bow, and my heart clutches the way it does every time the gravity of my loss rises to the surface. I press a fist to my chest and speak to the ashes. "Your peace will come soon, I promise."

Peace is key here. I can't send these spirits off with bitterness in my gut. It's wrong of me to be angry with Emerson. He's dealing with death in his own way. He lost a child, a potential son-in-law, and dear friends. Pushing people away is his coping mechanism. I, on the other hand, am lost, a man floating through each day while I wait for reality to define its edges instead of keeping me adrift in the shapeless blur my life has become since the fire.

My gaze follows the silver-white path painted by a near full moon on the sea. The night is a melody, punctuated with flashes of moonlight catching the tops of swells. I welcome the lunar energy flowing through me, a river of the peace I desperately need. The moon is the spiritual touchstone I feel most connected to. I crave its presence tonight. Away in the distance, I see the Santa Barbara shore. Behind me rises the familiar shape of Lalale Island. It's time to begin.

First, I cradle the matching, deep red ceramic urns of my parents in my arms. Their wedding rings hang on thin silver chains around the tops. "Thank you, Mom, for making Lucas my father and Piyo my brother. Thank you, Mom and Dad, for giving me a cool life surrounded by love and belonging. I will always cherish the connections you taught me to find with island, sea, sky, and the creativity within me."

One at a time, I raise each urn to the moon and snap a mental picture of its silhouette against the bright disk before I dip my parents' urns into the water. "I gift you to earth and sea under a watching moon. Walk the Cloud Path to your next adventure."

I'd be lying if I didn't admit to hoping for an otherworldly surge or some other sign of connection to the spirits of my parents as I sink the urns. Nothing ethereal or supernatural goes down as they disappear. Disappointing.

Next, I tell my brother how much I love him and send him on his adventure. The moment Piyo's urn is out of sight, tears blur my vision. I've said so many good-byes to my family before I fall asleep and again when I meet each new dawn alone. Giving them to the sea is the deepest cut.

I wipe my eyes to find a darker sky. Lines of flat-bottomed, gray clouds cut across the moon. Beneath me, the canoe pitches left and right as swells smack its sides. I check to make sure the oars are secure in the locks.

I'd settle for a much calmer sign of my family's spirits finding their Cloud Path than an agitated ocean.

Tani's urn rattles. I lunge forward to grab it before it spills.

The moon, wearing a red ring, reappears from behind storm clouds. In the commune, Old Granny Blossom, our resident green witch, read signs of nature and conversed with the unseen. She gave me a moonstone charm to represent my spiritual energy, which I planned to give to Tani but never did. Before Piyo and I started school, Granny Blossom watched us while my parents poured crazy hours into creating Cloudpath Music. One night, she dragged us out to see a moon with a red ring. The wise witch called it a killing moon and warned us to take shelter whenever we see one.

I'm looking at the same creepy moon now.

Did I summon a freaky red ring and clouds that look like they want to squash me with my self-created ritual? Totally not my intention. This is the good-bye I crafted to please my family. I meant no offense. Tutu would tell me to get out of my head and finish.

The plank canoe stills its choppy dance. Rowing out to the middle of the channel at night doesn't feel as poetic as it did when I planned the ceremony. I'll say my good-bye to Tani and get my ass back to the island.

I look at the green sea glass urn adorned with a delicate gold leaf pattern and pause, unable to speak. As soul scarring as it was to commit my parents and brother to the deep, it's worse letting Tani go. She was my first love. My only real love to date. We told secrets. We laughed until we couldn't breathe. We dreamed together. We shared first kisses and fumbling explorations of each other's bodies. We moved together from childhood to adulthood on the island.

And then she chose Piyo.

They loved in a language beyond what I understood. She was better off with the steady Cloud brother instead of the one who listens for the songs of trees. Tani and Piyo moved past me in the ebb and flow of life, and I accepted it.

At least, I thought I had. I clutch the urn to my heart. "I love you, Tani." There are no other words that matter. I raise her urn to the moon as forks of lightning slice through clouds to bury the tips of their sabers in a circle around the canoe with an unnerving *sizzle.*

The storm breaks above and around me like a beast on the hunt. I am powerless prey. I wedge Tani's urn between my knees and try to take up the oars. The boat shimmies, twisting my insides. The bow rises only to thwack down with teeth-shattering violence as it rides the swells. I attempt to pull the oars in, but the sea bests me.

I hunch over the urn, my mind searching for the best strategy not to get killed. I wedge my body as low in the canoe as possible. The next wave nearly topples the tomol. The possibility of riding out the storm looks grim. Tani and I may be fated to find our Cloud Path together after all.

I listen for a song in the storm to calm myself. I hear only fury. Spray drenches my hair, the bare skin of my chest, and my trunks. The stern of the canoe lifts. Under a cascade of lightning, the Santa Barbara cliffs rise in sharp relief. Suddenly, to the south, a blinding burst of gold splatters across the sky like a gilded lace curtain. The shine is beautiful, and I wonder if it's the gate to my next adventure, opening to receive Tani and me.

Instead of the canoe slapping down, it's catapulted upwards by an unforgiving wave. I'm airborne along with Tani's urn. I reach for it, but green glass meets bow. The urn shatters, its fragments mixing with spray.

"Tani," I scream in the instant before my head collides with the curved stern of Juan Luna's tomol.

Don't stop now. Keep reading with your copy of WILD AZURE WAVES, available now.

Don't miss WILD AZURE WAVES, book three of the *Rockin' Fairy Tales* series, available now, and find more from Leslie O'Sullivan at www.leslieosullivanwrites.com

He lost his music. She lost her life.Now love may be their only encore.

Rai Cloud was once rock's brightest rising star—until scandal, heartbreak, and creative silence cost him everything. With his record label slipping through his fingers and a storm raging inside and out, Rai nearly drowns at sea... until a mysterious woman pulls him from the waves and sings him back to life.

Her voice is haunting. Mesmerizing. Magical. And gone by morning.

Desperate to find the woman whose song reignited his soul, Rai becomes convinced she's the missing harmony he's been searching for. But his first love, Tani Emerson, isn't an ordinary obstacle— she's a spirit lingering on the threshold of the afterlife determined to win Rai back at any cost.

The enigmatic Sea Witch, Sulaa Kylock, offers Tani an impossible bargain: complete a series of trials to prove Rai still believes in their love, and she may earn her way back to the living—and into his arms.

There's only one problem.

In spirit form, Tani must convince Rai she's more than a dream... while watching another woman capture his affection. Azure Tempesta—sweet, sexy lead singer of the chart-topping sister group, *The Mermaids*—is inspiring Rai to create again. And the closer they grow, the more Tani's second chance slips away like sea foam at dawn.

Now Tani must decide how far she'll go to reclaim the life—and the love—she lost. Because true love doesn't sink without a fight. And some songs are meant for an encore.

Please sign up for the City Owl Press newsletter for chances to win special subscriber-only contests and giveaways as well as receiving information on upcoming releases and special excerpts.

All reviews are **welcome** and **appreciated**. Please consider leaving one on your favorite social media and book buying sites.

Escape Your World. Get Lost in Ours! City Owl Press at www.cityowlpress.com.

ACKNOWLEDGMENTS

In "The Merchant of Venice," Shakespeare said, "All that glitters is not gold." I can unequivocally share I have indeed found treasures more valuable than gold in the many people who have made this book possible.

It's an honor to be part of the creative community at City Owl Press and Mystic Owl Books. Shiny gratitude to Tina Moss, Yelena Casale, Heather McCorkle, Lisa Green, Theresa Cole, and the amazing authors at City Owl for building a compassionate nest for this writer. Thank you, MilblArt, for a scrumptious cover.

Much gratitude to my kickin' editor, Lisa Green, for your layers of polish that allowed Gilded Butterfly to shine.

Publicly embarrassing squeezy hugs to Sarah, Lizzy, Julie, Katharyn, and Shona for your golden friendships, encouragement, and nights at the pub.

A Scrooge McDuck treasure vault to Robert, Tiffany, Shannon, Laurie, Flo, and Diane for always being there.

Golden glittering appreciation to Lora O'Brien for her wonderful book, IRISH WITCHCRAFT FROM AN IRISH WITCH, that taught me so much and launched me to start learning Irish. Reverence to The Mórrígan because even though I put you in cahoots with the ill-intentioned Lear sisters, I think you're awe inspiring.

To my dearest Melissa, Cameron, Rich, John, and Elizabeth, there are no amount of riches in the world that could equal my love for you.

Thank you, Mom, for sparking my appreciation for

Shakespeare, and allowing my brothers and I to reenact Macbeth Act 5 Scene 3: "Birnam Forest comes to Dunsinane," every January with our dried-up Christmas trees.

To the readers who rooted for Adair and Chorda, may your lives sparkle with a golden glow. I look forward to continuing our online connections.

ABOUT THE AUTHOR

LESLIE O'SULLIVAN is the award-winning author of *Fae Destiny*, a romantasy series that explores the collision between the real world and the Irish Faerie realm. Her *Rockin' Fairy Tales* romantasy stories shine a new spotlight on favorite fairy tales set against the backdrop of a fictional Hollywood music scene. The completed *Behind the Scenes* contemporary romcom series peeks into the off-camera sizzle of a wildly popular Irish television drama. She's a UCLA Bruin with a BA and MFA from their Department of Theater where she also taught for years on the design faculty. Her tenure in the world of television was mainly as the assistant art director on "It's Garry Shandling's Show." Leslie is a voracious reader who loves to connect with other book lovers and indulge her fangirl side at cons.

www.leslieosullivanwrites.com

[f] facebook.com/leslie.osullivanauthor
[ɪɢ] instagram.com/leslieosullivanwrites
[♪] tiktok.com/@leslieosullivanwrites

ABOUT THE PUBLISHER

City Owl Press is a cutting edge indie publishing company, bringing the world of romance and speculative fiction to discerning readers.

Escape Your World. Get Lost in Ours!

www.cityowlpress.com

facebook.com/YourCityOwlPress
x.com/cityowlpress
instagram.com/cityowlbooks
pinterest.com/cityowlpress